Thg

Lynn Chandler-Willis

The Rising

Contact Information: titleadmin@pelicanbookgroup.com

Scripture quotations, unless otherwise indicated, are taken from the Douay Rheims translation, public domain.

Cover Art by *Nicola Martinez*

Harbourlight Books, a division of Pelican Ventures, LLC
www.pelicanbookgroup.com PO Box 1738 *Aztec, NM * 87410

Harbourlight Books sail and mast logo is a trademark of Pelican Ventures, LLC

Publishing History
First Harbourlight Edition, 2013
Paperback Edition ISBN 978-1-61116-274-5
Electronic Edition ISBN 978-1-61116-273-8
Published in the United States of America

Dedication

To my children and their spouses, Garey and Ellen Willis and Nina and Allen Jones, and to the wonderful nine grandkids they've given me: Jeana, Landon, Emma, Ava, Paisley, Aiden, Ivy, Casey, and Ireland. Thanks for letting me follow this dream. And to my sister, Rae, whom I love dearly.

1

"The kid's not dead."

Despite the middle-of-the-night grogginess, Ellie Saunders bolted awake at Sergeant Jack Walker's announcement resonating through the telephone. She adjusted the receiver cupped to her ear and shoved away the comforter. "How can he be *not dead*?" She swung her legs over the side of the bed.

"The hospital just called. They said we might want to come down there. Our homicide victim isn't a homicide victim after all."

Ellie brushed the tangled hair from her eyes. "What did he do, come back to life?"

"Apparently."

She had meant it as a joke, but by the tone of Jack's voice, her boss was dead serious.

Ellie's back straightened. A sudden chill wrapped itself around her, and it had nothing to do with her freezing cold bedroom. The dead kid had been found in an alley, no identification. From the looks of him, he had been beaten to death. Blood matted his blond hair into sharp clumps, and purple bruises the size of Ellie's fist covered his little body. About four or five years old, maybe thirty-five to forty pounds, he was wearing a blue t-shirt with a red Superman emblem and green nylon shorts, no socks, and untied sneakers that were too big for his tiny feet. The brutality of his beating was hard for Ellie to comprehend—or forget.

"Ellie? You there?" Jack asked.

"Uh...yeah, sorry." Her mind was reeling. That kid was dead. There was no way he could suddenly be *alive*.

"Meet me at the hospital in thirty."

She started to ask for forty-five, but he had already hung up. She sat for a minute, trying to make some sense of what Jack had just told her. There was no way. The kid was DOA. At least he had been thirty-six hours ago. She'd worked a thirty-hour shift gathering what little information and evidence she could before falling into bed sometime after midnight.

Ellie forced herself to stand and then padded to her closet. She took out a white linen blouse and a pair of dark colored jeans. She tucked her blouse into her jeans then pulled on her navy blazer. Jack would probably fuss about the jeans, but at four o'clock in the morning, this was the best she could do.

She returned to the bed and pulled her holstered Glock and badge from the nightstand drawer. She wrapped the holster around her waist then instinctively touched the butt of the Glock resting at her hip.

A few minutes later, she was speeding through town on her way to Burkesboro Regional Hospital. The town tucked into the foothills of the North Carolina mountains was dead at this time—much the same way the kid was hours ago.

How could this kid *not* be dead? There was no pulse, no heartbeat. Nothing. His little body had already gone cold and stiff. And now she was supposed to believe he *wasn't* dead? She'd believe it when she saw it. Maybe.

Perhaps there'd been some confusion. Maybe they

had her little blond-headed, blue-eyed kid mixed up with some other kid. It wasn't like blond-headed, blue-eyed kids were a rarity.

That was probably it. The kid was still dead and some other little kid who looked like him was alive and well.

She whipped her Ford Taurus into the hospital parking lot and parked beside Jack's Crown Vic outside the emergency room.

Jack stood at the admitting desk, dressed in coat and tie even at this awful time of morning, tapping his foot in a heavy rhythm, glancing first at his watch then at the clock on the wall then back to his watch. *Tap, tap, tap.* Glance. *Tap.* He was fifty years old with a slight paunch and high blood pressure, and Ellie wasn't looking forward to the day he dropped dead of a heart attack. She knew of no other supervisor that would put up with her.

"Sorry," she said as she hurried to the desk. "I was—"

"Save it." He motioned for the admitting nurse to buzz them through and then took Ellie by the elbow and guided her through the door to the treatment area.

She had to work to keep up as he marched ahead down the near-empty hall.

"I must have missed the memo that they changed the dress code." He cut his eyes toward her jeans then shook his head.

She let the remark slide. "How can the kid not be dead?"

"According to Cynthia Terry, he's alive and well."

"That's impossible. I know dead when I see it, and this kid was dead. Remember? I even called you and asked if I needed to follow them to the hospital. You told me no. You told me—"

"Ellie—" Jack stopped and turned to her. "Calm down. You did your job. Whatever's happened here isn't your fault."

Although she knew that in her heart, she wanted to hear Jack Walker say it. She'd been under his supervision in the Criminal Investigations Unit for over a year, but with the rest of the unit being seasoned veterans, she still felt the need to prove herself. The fact she was just twenty-nine and the only woman in the unit didn't help matters.

"He was dead, Jack," she said again.

Jack sighed. "And now he's not. Probably just a mix up." He returned to his break-neck pace toward the treatment area.

The hub of the ER was a circular corral of desks, computers, and medical monitors. Treatment rooms were located around the corral, some with curtains pulled for privacy, others wide open for public viewing. The smell of vomit hung in the air like a toxic cloud. A man from housekeeping was mopping up what appeared to be the source of the odor as a cluster of nurses and doctors in green scrubs gathered around the main desk. They were so engrossed in conversation—Ellie heard words like *kid* and *dead* and *morgue*—they barely noticed Jack and Ellie.

"Hey! I need something for pain!" a scraggly looking man in treatment three yelled. He stared at Ellie through glazed eyes.

Ellie and Jack stopped at the corral and smiled at the doctors.

"Ah, the troops are here," Peter Bryson said. He was a third year resident and it seemed every time Ellie had a case that involved a trip to the emergency room, Bryson was on call. "Guess you're here about the Lazarus kid."

The doctors and nurses focused on Jack and Ellie, their eyes anxious and excited.

"The Lazarus kid." Jack half-smiled. "Could you keep that title in-house for a while? The media's going to be all over this as it is."

Bryson handed Jack a manila folder. "They're still running with the idea we had a DOA. Our services are no longer needed in their books. It's all you guys from here on out."

"We'll return the favor one day." Ellie smiled and peered over Jack's shoulder at the file.

There were several photos stapled to the inside cover. Ellie took in a deep breath and pulled her blazer tighter around herself, warding off the chill. The pictures were similar to ones she took in the alley. Same Superman t-shirt and green shorts. Same bruises, same matted blood-soaked hair. The only difference was in these snapshots, the kid was lying on a gurney with fluorescent lights beaming down on him; in Ellie's pictures, he was lying among discarded needles and broken beer bottles, with the flash from her camera and red and blue strobes punctuating the approaching darkness.

"Leon's got some current shots of him," Bryson added.

"Leon as in wild-man Leon?" Ellie asked. Leon's reputation preceded him.

"It *had* to happen on his watch." Bryson shook his head. The doctors and nurses gave a collective chuckle.

"Where's the kid now?" Jack asked.

"With Leon."

Jack raised his eyebrows. "The kid's still in the

morgue? Has he been examined?"

"Oh yeah. We brought him back up here and checked him out thoroughly."

"And?" Ellie asked. She glanced at the photos again. There was no way this kid could be alive.

Bryson slowly shrugged his shoulders. "The kid is... *fine*. There's not even a bruise on him."

Ellie stared at Bryson, wide-eyed. "I saw the bruises. That kid was beaten to death."

"Or so we thought," Jack said. He handed the folder back to Bryson.

"No. That kid was *dead*," Bryson said, matter-of-factly.

"Why'd you send him back to the morgue after you examined him?" Ellie asked. The morgue wasn't exactly the best place for a child to hang out, and Leon wasn't exactly someone you'd want babysitting.

"We had a pretty bad accident with a carload of teenagers come in. A lot of hysteria. Screaming kids, crying parents. Dr. Terry thought it would be best if we got him out of the middle of it."

"Why didn't you just take him upstairs to the pediatric unit?"

Bryson shrugged. "For some reason, he really bonded with Leon."

That was understandable, Ellie thought. Leon was fun, if nothing else. "Who examined him when he was first brought in?" Ellie asked.

"I did. There was no pulse and no respiration. We checked for brain activity and, well..." Bryson arched his brows and scrunched his face. "When there's no brain activity, there's not much use in attempting resuscitation."

"Who called it?" Jack asked.

"Dr. Terry."

"Was she assisting?" Ellie asked.

Bryson shook his head. "No, but she makes the call on all DOA's. Standard procedure."

Ellie jotted the information in her notepad then asked, "What time did he arrive and what time was he pronounced?"

Bryson referred to the folder. "Arrived at six-thirty and was pronounced at seven o'clock. I called Leon and it looks like he signed off on the transfer at seven twenty."

"There's a thirty-minute time lapse between the time he was brought in and the time he was pronounced." Ellie had her pen poised and ready to jot down the explanation. When no explanation came, she glanced up at Bryson who looked as though he didn't understand the statement was a question. "What happened during those thirty minutes?"

Bryson glanced around at the other doctors. He was at a loss for words. He finally turned his attention back to Ellie, still with a puzzled expression. "Well, about fifteen minutes of it was spent checking for a pulse, any respiration, brain activity. Once we knew there wasn't anything we could do, he was covered; we pulled the curtain and…went on to other patients."

"Did anyone check on him?" she asked.

Bryson pursed his lips and shrugged. "Not that I'm aware of."

"So he was left alone?"

Bryson glanced around at the other doctors and nurses again for confirmation. "Sure, he was left alone. I mean…there was nothing else we could do for him. We moved on to other patients."

And that was that, Ellie thought. Poor kid. Left

alone to die in a stinking, muck-filled alley then left alone in the ER. It didn't seem right for even an adult to die that way, let alone a child.

"Were there any other children in the ER during this time?" Ellie asked.

Bryson again turned to his colleagues. One of the nurses spoke up. "We had a Hispanic kid with a fever and cough and a little girl that needed sutures. There was one white male—I think he was around twelve. Snow skiing accident, broken collar bone."

Ellie scribbled the information in her notepad then looked at Bryson. "Can I get a list of everyone who was seen in the ER in the last forty-eight hours?"

He gnawed on his bottom lip with a look of regret.

Ellie sighed. "I know. Court order."

"Honestly, there hasn't been that many kids in here in the last few days. And when we get one in the condition little Lazarus was in, it kind of sticks out so we tend to remember them."

"What about general admitting?" Jack asked.

Bryson shook his head. "You'd have to check with them."

Jack nodded. "Thanks for all your help. Is Dr. Terry in her office?"

"Should be. If she's not, let me know and we'll page her."

Jack and Ellie turned away from the corral and headed down the hall to Dr. Cynthia Terry's office. "Go ahead and get a court order for the general admitting list for the last ten days. And get one for the ER while you're at it," Jack said.

"You don't trust Bryson?"

"Just covering our butts, dear."

The door to Dr. Terry's office was open so Jack

poked his head in. "Good morning."

Cynthia Terry was a bone-thin, take-no-prisoners woman who looked harder than a high school principal ready for retirement. "Jack. Detective Saunders. Come on in and have a seat." She motioned with a skinny hand toward two mismatched chairs in front of her desk. "Have you spoken with Peter Bryson?"

So much for small talk. "Yes. He was very helpful." Ellie smiled at the doctor who returned the gesture with a stoic glare. Maybe it *was* four o'clock in the good doctor's morning but it was four o'clock in Ellie's morning, too. Maybe the woman just needed a strong cup of coffee.

Jack cleared his throat. "Peter said you make the call on all DOA's. Do you personally examine each one?"

Dr. Terry shook her head. "Not usually. It depends on the doctor, but Peter's one of our best. When it comes to DOA, I trust his call."

"Is there any possibility–even a remote possibility –that Leon picked up the wrong body?" Ellie asked.

Again, Dr. Terry shook her head. "I reviewed the admitting list and the charts of every person that was seen in the ER in the last thirty-six hours, and he was the only DOA."

"Were there any other deaths during that period?"

Dr. Terry leaned back in her chair and crossed her arms. "You mean did we lose anyone? An eighty-three-year-old heart attack victim and a sixteen-year-old female in a car wreck."

"Was this the carload of teenagers?"

"Yes. As you can expect, things were a little chaotic, and I thought it would be best if the child wasn't right in the middle of it."

"That's when you sent him back down to the morgue?"

She nodded. "Probably isn't the ideal place to send a child, but he was comfortable with Leon."

"Dr. Bryson said when he was examined, there were no... injuries, or—" Ellie began.

"There was nothing. No bruises, no scrapes. His heart rate was normal. His respiration was normal, no indications of internal injuries. We even took him down to X-ray, and there were no broken bones. There was *nothing* out of the ordinary." She sat up and leaned into her desk.

"What about signs of previous abuse," Ellie asked. "Any old fractures in the X-rays?"

Dr. Terry shook her head. "None."

At least that part of this whole ordeal was a blessing.

"There has to be some medical..." Ellie struggled to find the right word.

"Explanation?" Dr. Terry shook her head. "Trust me. I've been racking my brain since Leon called and... well, I've never seen anything like it. There is a rare... *phenomenon*... called the Lazarus Syndrome. But in the brief research I've been able to do so far, I haven't found a documented case of this nature."

Ellie wrote the words *Lazarus Syndrome* in her notes. She stared at the words wondering if there really was a clue in the name alone. She quickly dismissed the thought. It couldn't be. Things like that just didn't happen. Outside of the New Testament, anyway. And she had her doubts about those. "What do you mean *of this nature?*" she asked.

"The length of time between when the patient was

pronounced dead and when there were signs of life. It's usually just a brief period of time. Not two days."

"What time did Leon notify you he was... alive?"

"It was a little after midnight."

"And you're positive there wasn't some kind of mix-up? A patient misidentified, perhaps?" Jack asked.

"I'm certain, Jack. I can't really speak for Leon's department, but I did go over his procedures and reviewed the files on everyone that had been transferred to the morgue and there's still no explanation. Trust me—I'm a stickler for efficiency but I was *hoping* to find an error, a mix-up, something that would explain this." She leaned back again and rubbed her forehead like she was rubbing away a headache. She sighed then continued, "Although there appears to be nothing physically wrong at this point, we'd still like to admit him to the pediatric ward. Maybe *they* can come up with something."

"What about his emotional state?" Ellie asked. "Is he agitated or distraught?"

Again, Dr. Terry shook her head. "He's... fine. A little quiet, but considering he woke up in a morgue, I'd say he's your average kid."

"Can we see him now?" Jack asked.

"Sure. I'll walk you down."

2

The morgue of Burkesboro Regional Hospital was tucked into the far end of the basement, far enough away from anything else so anyone heading there was there for a reason. It would never be mistaken by wayward visitors for a restroom or the cafeteria. Except for the rhythmic *click-clack* of Dr. Terry's clunky heels, the hallway was eerily quiet. The smell of chemicals seeped from under the tightly sealed door.

Despite the silent voices that occupied it, Ellie had always found the morgue to be a rather lively place, especially when Leon was working. He usually kept the Beach Boys at full volume, classical on his moody days. As they approached, Ellie heard only silence.

"No music?" Ellie asked, surprised at the quiet filtering under the door.

"Even Leon was a little perplexed by this kid." Dr. Terry keyed in a code on the electronic door then waited for it to open. When it swung open, Jack and Ellie followed her toward the office on the far side of the room.

Through the glass walls, Ellie could see Leon sitting at a gray metal desk, and a child sitting on top of it, his back to the glass wall.

Dr. Terry stopped and motioned for Jack and Ellie to do the same. "Wait right here and I'll get Leon. I don't think it would be in the child's best interest at this point to hear all the details."

Ellie peered over Dr. Terry's shoulder, anxious to get a look at the child. He definitely had blond hair, and he was wearing a blue t-shirt but from the angle, she couldn't see the front of it, the Superman emblem. The child turned and gazed through the glass at the trio of visitors. When he did, Ellie's blood turned as cold as the temperature in the room.

That's him. That's the same kid that two days ago was dead. She gathered her blazer and wrapped her arms around herself to ward off the creepy chill. Her teeth chattered. "Are you cold?" She asked, turning toward Jack.

"It's always cold in a morgue, Ellie."

"No, I mean it's colder than *usual.* It's cold, cold. Weird cold."

Jack stared at Ellie then slightly grinned. "It's not that cold. I think you're a little spooked."

"You would be too if you'd seen him in that alley. And dead."

Leon came out of the office. He was wearing a Hawaiian shirt and cut-off khakis that hung below his knees. His red hair was a mass of loose curls that sprang in different directions when he walked. As usual, Leon had way too much energy. Especially at this time of morning.

"Jack, Ellie, it's been a while." Leon laughed and offered his hand to Jack then gave Ellie a grabby hug. "Looking fine, woman. When are you gonna leave this old man and come to work for me? We can dance all night." He grabbed her hand and twirled her around then dipped so low Ellie knew she was going to fall to the floor.

When he finished, he saluted Jack and pretended to stand at attention. Ellie straightened and smoothed her jacket. "Good to see you again, Leon."

"Good to see you, too, gorgeous. You ought to get down here more often."

"Well if I was here more often that would mean we both had too much work." She ran a hand over her hair, hoping to settle it back into place.

"Good point. Doc says you wanted to talk to me about *Johnny Doe*. Weirdest thing I've ever seen in my life, and I've seen some doozies." He shook his head back and forth for emphasis, sending his red curls into a bouncing frenzy.

"From the beginning, Leon," Jack said.

"Sure." He stuffed his hands in his pants pockets and rocked back and forth on his feet. He smelled like rose-scented room freshener. "Tuesday night I got a call around seven that the ER had a transfer—"

"Who called you?" Ellie asked, her pen poised at her notepad.

"Peter Bryson. I got up there around seven fifteen, maybe, and brought him down here to the dungeon." He glanced around his work environment and smiled.

"What did you do after you got him down here?"

He pointed to a row of three gurneys, two with army green drapes covering noticeable lumps, and one with the drape puddled beside it on the floor. "I parked him right there. There were instructions to hold for autopsy, so I didn't prep him or anything. I took all the information from his toe tag and went back to the office to catalog it."

"You didn't touch him or move him again after that?"

Leon shook his head. "Not for a while. I had four to catalog so I was in the office for about an hour and when I finished, I moved him to a drawer. I pulled the rest of my shift, and then went home."

"Who came in after you?"

"Vanessa. She works day shift. Dr. Jenkins had three autopsies scheduled yesterday, including your little Johnny Doe, but he called in sick – the flu, I think. I mean, like it really matters down here, ya know?" He smiled.

Maybe it was a good thing Jenkins was out sick. The Medical Examiner was known to be a little stressed and jumpy. Ellie could only imagine how jumpy he would have been if he had started an autopsy on a child that wasn't dead.

"Did Vanessa...*check* on him or anything?"

Leon stared at her a moment then chuckled. "Check on him how? Usually when we put 'em in a drawer, they stay put."

Ellie sighed. Leon was right. It was a stupid question, but considering the circumstances, she wasn't taking anything for granted. "OK, fair enough. When did you discover he was... alive?"

"Sometime around midnight. I went up to the coffee shop and got a cup of coffee and a couple of doughnuts. When I came back, I moved him out of the drawer and put him over there. Then went to the office to finish up some paperwork."

"Why'd you remove him from the drawer?"

"Dr. Jenkins is supposed to be in around six, and I was supposed to have all the prep work finished before he gets here."

"What happened next?"

Leon's eyes widened, and he spread his hands open. "Oh man, talk about weird. I was working in the office and he just...*walked up*. Asked where the bathroom was. Imagine that. The kid had to pee." He laughed.

"What did you do then?"

"I took him to the bathroom."

Ellie glared at him. "You didn't question who he was or where he came from?"

"The kid had to go bad. Real bad. He was doing that little pee-pee dance kids do. You know how they—" He began to illustrate but Jack interrupted him.

"Um—Leon, when did you get around to asking him how he got down here?"

"After we got back from the bathroom. I asked him who he was and how he got here, and he said he 'woke up' on that table over there. He pointed to that empty gurney." Leon did the same. "I'm telling you, I flipped out. He was still wearing the toe tag so I took him in the office and checked it against the paperwork and man-oh-man, the thing matched. Then I *really* flipped out."

Ellie glanced at the gurney and saw the same sneakers she had seen in the alley now lying underneath, partially covered by the drape. She looked at Leon and nodded understandingly. She would have flipped out, too. She shivered again. "Did he say his name, or what happened to him?"

Leon shook his head. "I asked him, and he said he didn't know."

"What happened to him or—"

"No, his name. He doesn't know his name."

Ellie furrowed her brows. Even a two-year-old usually knows their name. "Was there anyone in here while you were gone?"

Leon shook his head. "Not to my knowledge. The security camera at the door would know for sure."

"We'll need to get a copy of that tape," Jack said.

Ellie looked around the room, paying close attention to the upper corners. She wondered if she could get so lucky. "Are there any other cameras?"

"Just the one at the door. I guess they're not as concerned about what goes on in here as they are who comes and goes."

"Did anyone else come down while you were in the office?"

Leon shook his head. "Nope. Just me. We don't get a lot of traffic down here. There's an electronic log of each time the door's opened, time, date—stuff like that. I know 'cause they nailed me a few weeks ago. Came in late." He smiled. He was missing a tooth.

Ellie looked past Leon at Dr. Terry and the little boy. She wondered if he remembered anything. "Can you introduce us?"

"Sure. I've been calling him Johnny. You know, John Doe?" He bobbed his head again.

Ellie smiled. "Better than Lazarus."

Leon laughed hard enough his hair bounced again. Jack and Ellie followed him to the glass office. The kid turned and looked at them as they entered. Ellie forced herself to breathe.

It was the same kid; there was no doubt. The same blue t-shirt with the red Superman emblem, the same green knit shorts. The same blond hair—except now there were no bloody clumps. The same delicate features, except now there were no bruises. His fair skin was flawless. There were no scuff marks at his knees, no scratches on his little skinny arms. His blue eyes were bright and sparkled with life. New life.

"Hey, Johnny, this is Ellie and Jack. They're going to talk to you for a minute. OK?" Leon gently clapped the kid on his shoulder. "Now you be nice to him. He's my little buddy." He pointed a stern finger at Ellie and grinned.

Dr. Terry moved from the front of the desk and planted herself in the corner of the cramped office, making it clear she intended to stay. Ellie moved in front of the child and sat in the vacant chair. "Hey, Johnny. I'm Ellie Saunders."

The kid smiled slightly and looked at Jack. "Y'all are cops, aren't you?"

Ellie nodded. "Yes. We're police officers."

Johnny Doe nodded and continued to stare at Jack. "He looks like a cop."

Ellie glanced at Jack and fought back a smile. "I know. He's kind of a nerd. We're here to see if we can't find out what happened to you. Can you help us do that?"

"I woke up over there." He pointed to the gurney.

"When you say you 'woke up,' do you remember going to sleep?"

He slowly shook his head as if he were embarrassed at the answer. He glanced at Leon then looked downward toward the tiled floor. Ellie wasn't sure if he really didn't remember going to sleep or if it was something he was purposely trying to forget.

"Do you remember what you were doing *before* you went to sleep?"

"I was walking with my daddy. We were walking down a real shiny road."

"Do you know your daddy's name?"

He slowly shook his head.

"Leon told us that you don't remember your name, either." Ellie said, tilting her head slightly to catch his gaze.

"Leon said my name was Johnny." He lifted his head and smiled. His eyes were the color of sapphires and sparkled with a virgin brightness. "See, it says so right here." He lifted his foot and pointed to the dangling toe tag.

Ellie read the tag and smiled. "You are exactly right. It does say Johnny. Do you have another name? Do you remember what your name was before you went to sleep?"

He shrugged his shoulders then pulled his foot up again and examined the tag. "Johnny Doe."

"You're a very good reader. What are you in, the first grade?"

He furrowed his brow and stared at Ellie like she was speaking in a foreign language. He slightly shook his head. "I woke up over there." He pointed again to the gurney. "Leon says those are my shoes."

Ellie looked at the gurney, too, then nodded. "Those are nice shoes. Do you remember where you got them?"

"Leon gave them to me. I don't have any—see?" He kicked his feet, thumping the back of his bare heels against the metal desk.

"I like your t-shirt, too. Do you like Superman?"

He nodded. "But I like Spiderman better. He can climb walls to get away from the monsters."

Ellie glanced at Jack. "Wow. That's pretty cool, huh. What kind of monsters is he trying to get away from?" She asked.

With pleading eyes, Johnny Doe looked at Ellie then turned his head downward and watched his feet thump against the desk. "Just monsters. Can I play with Leon now?"

Dr. Terry softly cleared her throat.

Ellie looked up.

The doctor ran a finger across her neck, indicating it was time to cut the questioning.

Ellie pressed with one more question. "Hey, you know what? Tomorrow is Jack's birthday. Guess how old he's going to be."

Johnny Doe eyed Jack then leaned in to Ellie. "Old," he whispered.

Ellie laughed out loud. "Real old. How old will you be on *your* next birthday?"

He shrugged his tiny shoulders.

Ellie held up her hand, five fingers spread wide. "This many?"

He studied her hand a moment then shook his head.

Ellie added the index finger from her other hand. "I bet you're this many."

Again, he shook his head then yawned.

Fearing Dr. Terry would cut her off any moment, Ellie asked one more time, "and you don't remember anything else before you woke up?"

He continued to thump his feet against the drawer. "I remember talking to my daddy."

Ellie's heart jumped. "Do you know your daddy's name?"

He shook his head then looked over at Leon. "Can I play with Leon now?"

Dr. Terry stepped forward and placed her hand on the child's shoulder in a protective manner. "I think it's time we get you settled into a room upstairs."

The child looked unsure. "But I want to stay here. With Leon."

Dr. Terry's mouth twitched like she was trying to actually smile. "We have a nice room for you upstairs—and it's right down the hall from a big playroom."

"Can Leon come?"

Her mouth twitched again. "Maybe after you've had some rest. How about if Leon helps you get your shoes on? Would you like that?"

Johnny Doe watched with scared eyes as Dr. Terry snipped the dangling toe tag and dropped it in the manila folder. It was the only link to who he was, and he didn't seem too keen about parting with it. She lifted him down from the desk then mussed his hair, hair that a little while ago had been matted with blood. He turned once to look at the folder that held his lifeline as Leon led him out of the office.

Dr. Terry waited until the boy was out of earshot then turned to Ellie and Jack. "The chief of pediatrics will be here in about an hour. I'm sure Dr. Deveraux will let you question him again tomorrow after he's had some rest."

"Uh, with all due respect, Dr. Terry, time is of the essence with this. We need to find out as much about him as soon as possible if we hope to find out who *did* this to him."

Dr. Terry stared hard at Ellie. "I'm somewhat familiar with how investigations work, Detective Saunders. But until Dr. Deveraux says the child is stable enough to answer any more questions, no one is going to ask him anything."

"You said in the emergency room that he was fine. That you couldn't find anything wrong with him. That you were even *hoping* for—"

"Thank you, Dr. Terry," Jack said. "We appreciate all your help." He cut his eyes toward Ellie. She looked away and watched Leon help the child with his sneakers.

She wondered just how much help the boy would be. He didn't know his name, or how old he was. He didn't know his father's name. The idea of school seemed phantom to him, and he didn't remember anything prior to waking up on the morgue gurney except walking with his daddy along a shiny road. A *shiny* road? There had been some ice in the area the night he was found. Maybe he was referring to black ice? It wasn't much of a lead but it was something. The only other thing Ellie could gather so far was he was uncomfortable talking about monsters. She wondered if the monster he saw in his mind was the same one that tried to beat him to death.

3

Ellie opened her front door, dropped her keys and notepad on the side table then collapsed onto the lumpy sofa, one foot dangling on the hardwood floor. She thought about pulling her leg up, snuggling down on her side and catching a couple of winks before reporting to the office. "*Oh*... you can't." She moaned and then sat up. As much as she would love just one hour of sleep, even thirty minutes, if she closed her eyes, Jack would be calling reaming her for being late.

She was battling a headache, a severe lack of sleep, and a kid she'd thought was dead but now wasn't. Was she investigating a homicide or an assault? An array of thoughts bumped around in her head, making it throb all the more.

She pulled herself off the sofa and lumbered into the kitchen. The tiny house was old and drafty with creaking wood floors and a pull-chain light in the bathroom, but the rent was cheap. The Robins, the elderly couple who owned the place, lived next door and brought her homemade soup in the winter and vegetables from their garden in the summer. They were the closest thing she had to grandparents.

Ellie put a kettle on the old stove for coffee. She leaned against the Formica counter while she waited for the water to boil and stared at the dingy linoleum. No matter how often she mopped, which she'd admit wasn't often, the once-white floor was yellowed with age. No amount of cleaners could permanently erase age.

She was on the downside of twenty-nine and beginning to worry about things like frown lines and crow's feet. She'd never been one to spend money on expensive makeup and wrinkle-reducing creams but wondered if it was time to start. Maybe if she had had some instruction on how to use the stuff, the whole idea wouldn't seem so foreign to her. Maybe if her mother had been around to show her how....

The kettle's shrill whistle snapped her out of the "what-ifs." She fixed herself a cup of straight black coffee, drank it down, then headed to the shower.

When she was through, she pulled on her tattered bathrobe and padded to the bedroom, the bare wooden floor cold beneath her feet. She stared at the rumpled sheets. What few hours of sleep she had managed, had been restless. Her whole life seemed restless lately. She couldn't put her finger on why. Her biological clock was ticking, and she didn't know if she even really wanted kids. Of course, a husband would have to come first, and those prospects weren't hitting on much. The few dates she'd had lately weren't horrible, but they didn't take her breath away, either. She'd pulled so far away from God over the last few years, she felt like a total hypocrite praying for God to send her someone. She was a lot of things, reckless at times, stubborn, judgmental, but no one could accuse her of being a hypocrite. She jerked the sheets off the bed and piled them in the corner of the room to be washed. Nothing like clean sheets for a good night's sleep. When she got to sleep again.

She wished it were that simple. Throwing

something in the washing machine, or taking a hot cleansing bath, anything to wash away the dirt. Like being baptized, her father would remind her.

She carried the soiled sheets to the washer on the back porch, dumped them in and started the machine. The winter wind whipped through the screen door, which didn't exactly fit the frame, and made her shiver. After five years in the old house, she had grown used to the oddities—like windows that weren't standard size, molding that didn't meet in the corners, and doors that weren't level. Or either the house wasn't level. She hadn't figured that one out yet.

But it was home. Like a second skin, she was comfortable in it.

She hurried back in, into the natural warmth of her little house, and pulled a clean set of sheets from the cabinet in the bathroom. After making the bed, she arranged the pillows. Who was it that said loneliness could be measured by the number of useless pillows a woman kept on the bed? She had four. Not too bad. Maybe she was just a *little* lonely.

She looked at the clock on the nightstand then panicked when she saw it was 7:45. She was supposed to meet Jack at the hospital at 8:15. "Oh..." She hurriedly got dressed—gray twill pants, cream colored blouse and black blazer, a proper 'uniform'—then grabbed a towel from the bathroom and towel-dried her auburn hair. A short haircut came in handy when she was pressed for time, especially when the only outlet in the bathroom was attached to the pull-chain light. Blow drying in this house was both time consuming and risky.

Satisfied her hair was presentable, she ran back into the bedroom to slip on her shoes. The phone rang and she nearly tripped trying to get to it, afraid it might be Jack. She picked up the phone and stared at the name and number displayed. *Dad?* That was all she needed right now. The good Reverend Ferrin Saunders. What was he going to preach to her about this morning? Whatever it was, it could wait. After the sixth ring, it finally shut off. Moments later, the red voicemail indicator light flickered. She took a deep breath, returned the phone to the charger, and rushed out the door.

She pulled into the hospital parking lot at 8:10 and breathed a sigh of relief. Jack's car wasn't anywhere to be seen. She parked beside a police cruiser outside the emergency room, gathered her notepad, and headed inside. She flashed her badge at the admitting nurse and was buzzed through without question.

The hallway and corral were buzzing with morning activity. The faint smell of vomit still permeated the air. Peter Bryson still manned the helm, looking ragged and tired.

"Don't I know you?" he asked and smiled.

"Don't *you* ever go home?"

He half-laughed. "Home? What's that?"

Ellie leaned into the counter and whispered. "It's that place you go when you want to get away from work. Anything new with our little John Doe?"

Bryson shook his head. "Haven't heard anything. I know he's up on the pediatric floor. Other than that..." He shrugged.

Ellie smiled softly. "Go home and get some rest."

As she started to walk away, Bryson called to her. "Oh, by the way—Sara Jeffries from the *Bulletin* called."

Ellie groaned then turned around and glared at

Bryson. "What did you tell her?"

"Told her we didn't know anything more than we did last night, and if she needed further info to contact Burkesboro's finest." He grinned.

Ellie slowly nodded and forced a smile. "Thanks. I'll remember you at Christmas."

She turned and headed to the elevator, cursing Sara Jeffries and the Burkesboro *Bulletin* under her breath. This case was going to be tough enough without the media jumping on it.

The elevator doors opened to a whole different world. It was still a hospital, no doubt, but the walls resembled a giant canvas covered with colorful characters of every child's fantasy. The nurses wore brightly colored knit pants and t-shirts with "Team Peds" printed across the front. They were bouncy and walked and talked with a youthful energy that reminded Ellie of a cheerleading squad.

She found the main desk, showed her badge to one of the cheerleaders, and smiled. "Detective Ellie Saunders, Burkesboro PD. I'm looking for Dr. Deveraux."

"Are you here about Johnny Doe?" Her eyes were wide. She gnawed on her bottom lip, anxious for Ellie's answer.

"Yeah," Ellie said. "He was admitted to this floor, wasn't he?"

The nurse nodded. "Room 413. Dr. Deveraux's with him now. Pretty wild about him coming back to life and all, huh?"

Ellie slowly nodded and forced a smiled. "Yeah." Just as she was turning to go, her cell phone beeped. She again smiled at the nurse as she removed the phone from her jacket pocket. She was surprised to see it was Jack calling from the office. "Hey, where are you?" It wasn't like Jack to be on time—he was always early.

"Good morning to you, too," he said.

"Sorry. Good morning. Where are you?" She stepped away from the nurses' station.

"How'd the call come up?"

"What?"

"How did the call come up?"

She sighed. "From the office."

"Then that's a pretty good indication of where I'm at. Think, Ellie, before you ask a question you already know the answer to."

"Jack—I knew you were at the office—what I meant was why aren't you here at the hospital?"

"Ah. So you were on time." He snickered. There were times she wanted to strangle him, and this was one of them. "I forgot I've got an eight-thirty meeting with IT."

Jack Walker forgot something? Maybe the kid did come back to life through divine intervention because the world was certainly ending. "You want me to wait until you get here?"

"No. Just fill me in when you get back to the office."

Ellie's heart raced, and she couldn't help the grin curling her lips. Jack actually trusted her. With *this* case.

"Just mind your manners, and when the doctor tells you no more questions, no more questions. As long as he's in the hospital, we play by their rules. Got it?"

She hesitated a moment.

"Ellie?"

"Got it," she said reluctantly.

"Good. Keep me posted. And Ellie, try not to irritate the doctors. We are on the same team."

Ellie closed her phone and tucked it into her pocket. She stared down the long hallway, her new-found confidence slipping a little. She smiled at the nurse again, took a deep breath, then headed to room 413.

She read the room numbers posted on the doors along the corridor, but refused to glance inside as she passed each room, afraid of what she would see. Sick kids tethered to mechanical beds by IV tubes, tiny hollow eyes glaring at her as if she offered salvation from their ravaged little bodies. She stared straight ahead.

Room 413 was at the end of the hallway with the door partially open. She knocked once then poked her head in. Johnny Doe was sitting on the side of the bed, laughing at the doctor standing in front of him. His eyes were as bright as before, his smile as pure.

"Am I interrupting?" Ellie asked as she stepped into the room.

"That depends," the doctor said and smiled. He offered his hand. "Dr. Marc Deveraux. And you are who?" He spoke with a heavy accent but Ellie couldn't pick up on the dialect.

She smiled and shook his hand. "Ellie Saunders. Burkesboro PD."

"Ah. Dr. Terry told me you were coming."

Ellie didn't know if that was a good thing or a bad thing.

"She's a cop," Johnny Doe said. The Superman t-shirt had been replaced by a pint-sized hospital gown.

There was something about the way the kid said

"cop." Most kids around his age would have said "policeman," familiar with the more honorable term. He had picked up the word "cop" somewhere, and Ellie doubted its usage had anything to do with honor.

"How you doing?" Ellie approached the bed and lightly touched his hair.

"They have a big truck in the playroom. Leon's gonna come play with me later. You can come, too, if you want to."

"I just might do that." She stroked his hair again. "How you feeling?"

He looked at her, his tiny brows furrowed. "Why does everyone keep asking me that?"

Ellie glanced at Dr. Deveraux and hem-hawed before answering. "Well, because everyone cares about you so much. We just want to make sure you're OK, you know?"

He scrunched his button nose then bobbed his head up and down. "Can we go play now?"

Dr. Deveraux cleared his throat. "We'll go down to the playroom in a few minutes. Right now, I need to talk to Ms. Saunders. You use those new crayons I brought you and color Ms. Saunders a picture, OK?"

Ellie stared at the doctor a moment, still unable to catch the dialect. She turned back to Johnny and smiled. "Will you color me a picture? I'd like that." She pulled the tray table up to the bed and skimmed through the coloring book. "How 'bout a ladybug? I like ladybugs." Except when they colonized in the corners of her ceiling when the weather turned cold.

While Johnny Doe took a red crayon from the box and went to work on his masterpiece, Ellie followed Dr. Deveraux outside to the hallway.

He looked to be in his early thirties, but Ellie

figured he was older—there weren't many thirty-year-old department heads in the medical profession. His mocha-colored eyes were warm and sincere and radiated compassion. His hair was blacker than midnight and his smile brighter than fresh snow, and the only imperfection Ellie could find was a scar that ran from the outer corner of his left eye downward, stopping just below his perfect cheekbone.

"I've ordered a series of tests. It could be days before we have all the results, but so far, there doesn't seem to be anything at all wrong with him. You're still looking for his parents?"

"His parents, grandparents... anyone who could tell us who he is. Have you been able to get any information out of him?"

Deveraux shook his head. "We haven't really pushed him too hard. I've arranged for a child psychologist to spend some time with him this afternoon, so maybe we'll know more after that."

Ellie peeked into the room and watched Johnny Doe as he colored her ladybug. "And until then?"

Deveraux twisted his mouth into a tight knot. "I suppose we wait."

"What then?"

"We wait some more." He smiled. It was a beautiful, soft smile, and Ellie thought for a moment the gorgeous doctor should be counseling adult patients, delivering life-altering news to grown-ups who could find comfort in the warmth. Or at least be distracted enough by his looks to not care about the bad news he was delivering.

"What do we do when we're through waiting? There has to be a point when you've done all you can."

Deveraux leaned against the brightly painted wall,

his shoulders resting between a cartoon bear and a tiger. A slight look of resignation crept over his face. "You mean child services. When do we reach the point that, as a hospital, we've done all we can do and turn him over to the court system?"

Ellie peered in the hospital room. Johnny Doe had finished the ladybug and moved on to a dragonfly. Poor little guy. Ellie's heart ached knowing unless they found his parents soon the kid would probably end up shuffled back and forth in the system.

"It's going to be a while before the hospital releases him," Deveraux said, his voice soft and comforting. "He's not going anywhere until we know what happened to him in the morgue."

Ellie pulled her attention away from Johnny Doe and stared at Deveraux. "Have you seen the pictures?"

"The before and after? Yes, I've seen them. Quite a miracle if you ask me."

Ellie laughed. "I didn't think doctors believed in miracles."

Deveraux shrugged his shoulders. "Depends on the doctor. I've always thought it a bit arrogant to think there has to be a scientific explanation for everything."

A scientific explanation sure would help at the moment. She removed a business card from her pocket and handed it to him. "This has all my contact information. Can you call me as soon as you get the test results?"

Deveraux slipped the card into the pocket of his lab coat and nodded. "I've instructed the lab to call as the results of each test come in. We should start getting them in a few hours."

Ellie nodded. "Can I sit in when the psychologist

examines him?"

Deveraux frowned. "Probably not a good idea. The fewer the distractions, the more Doctor Mertzer will be able to get out of him."

She peered in the room again. Johnny Doe had finished the dragonfly and had started on a bumblebee. She wondered how many other kids his age would be content to sit and color picture after picture while the adults around them talked in hushed voices. Not many, she guessed.

She stepped back into the room to collect her artwork and to tell Johnny Doe she'd see him later.

"You like it?" he asked as Ellie carefully tore the ladybug picture from the coloring book.

"It's the most beautiful ladybug I've ever seen, and I've got the perfect place for it."

Johnny Doe's tiny face lit with pride. He held his hand up to Ellie, offering a high-five.

Ellie lightly slapped his hand. "I'll be back this afternoon, OK?"

"OK." He pulled a green crayon from the box and went to work on a lizard.

Ellie leaned into Deveraux and whispered. "Tell Doctor Mertzer Johnny's very good with his colors."

In the elevator, Ellie stared at the ladybug. Swooshes of red colored the body while jagged streaks of black made up the dots. The ladybug's eyes were colored bright blue. It was perched on a dark brown tree limb with a few brown leaves jutting from the sides. The little house in the background was dull, cinderblock gray. Although there was an outlined sun high above the house, it was untouched. No lemon-yellow or orange color to bring it to life. Nothing but a black outline.

Ellie folded it neatly and slipped it in the pocket of her jacket.

4

Ellie left the hospital and headed to the Burkesboro Police Department. Rush hour traffic along Main Street had died down, but the everyday traffic was still pretty heavy. The morning sun was glaring through the windshield, blinding her to the color of the light at the intersection of Main and Baker Street. A horn honked behind her, and the woman driver gave her an exasperated look, hands spread wide, mouth hanging open. Ellie slowly pressed the gas and crawled forward then offered the woman a smile as she jerked around Ellie and sped by in the other lane. Ellie threw her hand up in a mock wave.

She fished her sunglasses from the glove compartment and wondered about Johnny Doe's colorless sunshine. Was it an indication of a sun-less world, or had he simply forgotten to color it? And what was with the little gray house? Prisons were made of cinderblock, not homes.

Ellie turned into the department's parking lot and pulled around to the back. The morning shift had already checked in and headed out, while a few of the night shift's squad cars were still lingering, taking up valuable parking spaces. There was an empty spot between the Crime Lab van and Jesse Alvarez's red Camaro, and one at the far end of the lot. She opted for the one at the end of the lot. Walking a little farther would be less painful than an encounter with Jesse

Alvarez.

He must be behind in his paperwork, she thought as she locked up her car. Working vice, his appearances at the station were few and far between. Probably just as well. Jesse had been a one-night stand during a bout of reckless abandon a few years back. He'd been the only one she wished had called back, but when he didn't and started ducking behind corners whenever they were within a hundred feet of each other at the office, she pretty much knew where she stood. Just as well, he was different now. She was different.

The Burkesboro Police Department was a sprawling, six-story building of black-paned glass and chrome, and looked terribly out of place among the older, more traditional buildings jammed up around it. Over the years, Burkesboro's population had spiraled upward with new residents coming in who longed for a "small town" atmosphere but weren't quite desperate enough to make a total escape of city life and head to the mountains proper. With all the new residents, the small town atmosphere had blossomed into a busy little city.

That was fine with Ellie. She liked the convenience of having a Starbucks around the corner and a movie complex that showed first-run movies. The community where she grew up was nestled in a valley tucked into the Blue Ridge Mountains about fifty miles west of Burkesboro and opened its first movie theatre when she was well into her teens. It probably wouldn't have mattered if it had been built earlier, anyway, as her father was a preacher and didn't approve of too many movies. She was twenty-three before she saw the *Wizard of Oz*. She liked the scarecrow best and still had nightmares about the flying monkeys.

Ellie slid her ID card into the electronic card reader at the back door then sprinted up the first three flights of stairs. Next, she took the elevator to the fifth floor. Three flights were all she could do without breaking a major sweat and having everyone in the office wonder if she ever showered. Her New Year's Resolution had been all five flights, and she had conquered three. It was mid-March, so she figured she was doing pretty good.

The elevator doors jerked opened and as Ellie was stepping out, Jesse was stepping in. He had a three-day growth of beard and was wearing a ragged flannel shirt and jeans torn at the knees. His black eyes were rimmed with red. Six months ago, Ellie would have been tempted to step back in the elevator with him. Now, she just wanted to run and hide.

"Hey," he said. "Haven't seen you in a while."

"Yeah. Been pretty busy. You know how it is." She rocked from one foot to the other, anxious to get to her desk and away from Jesse and away from her past.

"Yeah, I heard about the dead kid. Something, ain't it?"

She nodded in a jerky motion. "Yeah. It's ah…really something."

He smiled slightly. "Well, good luck with it."

"Yeah. Thanks. Look, uh, I've got to get. You know, got to check in then get back up to the hospital."

"Yeah." He bobbed his head up and down. "Well, good seeing you again. I'll see you around." He stepped into the elevator, and Ellie didn't wait for the doors to close. She was already at her desk by the time the elevator and Jesse disappeared.

See you around, yeah right. That's what he said the

morning he stumbled out of her house. Jerk. If he just wasn't so good looking. And charming. And man, he had a smile that could light up a room! *Jerk*. She didn't know if she was mad at him, or angry with herself for having been so weak. She still was. It was a constant struggle. The memories of her father's sermons were fading like an old photograph.

The Criminal Investigation Department was located in the south-side corner of the fifth floor, lackluster in appearance and cluttered with too many desks jammed into too small of an area. Half of the CID's designated real estate was occupied by a seldom-used conference room big enough to hold a United Nations meeting. The room was designed for detectives to use as an interview room, but Ellie often wondered who the builder thought they were supposed to be interviewing in a room that size. An entire football team? Jack's hole-in-the-wall was at the back of the office area, which consisted of eight desks, separated into two rows. The four lining the outside wall were blessed with a window overlooking the drab parking lot while the other four, including Ellie's, were pushed against the inside wall. A fake ficus tree that shimmered with dust was the lone decoration.

Ellie removed the ladybug picture from her pocket and pinned it to the corkboard on the wall beside her desk. Five investigators were at their desks, on the phone, transcribing notes into the computer, or, in Mike Allistar's case, surfing the Internet.

"Heard about the dead kid," Chip Craven said. He stopped typing and referred to his scribbled notes. "Anything new?" He resumed his pecking at the keyboard.

"They did a bunch of tests this morning. It'll be

awhile before we get the results, though."

"Anyone mention testing Leon?" He looked at Ellie and half grinned.

"I thought about that, but...I mean, certainly he wouldn't while he's on duty, would he?"

Both Craven and Allistar burst out laughing. Craven shook his head, still laughing. "Did the room smell like rose air freshener?"

Ellie closed her eyes and massaged her forehead with her fingertips. "Really? I thought he used it to cover the smell of the chemicals."

Craven's laugh finally settled into a crusty cough. "Run a drug test on Leon. It could explain a lot."

Ellie fell into her chair and shook her head. Even if the kid's "rebirth" could be explained by Leon's high, it didn't explain who nearly beat the kid to death. She powered up her computer then checked her voicemail. She had three messages: one from Mrs. Hilda Thompson, a B & E victim with additional information; one from her dentist reminding her of a three o'clock appointment; and one from her dad.

He'd called her at work? She erased the message, grabbed her mug with the Burkesboro PD emblem and headed for the coffee pot.

Why was her dad calling her at work? Why was he calling her at home, for that matter? She hadn't talked to him since Christmas, and that was fine with her. The conversation had been brief and strained as usual.

"Merry Christmas to you, too, Dad. No, I can't make it home. I'm tied up at work. Tell Aunt Sissy I said hello. I've got to go now, but I'll call later."

She never did. She spent Christmas day in her little drafty house watching a light snow brush the ground then watched *It's a Wonderful Life* and cried herself to sleep.

Ellie set her coffee on her desk then pulled the missing persons binder from the department bookshelf. She carried it back to her desk and called Hilda Thompson.

"I've been making a list of other things that's come up missing, just like you told me to do," Hilda said, her voice creaky with age. "I can't find my remote. You think they took it when they took the TV?"

Ellie took a sip of coffee. "It's possible, but not likely. They'd probably have no use for a remote and besides, most televisions now days work with those universal remotes."

"So you're not going to add it to the list?"

"I'll add it, Mrs. Thompson, but in the meantime you continue to look around the house for it, OK? Call me if you find it." Ellie wished her a good day then told the woman goodbye and hung up.

"Ten dollars says it's underneath the couch," Allistar said. His beak-like nose was buried deep in NASCAR collectibles offered on an online auction site.

"I found mine one time in the john. Who takes the remote to the john?" Craven spit out a laugh then coughed again.

Ellie flipped open the binder and turned to the children's section. There were only two in Burkesboro: a twelve year-old Hispanic runaway, and a little red-headed girl abducted by her father. The Feds had taken over the abduction.

She picked up the phone and dialed the Tolson County Sheriff's Department's Detective Division.

Carson Fink answered. He rattled off a string of pleasantries and invited Ellie to go skiing with him at Beech Mountain next weekend.

She politely declined. In part, because he was married, and she did have standards, and also because his breath smelled worse than goat cheese. "Hey — we've got a kid, no ID, found in an alley. You have any reports of missing children around the area?"

"None in Tolson, but I think Avery County's got one. Got the bulletin yesterday."

Ellie's ears perked up. "Male or female?"

"Male I think. Hold on a sec and let me go pull the bulletin." He returned a moment later and read the description. "Eight-year-old male. Fifty pounds. Blond, blue. Went missing from the Mountain View community two days ago."

Ellie's breath caught in her throat. "Does it have a picture?"

"Yeah. It's a photo copy so it's kinda grainy."

Ellie's mind raced with a thousand questions. "What's he wearing?"

There was hesitation on the line then Fink finally answered. "Ummm — it's hard to tell. I can't say for sure."

"OK, never mind. Can you fax me the bulletin?"

"Sure. No problem. I can't believe y'all didn't receive it in the first place."

Ellie rolled her eyes, willing to bet it was lying in a heap of other unread faxes at the machine. When it came to faxes, every man, or woman, was on their own. "Why wasn't an Amber Alert issued?"

"I don't know. You'll have to check with Avery County on that."

Ellie thanked Fink, hung up and raced over to the fax machine. She didn't know whether she was going to shoot herself or jump for joy if the fax was there, if it had been lying there the whole time. And what if the missing Avery County kid was her Johnny Doe? Could she get that lucky?

She separated the faxes and found the bulletin near the bottom of the pile. Fink was right. The picture was really grainy. She stared at it, brought it closer to her face, held it at arm's length, but in the end didn't think it was him. Her heart sank to her toes as she let out a long, slow breath.

She carried the bulletin back to her desk and continued to stare at it, willing her eyes to see something she didn't think was there.

Craven peered over her shoulder. "Is that him?"

Ellie shook her head. "I can't tell from the picture. The description matches, though. You can't tell me this is the best picture the parents have of their child."

"Probably has older siblings," Craven said. "You know, the second-child syndrome. There's never as many pictures of the second kid as there is of the first."

Ellie continued to stare at the picture and sighed. "There still should be a better picture."

"Get Avery to email you the original."

She was just about to pick up the phone when Jack came sprinting by on his way to his office. "Ellie—my office. And bring a picture of the kid."

He was already behind his desk and comfortable in his chair by the time she got in there. "I've got a lead from Avery County. I was—"

"Chief wants it on the news." He held his hand out for the photo.

Ellie handed it over, sighed, and plopped into the chair in front of Jack's desk. "Can we wait until I check on this Avery County lead? It could pan out, and we wouldn't have to notify anyone of anything." She was hoping. Her experience with the media had been a long time ago. She was a kid at the time, and the lights and microphones and probing questions had left a scar she couldn't gloss over. The exposure, the humiliation had driven her mother to….

Johnny Doe had the potential to be a major headline, and Ellie was already dreading it. "Can't we wait until tomorrow?" she asked softly.

Jack slowly shook his head. "The sooner we get it out there, the sooner we can find out who he belongs to. He wants it on the noon news."

"But I've got a good lead. We could wrap it up this afternoon."

"*If* it pans out. And whether it does or not, we've still got a major investigation on our hands, Ellie. That little boy was beaten and left for dead."

She wanted to correct him and say that little boy *was* dead. He was as dead as dead is.

Ellie's stomach churned until bile burned her throat. "Jack, the whole Lazarus thing. The media's going to have a feeding frenzy."

"The Lazarus angle may actually help us. Whoever beat that kid, left him for dead. If they hear the kid survived, they may panic thinking the kid can tell us something. There'll be some movement somewhere." He leaned back in the chair and rested his hands behind his head. "What'd you find out this morning?"

"Deveraux's got a child psychologist coming in this afternoon." She filled him in on the Avery County lead and threw in a gripe about the faxes piling up.

Jack nodded and Ellie knew it was more an acknowledgment of the possible lead than the fax situation. Nothing would change there. "Keep me posted on Avery County, and in the meantime, get his picture to the National Center for Missing and Exploited Children."

Ellie's eyes widened. "You want to go national? If the national media picks this up, it'll be a nightmare, Jack." Her voice rose as high as her brows were raised.

"You'll look good on Oprah. Now get outta here and get over to the alley where he was found. There has to be someone who saw something."

Ellie rose and started out then stopped. "Why would an agency not post an Amber Alert for a missing kid?"

Jack shrugged. "Different reasons, I suppose. Could be they suspect foul play right off the bat and have a person of interest nearby."

Foul play. There was definitely foul play involved with her little Johnny Doe. She wasn't sure about the poor kid in Avery County. Could they really be one and the same?

****

The alley where Johnny Doe was found was a narrow cut-through between a dilapidated wholesale fish market and a dive called Marisol's that reeked worse than the fish place. On the other side of the fish market was an abandoned three-story building, its front door and windows boarded up. The alley was littered with grease-stained food wrappers and used hypodermics and smelled of urine, courtesy of the drunks stumbling out of Marisol's. The area was mostly industrial with a few small office buildings housing questionable small-time insurance agents and smaller-time lawyers who paid the rent with fees from petty crooks and frivolous lawsuits. It was a forgotten area, a blip on the Burkesboro planning map that had been continually overlooked each budget year when the city doled out funding for what they liked to call *economic development*.

The sleazy insurance agents and small-time lawyers didn't care; their clients felt at home among the muck and stink.

Ellie parked in front of the fish place. She gathered her notepad and the photos of Johnny Doe. The wind whipped up the stench and dropped the temperature ten degrees. Ellie buttoned her blazer and hurried inside, anxious to escape both.

"Hello?" She yelled into the seemingly empty warehouse.

"Be right there," a slight voice yelled from the back of the building.

The dull metal coolers against the walls were the length of coffins and lined end to end. Condensation gathered along their outsides and dropped splatters of water on the concrete floor. A cheap partition near the back separated a small office from the dead fish. A tiny man wearing a blaze orange jumpsuit and a toboggan with fluffy fur surrounding his prune-like face emerged from behind the partition. He removed a fat glove and offered his hand to Ellie.

"Shorty McCorkle. What can I do for you?" He stared at Ellie and sniffled against the cold.

His firm handshake made up for the slight size of his hand. "Detective Ellie Saunders, Burkesboro PD."

He eyed her up and down then nodded approvingly. "Cops sure didn't look like you back in my days." He chuckled, and it was a mouse-like sound.

Ellie slightly smiled. "Are you the owner?"

"Owner, marketing manager, and chief bottle washer. That's me." He put the glove back on his wrinkled hand then pushed a clump of toboggan fur from in front of his face.

"A small child was found Tuesday night in the alley, and I'd like to ask you a couple of questions."

"Yeah, I heard about that. Dwayne said he thought the kid was dead."

"Dwayne?" Ellie took out her pen and opened her notepad.

"Dwayne Andrews. Comes in around three. Helps me out a little."

"So you weren't here when the child was found?"

McCorkle shook his head, and the fur swished back and forth. "Left about five to grab a burger."

"Did you return at any time that day?"

He shook his head again. "Dwayne closed up about eight. Called me when he got home to tell me all about it. He's a bit of a gossip, you know—loves drama. Gets real excited when he sees blue lights." He chuckled then sniffled again.

"Is Dwayne working this afternoon?"

"As far as I know. He should be in around three if you want to check back."

Ellie nodded and said she would. She showed McCorkle one of the pictures of Johnny Doe, one where he was sitting on the gray metal desk in Leon's office, smiling and full of life. "Have you ever seen him around here?"

McCorkle studied the picture then shook his head. "Nope. Cute kid. So he wasn't dead?"

Ellie didn't quite know how to answer. "Obviously not."

McCorkle looked as confused as Ellie had been

feeling since discovering Johnny Doe. He pushed fur out of his eyes and frowned.

"Did you see or hear anything out of the ordinary Tuesday?"

McCorkle pursed his lips as though he was in deep concentration then shook his head.

"What about your customers? Did you have many come in on Tuesday?"

He laughed then sniffled again. "I can count on one hand. Mostly regulars, two or three new ones looking for trout. Made me wonder what was up with the trout, you know? I mean three in one day, what's up with that? Something you might want to look into." He blinked away a stray piece of fur.

"Do you have a log of customers? Credit card receipts perhaps?"

"Yeah, sure. They're back here in the office."

Ellie followed him to the back where McCorkle ducked behind the partitioned wall. A cheap wooden desk was littered with various generic store-bought inventory sheets and sales receipts. McCorkle thumbed through a scattered pile of papers then handed them to Ellie. "I haven't posted those yet so you can't take them with you but I can make you copies."

"If it wouldn't be too much trouble that would be helpful."

He removed his gloves then powered up an ancient copier that sounded more like a lawn tractor than an office machine. McCorkle blew a breath into his balled fists while he waited for the copier to awake from its hibernation.

Ellie scanned through the receipts, studying one in particular, a delivery receipt from an outfit near Boone. "What about this delivery? Are they local?"

McCorkle glanced at the receipt. "Bekley's? Naw, they're not from around here. Up around Avery County I think."

Ellie raised a brow and stared at McCorkle. "Been dealing with them long?"

He shrugged. "Couple years. Home office is down along the Mississippi. They bring up most of my gulf water fish."

She looked over the receipt for a delivery driver's name. When she didn't find one, she asked.

"It was a new guy. I didn't catch his name. Big fella."

To McCorkle, that could be anyone over five-foot-six. Ellie handed him the receipts and waited for the copies. McCorkle stuffed them in the machine then punched a button. He blew air into his hands again while they waited.

Afterward, Ellie put the copies in the car then headed into Marisol's. The walls were dark-paneled with lopsided dart boards hanging on for dear life every few feet. The numbers around the circles were worn and unreadable, some punctuated with holes big enough to drive a truck through. Green-covered lights hung from the low ceiling and cast an eerie glow over the few scattered tables and wooden bar that had lost its sheen a long time ago.

A woman with a masculine haircut and biceps bigger than McCorkle's body was stocking bottles of whiskey behind the bar. "Can I help you?" she asked, eyeing Ellie suspiciously.

Ellie navigated around discarded peanut hulls and sticky-looking liquid spotting the floor and approached the bar. "Ellie Saunders, Burkesboro PD." She offered her hand but the woman stared at it as if it were spurting blood.

She continued with her restocking. "We don't want any trouble."

"And I'm not here to offer any. A little boy was found in the alley Tuesday night, and I'd like to ask you a couple questions if that's OK."

The woman put up the last bottle of liquor then busied herself wiping down the bar. Ellie held the picture of Johnny Doe in front of the woman. The woman squinted against the dim light for a better look then shook her head. "We don't get too many kids around here. It's not exactly a family-friendly neighborhood."

"Were you working Tuesday night?"

The woman continued wiping away at the bar, removing spots apparently only she could see. "Yeah, I was here. I'm here all the time."

"And your name is?"

The woman eyed Ellie then after a moment offered her name. "Marisol Bowman."

Ellie jotted down the name. "Did you see or hear anything out of the ordinary?"

Marisol snickered. "Honey, ain't anything around here *normal*. It's a full-time job just keeping some of these yokels straight. Know what I mean?"

"Some of the clientele's a little rough around the edges?"

She laughed then shook her head. "A little rough? They make longshoremen look like sissies."

"Think any of them are capable of —"

"Hurting a kid?" She shook her head again, thin lips drawn together tight. "They're a bunch of brutes but hurting a kid...naw. Kids, dogs, and mommas are off limits."

"The 911 call came in around six from a pre-paid cell phone registered to...." She referred to her notes, raised her eyebrow then sighed. "It was registered to a *Mickey Mouse*." Of course the name was bogus, so she hadn't made any effort to remember it.

Marisol grinned. "Mickey. He's a regular. He'll be in later if you want to talk to him."

Ellie stared at her. She couldn't be serious. "Mickey Mouse?"

"His name's Mickey Makowski."

Ellie had interviewed several gawkers standing around that night, but no one saw anything, heard anything, or knew anything, and no one owned up to having placed the 911 call. She'd bet money Mickey was standing in the crowd, probably one of the gawkers who hadn't seen or heard anything, either. "What time does Mickey usually roll in?"

"Three thirty, four."

"What time did he leave that night?"

She shrugged. "He was here at last call so that was around midnight."

"And he didn't say anything about finding a kid in the alley? Seems like that would be a topic of conversation."

Marisol shook her head. "You've got to know Mickey. Been coming here five years, and we ain't figured out if he's a genius or just plain stupid."

Wonderful. So far, the only witness was either a freaking genius or an idiot. Ellie handed Marisol a contact card and asked her to call if she heard of anything.

As she was leaving, Marisol called out. "Hey, the kid—was he dead?"

Ellie gnawed on her bottom lip a moment then

finally answered. "He was pretty close."

Marisol slowly shook her head. "What a shame."

Ellie nodded her agreement. "Yeah."

She spent the rest of the morning hoofing it between grungy insurance salesmen and pudgy lawyers wearing cheap ties and cheaper shoes. No one saw anything. No one heard anything, and no one knew anything. An insurance salesman, Stan Kellum, said he saw the blue lights and the ambulance and figured there had been a pretty good bar fight and didn't want to get involved. One of the lawyers, a bulky guy named Alvin B. Kepler, III, said his last client, a girl with a habit of writing bad checks, left around three then he closed up shop and headed to the gym. Guy's got to keep in shape, you know. Wink, wink.

Around eleven, Ellie headed back to the office. She had one more stop to make and turned into the Market Street Plaza. She found a spot in front of Wal-Mart, went in, and headed straight for the clothing department. She couldn't decide between the blue, red, or black, so she grabbed all three and marched to the checkout line.

The cashier grinned as she scanned the items. "Guess your little guy likes Spiderman, huh?"

Ellie smiled.

5

Ellie rushed up the stairs, stretching her limit to four flights, and hurried to her desk. Partly because she was anxious to check her email and partly because she was ready to collapse. She thought of Alfred B. Kepler, III—the pudgy lawyer—and willed her legs to stop throbbing and her heart to slow to a normal rate.

The message light on her phone was blinking red. She punched in her passcode and listened. She had five messages, and four of them were from Detective Brady Mitchell with the Avery County Sheriff's Department; the fifth was from her father again. She deleted the messages and clicked open her email. Her heart raced when she saw a file with attachment from Avery County. She downloaded the file then clicked it open, her breath backing up in her lungs. "Please let it be him," she whispered as the pixels danced across the screen until they united to form a picture. She let out her breath and stared at the screen.

The quality still wasn't great. It was still grainy and had been taken from an odd angle, making it difficult to get a good look at the kid's face. She honestly didn't know if it was him or not. Deep in her heart, she didn't think it was, but there was too much similarity to not pursue it.

She picked up the phone and called the Avery County Sheriff's Department. "Detective Brady Mitchell, please."

After a moment, Mitchell answered.

"Brady—it's Ellie Saunders, Burkesboro PD."

"Man, you're hard to track down. Burkesboro too cheap for cell phones? Did you get the picture?"

"Yes, and thanks for sending it. It's still pretty hard to tell if it's the same kid."

"Yeah, it's a crappy picture. It was the only one they had, though."

Ellie held the hospital's photo up to the computer screen to compare them side-by-side. "You mean this was the only picture these parents had of the kid in the whole entire house?"

Brady grumbled. "They had some baby pictures, but none recent. Has your kid got any birthmarks? Scars? Anything like that?"

"He has a birthmark on his upper left back, triangle-shaped, right above the shoulder blade. About two inches in length."

Mitchell let out a long slow breath. "Our kid has a triangle-shaped mark on his *right* upper back." Disappointment registered in his voice.

"That's too much of a coincidence to not pursue. And, oh yeah, I canvassed the neighborhood where he was found this morning, and one of the businesses received a truck delivery yesterday from Avery County. Maybe your kid was a stowaway, or kidnapped, or killed there and transported here?"

"The kid's dead?"

Ellie bit down on her bottom lip. It was hard enough for her to understand; explaining it was even more difficult. "Not exactly."

There was a deafening pause on the line. Mitchell cleared his throat. "Either he's dead or he's not. There's not much in between."

Ellie resigned herself to the truth. She might as well get used to trying to explain it. "He was pronounced dead at the scene and at the hospital but somehow...recovered." Yeah. That was a good word. *Recovered.*

There was a long pause again then Mitchell finally responded. "The kid came back to life?" His voice raised a whole octave. "How long was he dead?"

Ellie cleared her throat. "A couple hours." She was anxious to move on to the similarities between Mitchell's missing kid and her Johnny Doe. "Can you arrange for the parents to come up and take a look?"

"Yeah, sure." They arranged to meet at the hospital at three o'clock. Ellie was about to hang up when Mitchell asked, "What was the name of the company that made the delivery? I'll check it out before heading your way."

Ellie referred to her notes. "Bekley's Wholesale Seafood. I don't have the name of the driver. He was a new guy."

There was silence on Mitchell's end of the line. After a long moment, he spoke. "Hmm. Interesting."

"Interesting how?"

"The dad of my missing kid works for Bekley's."

Ellie's breath backed up in her lungs. She glanced at the clock; it was 11:45. She told Mitchell goodbye then headed straight for Jack's office. "OK, the lead from Avery County is looking really good." She spit the words out, battling a time-clock and an overzealous Chief of Police.

Jack stared at her as she rattled off the new developments, obviously not as impressed with the similarities in the two cases as she was.

"So, what do you think?" She sat on the edge of

54

the chair in front of his desk, her hands gripping the side arms, ready to spring into action. "Are you going to call the chief? Maybe he could hold off until the six o'clock news? I mean—this *is* a pretty good lead, right?"

Jack continued staring at her. After a long moment, he leaned up, folded his arms and rested them on his desk. "Why are you so afraid of the press? They *can* help us in situations like this, you know."

"I'm not afraid of the press." She lied. She sat back in the chair and sighed. "It's just I don't see a need in plastering the poor kid's face all over the news when we might be able to wrap this whole thing up this afternoon."

"You're afraid of the press. You were terrified when they interviewed you about the Smithfield robbery, and you're terrified now."

"I'm a private person, Jack. I'm not comfortable in the spotlight."

Jack laughed. "*You* won't be in the spotlight. You won't be the focus of their story; the kid will."

She knew what *that* was like and wouldn't wish it on any child. "Don't you feel an obligation to protect him? To shield him from this circus?"

"What circus? All we're trying to do is find out who the kid belongs to and what happened to him. Like it or not, we need the public's help for that. You're just going to have to suck it up and get used to it."

He dug the remote from under a case file and clicked on the small television perched on a bookshelf in the corner. He turned the channel to the twelve o'clock news and punched up the volume.

Kristen Conrad stared into the camera from behind the anchor desk, her face expressionless.

"Burkesboro police have a highly unusual case on their hands. A little boy found Tuesday was pronounced dead on arrival...."

And so it begins, Ellie thought as she tuned out Kristen Conrad. Ellie stared at the picture over Conrad's left shoulder. There was little Johnny Doe, sapphire eyes and bright smile, staring back at Ellie.

6

Ellie could hear the clatter of dishes and yelling before she walked in Caper's Deli. If one wanted a quiet lunch, Caper's wasn't the place to go. Jedimiah Caper was a barrel of a man who roared food orders like a drill sergeant while the cooks and waitresses slung dishes like they were Frisbees. The place was usually packed, and customers wanting conversation resorted to yelling at one another so they could hear over the racket.

She found an empty stool at the counter and squeezed herself between a city fireman and a guy in an expensive business suit. She ordered her usual: a ham and turkey club with spicy mustard, no mayo, an extra pickle, and a large sweet tea.

Jack was wrong. She wasn't afraid of the press. She was terrified. It was a long time ago but she remembered the cameras and the lights and the microphones jammed in their faces like it was yesterday. To an eleven-year-old, seeing hordes of strangers camped out on your front yard left its mark. Seeing vans with flashy logos and satellite antennae that disappeared high into the night parked end to end in front of the place you called home was as disturbing as a nightmare that left you afraid to close your eyes. It was a nightmare she couldn't wake up from. A nightmare that led her mother to disappear into the fortress of her bathroom and chop away at her hair with a straight razor before slicing her wrists open.

Ellie sipped on her tea while she waited for her sandwich, replaying the scene over and over again in her mind as she had done countless times before. The blood, her father's wailing screams, the sirens, and the throngs of reporters already in place moving into action like a disjointed army.

"Hey. I've been thinking about your dead kid and—"

"What?" Ellie stared at Jesse Alvarez as he wedged himself between her and the fireman.

"I've been thinking about your dead kid," he shouted.

The fireman turned and shot him a questionable look. Ellie massaged her forehead with the tips of her fingers and slightly smiled. "Burkesboro PD," she mouthed to the fireman.

He stared at them a moment then went back to his burger.

"What are you doing here?"

"Jack told me you were at lunch. Caper's is one of my favorites, so I thought I'd take a chance." He winked at her then sidled closer. "Anyway, I was thinking about your dead kid—"

"He's not dead."

A waitress slammed a sandwich down in front of Ellie, and Jesse helped himself to a homemade chip.

"OK, so he's not dead. You have sent his picture to the National Center for Missing and Exploited Children?"

She huffed. "Did Jack send you?"

"No, Jack didn't send me. I was just thinking if the center didn't get a hit, I've got a few connections with the FBI, and they've got some really cool equipment."

Ellie pulled a piece of bacon from her sandwich and chewed on one end. "Thanks, but no thanks. I really don't want the Feds involved."

Jesse snatched another chip and shook his head. "No black suit with shades is going to swoop in and take your case, Detective Saunders." He grinned and helped himself to another chip. "I thought we could get them to run his picture through the facial recognition scanner. Maybe we'll get a hit."

What was with all the *we* stuff? The case was complicated enough. The last thing she needed was Jesse involved. She didn't need a constant reminder of her downward spiral.

"So what do you think? You want to give it a try?" he asked.

Ellie sighed. "We're going to get a hit on every kid with blond hair and blue eyes. Do you know how many kids have blond hair and blue eyes?"

"No, sweetheart. That's not how it works. There has to be something like a ninety-eight percent match in characteristics. It's real technical. It measures the size of the nose, the distance between the eyes, stuff like that. It's used a lot with missing persons."

Ellie took a bite of her sandwich then grabbed a chip before they disappeared. "I know what a facial recognition scanner is, Alvarez."

Jesse rolled his eyes and snagged another chip. "Touchy. Sorry if I insulted your intelligence. But look, if the kid's been reported missing, he's somewhere in the system."

Ellie took a sip of tea and considered what Jesse was saying. "But what if he's not in the system?"

"He has to be. I mean, he's a missing kid. People usually report missing kids. Although I do have a couple little maverick nephews I'm not sure their parents would report." He burst out laughing, and Ellie remembered why she let him come home with her that night.

Jesse was just grungy enough to make a woman swoon without making her wonder if he ever bathed, and he was soft enough to make you want to mother him. He was someone she wouldn't have minded getting closer to, if she hadn't fallen in bed with him. How can you want to see someone again when you can't look them in the eye.

"Earth to Ellie. It'd be worth a shot, don't you think?"

She pushed her remorse and the thoughts of what could have been from her mind and sighed. "Of course it would. But like I said, I don't really want the Feds involved."

"They're probably going to get involved anyway. Especially if it turns out to be a multi-jurisdictional kidnapping. But for now, we won't worry about that. All we're asking them to do is simply run a scan."

When had Jesse been assigned to this case? Last she heard he was pretending to smoke dope with hookers.

"Look," he said as he finished off her chips, "all the scan is going to do is give us a possible lead on his identity. It ain't going to tell you who beat the crap out of him. But once you know who he is and where he came from, you can start narrowing down the how and why. Know what I mean?"

"Is there a cost involved?"

"For you dear, my services are free."

Ellie couldn't help but laugh. She shook her head. "I meant is there going to be a cost involved to the department. If so, Jack will have to approve it. Unlike *vice*, we don't walk around with wads of department cash in our pockets."

"No cost. I got connections, baby." He winked and she laughed again.

Ellie stared at him a moment wondering about those connections. She shook her head then finished off her tea and picked up her ticket. "Why are you so interested in this case? Shouldn't you be hanging out with dope dealers?"

He shrugged. He watched Jedimiah Caper bark orders to the kitchen while punching numbers into the register at marathon speed. "I was reassigned."

"To this case? Why would vice work this case?"

"I haven't been in vice for a month now. Guess you didn't get the memo."

If there were such a memo, it was probably lying with the stack of unread faxes.

"They started up a new unit and thought I'd be perfect for it. The pervert beat." He shrugged again.

Ellie chuckled. "You're working sex crimes?"

Jesse sighed and rolled his eyes. "Pedophiles in particular. Lovely job. Meet you back at the office."

****

Ellie left Caper's and swung by the hospital. She headed straight for the pediatric floor with her bag of little boy clothes, all decorated with spiders and webs. If he was going to be in the hospital for a while, there was no need in him having to wear those silly little hospital gowns, and there was nothing more comfortable than a good pair of sweats.

She found Deveraux outside Johnny Doe's room

with his nose stuck in a report of some kind. The door to the room was partially closed.

"Hey. How is he?"

Deveraux looked up and smiled. "Good. He's doing very well. They're taking some tissue samples." He bobbed his head toward Johnny Doe's room.

Ellie's eyes widened. "Tissue samples? That sounds painful."

Deveraux shook his head and that comforting smile spread gently across his face. "It's not. Just a skin scrape, really."

Ellie let out her breath and relaxed. Although Johnny Doe appeared to be in perfect health and seemed to be suffering no pain, she couldn't shake the images of his tiny beaten body in that alley. He suffered pain then, and she would do everything in her power to prevent him from suffering more.

"We have some parents coming in this afternoon to take a look at him," Ellie said.

"So, you've got a lead?"

She shrugged. "I'm trying not to get my hopes up."

He smiled that brilliant smile. "Sometimes hope's all we've got."

Ellie grinned. "I'm not real good with hope."

He nodded, understanding. "It would probably be best if they observed him in the playroom. It's one-way glass. They can see him but he won't be able to see them."

"I'd like to gauge his reaction, though. Even if it turns out they are his parents, there's a lot of explaining to do."

Deveraux nodded again. "I understand. If they make a positive identification, then we'll invite them to join him in the playroom. A parade of prospective parents could traumatize him. Especially if the parents have questionable intentions."

Ellie thought about the parents coming up from Avery County. No Amber Alert. No decent picture in the house. Thin shorts and an even thinner t-shirt. There was snow on the ground for goodness sake.

"I don't want him traumatized any more than he already is." She pulled one of the sweatshirts out of the bag and held it up for Deveraux's approval. "He can wear these, can't he? Maybe I should have asked first, but, I just thought he'd be more comfortable."

Deveraux smiled. "I'll make sure he gets them."

Ellie handed him the bag and nodded. "He likes Spiderman. He told me that down in the morgue when I spoke with him earlier this morning. He told me he liked Spiderman. I'm an Ironman girl myself. I mean, not that I really enjoy any of that…" She chewed on her bottom lip like a nervous school girl. "I need to get down to the basement to pick up some security tapes. I'll see you around three."

Deveraux grinned. Ellie figured he was used to women blabbering like idiots in his presence. She felt the heat rise to her face and knew her cheeks were blood red. She took a step or two backwards hoping to put some distance between them. Maybe from a distance, the glow of her cheeks wouldn't be as obvious.

She smiled through her embarrassment and slowly backed away then walked quickly to the elevator. She tapped her foot impatiently while she waited, afraid to glance back down the hall. Deveraux was probably staring at her wondering what planet she fell off of. Where was that elevator? There were only six floors in this hospital—it couldn't take that long to call it to a floor. Finally, the doors opened and Ellie rushed in, leaning hard against the back wall.

The hospital's security room was at the opposite end of the basement from the morgue, which Ellie was glad for. She didn't want to run into Leon. Her back was still aching from the dancing dip.

She rang the bell, expecting the Great Oz himself to peer through the peephole. The small window slid to the side and she showed her badge and smiled. The door opened and a stocky man in a blue uniform ushered her into the room. He had a seriously thin mustache that looked out of proportion on his seriously fat face. He waddled over to a bay of color monitors and sat in a cheap office chair on wheels. Half a million dollars' worth of security equipment and the hospital sticks the poor guy with a twenty-nine-dollar chair.

Images of every entrance and exit into and out of the hospital, every elevator, every floor, and the door to the morgue glowed across the bay in living time and in living color. Burkesboro Regional Hospital had a better security system than the county jail.

"I pulled tapes from every camera for the last ten days. They're date, time, and camera stamped so I made you a reference copy of the camera locations. If you find something, just note the camera stamp on the tape then cross reference that to the sheet." He spoke in a high, nasally voice.

He picked up a list and pointed to one of the numbers. "See—your reference sheet refers to camera fourteen. You follow along here, and you'll see camera fourteen is in the east wing, fifth floor." He pointed to the camera fourteen monitor.

Ellie glanced at the monitor and her heart stopped. Her hand flew to her mouth as she leaned in for a closer look. She stared at Aunt Sissy leaning against the wall outside a patient room, one foot pulled up and propped against the wall. There was no doubt it was Aunt Sissy. She was wearing a flannel shirt with quilted lining over a t-shirt, jeans, and hiking boots—her 'uniform' as she called it. "What floor is that?" Ellie asked.

"I just said it was the fifth floor."

"No, I mean *what* floor? Cardio, ortho?"

"That's the oncology floor. Cancer." He made a tsk-tsk sound and shook his head.

Ellie grabbed the box of tapes and hurried out. Sissy didn't look like a patient, so why was she here? It had to be Ellie's father. She thought of all the messages he had left over the last few weeks, messages she had ignored.

She rushed to the elevator, waited forever for it to drop to the basement then hurriedly punched the button for the fifth floor. "Come on, come on...." she said as the carriage slowly rose.

When it settled into a stop, Ellie burst through the door, found the sign pointing out the east wing and hurried in that direction. The wing's entrance was decorated with pictures of smiling faces and bald heads. Their darkened eyes held the slightest hint of a sparkle. Above the pictures was a colorful banner proclaiming it as the "Wall of Fame," below the banner, a cartoon picture of a bruised and battered prize fighter with gloved hands raised in the air victoriously and the words "I beat cancer" written in a balloon hanging in cartoon space beside his head.

Ellie glanced down one empty hallway. She

turned and headed down the second hallway, and there was Aunt Sissy, still propped against the wall.

"Aunt Sissy…" Ellie bolted down the hallway toward her aunt.

Sissy met her with a long embrace then stepped back and ran a hand over Ellie's hair. "Hey, sweetie. Your daddy's going to be so happy you came." Her smile was as warm as ever.

Sissy carried her seventy years well and had only over the last few years begun to show a wrinkle. She lived alone in a log cabin overlooking a stream where she fished daily for trout and bream. She chopped her own firewood and could handle a hammer and nail as well as a trained carpenter. She had her share of suitors but had never married, saying she wanted to be madly in love with her husband and had yet to find anyone who "tripped her trigger."

"Guess you got your daddy's messages?"

Ellie nodded, ashamed to admit she hadn't actually listened to any of them. "How bad is it?"

Sissy shrugged her shoulders then shook her head. "We thought they had got it all during the surgery, but it looks like it spread."

"When was the surgery?"

"Right after Christmas. Your daddy thought you'd be home, so he wanted to tell you then."

Yeah, and Merry Christmas to you, too. Ellie picked at a phantom cuticle, embarrassed to look at Sissy. "Can they operate again? Maybe they can get it all if they operate again."

Sissy stroked Ellie's hair. "They can't sweetie. It's spread too far. All they can do is make her comfortable."

Ellie pulled away from her and stared at Sissy.

"*Her*? As in Peggy?"

Sissy cocked her head to the side and scowled at Ellie. "You didn't listen to the messages, did you?"

"I was going to call him back. It's just I've been real busy. You know, with work."

Sissy eyed her suspiciously. "Uh-huh."

Ellie dodged the penetrating stare by glancing at the ceiling, at the nurses' station, anywhere but at Sissy.

After a moment, Sissy dismissed the lie with a wave of her hand. "Well, anyway, Peggy is very sick, and your daddy could use your support right now."

Ellie scratched at her neck, still avoiding Sissy's glaring eyes. "I don't know, Aunt Sissy."

"Regardless of the past, she is his wife, and he loves her very much. You need to get over whatever problems you have with her and be there for him."

"She killed my mother."

Sissy rolled her eyes. "You do have a flair for the dramatic, don't you, kid?"

Ellie shifted the box of tapes to her hip; they were growing heavier by the minute. "I really do need to get back to the office, but I've got to come back later this afternoon. Tell Daddy I'll try to see him then."

Sissy slowly nodded, a hint of suspicion still burning in her eyes.

Ellie sighed. "She's not going to die like within the next hour, is she?"

"You should get so lucky." She shook her head. "No, it may be days; it could be another month."

"Then tell Daddy I'll see him later today." She gave Sissy a kiss on the cheek then hurried to the elevators.

The oncology floor was on the east wing of the

hospital, and the ER, where she always parked, was on the west. She took the central elevator, figuring it would cut down on her time traipsing through hallways, but when the central elevator doors opened in the main lobby, she wished she hadn't taken any elevator at all.

The lobby was packed with reporters and cameras and blow-dried evening news anchors clamoring over one another at the main desk. She recognized a few of them from the local network affiliates and a couple from local papers. A wave of sheer panic hit her like a sledgehammer while hot-burning bile churned deep in her stomach.

"Detective Saunders—" Sara Jeffries from the Burkesboro *Bulletin* pushed her way through the crowd. She pointed a palm-sized digital recorder straight at Ellie as if it were a gun loaded and cocked. "Can you give us an update on Little Lazarus's condition?"

Ellie jammed her shoulder to the wall and rushed down the hallway. Several of the others took their cue from Jeffries and tailed the moving target.

"Are there any leads in the investigation?"

"What was his condition when he was brought in?"

"Will the FBI be called in?"

Ellie felt like little Joey Tansley, a kid she grew up with who fell in a beehive. She remembered the sound of the angry bees as they swarmed around him, engulfing him in a cacophony of pure horror. She remembered seeing him twisting and turning and knocking at the swarm with his tiny fists as he fought to get away.

Sara Jeffries, the queen bee, was now side-by-side

with Ellie, the recorder inches away from her face.

"What steps are you taking to identify the boy?" She took a wide step and planted herself in Ellie's path.

Ellie had to stop or else run over the woman. She took a deep breath to steady her nerves. "I'm not at liberty to answer any questions right now. I'm sure the chief will let you know as soon as any information becomes available. If you'll excuse me, I need to get back to the office." She sidestepped around Jeffries and ducked through a door with a sign that read "Emergency Room Personnel Only."

Her eyes wet with tears, she pressed her back to the door and forced herself to breathe.

7

As far as Ellie was concerned, Peggy had played a part in her mother's death. The woman may not have held the razor, but the blade was laced with the humiliation Peggy had caused. Humiliation, betrayal, ruined public image. They all played a part, and Peggy had been at the root of it all.

Ellie parked beside Jesse's Camaro and lugged the box of tapes up two flights of stairs. She didn't feel up to her standard three and sure didn't feel like pressing for the fourth flight.

Jesse was at her desk, in her chair, on her computer. She dropped the box beside the desk and fell into the other chair.

"I've already emailed the picture," he said, his nose buried in the National Center for Missing and Exploited Children website. "Remind me again why you don't want the center involved?"

She ignored him. "How did you get into my email?"

"Connections." He glanced up at her and raised his brows. "What have you been crying about?"

Ellie quickly wiped at her face. "It's windy outside."

"You're crying because it's windy?"

Ellie huffed then sniffled. "I haven't been crying. How long will it take for the Feds to get back to us?"

Jesse shrugged. "They said they'd call me today."

Me? She wondered if there was a memo back there with all the un-read faxes informing the department Jesse Alvarez was now a part of this investigation. She glanced at the box of tapes, figuring if he was going to continue to involve himself in her case, she might as well use it to her benefit. "Want to take a look at these tapes while you're waiting?"

He glanced over the desk at the box on the floor. "You know the kid's probably between four and six years old, and you've got about twenty years' worth of tapes there. I think we can safely cut out the ones prior to 1998."

Ellie grinned. "Actually, it's only the last ten days. But fourteen cameras."

"Is hospital security a little paranoid?" He rose from her chair at her desk and picked up the box.

"We're particularly interested in the morgue. The last forty-eight hours."

"How do I know which camera's the morgue?"

She dug out the reference sheet and handed it to him. "They're very thorough."

"But they still can't explain how a dead kid's not dead anymore." He smiled and then disappeared into the audio/video room.

Ellie sneaked a peek at herself in a chrome clock on Mike Allistar's desk. Satisfied she could get by with the wind story, she headed into Jack's office.

He was on the phone and motioned for Ellie to sit.

"I agree we need security up there, but I don't think it should come out of CID's budget. The chief's the one that wanted to go public." He glanced at Ellie and rolled his eyes. "Well, see what he says and get back to me. Yeah, OK, I will." He hung up and blew enough air through his nose that Ellie felt the breeze ruffle her hair. "Hospital's wanting extra security."

The weight of her brief encounter with Sara Jeffries drove Ellie deep into the chair. "I swung by there after lunch, and the place was swarming with media."

Jack removed his glasses and massaged his eyes. He picked up a stack of pink phone messages and handed them to Ellie. "Some are requests for interviews; some are people claiming he's their kid."

Ellie's mouth fell open as she skimmed through the pieces of paper. "There must be thirty messages here."

"I'm going to have the tips routed to Mike. He can tell the difference between the crackpots and the legits."

"You know you're going to be cutting into his on-line shopping time."

He almost smiled and leaned back in his chair, folding his hands behind his head. "You know not to release information like what he was wearing and his exact height and weight, right?"

She glared at him, wondering if he reminded all of his investigators of the rules of play before the big game. She doubted it. "Can I refer interview requests to the chief?"

Jack grinned. "You're going to try to weasel out of any contact with the media, aren't you?" He leaned forward, resting his arms on his desk. "Actually, yes. It's a big case, his department. He's going to want the face time on this one."

That was fine with Ellie. She could say "no comment" as well as any seasoned politician. "I'm meeting with the detective and parents from Avery County at the hospital at three. You think we could have security in place by then?"

Jack shook his head. "I doubt it. We're negotiating whose budget it's going to come out of."

"Wonderful."

"Also—you need to keep in mind news times. The chief's going to be wanting updates in time to get it on the different newscasts."

Ellie played it safe and held back the things she wanted to say. "Anything else the chief would like?"

"I'm sure he'll come up with something. Let me know how it goes at the hospital." He slipped his glasses back on, a sure indication he had said all he intended to say.

Ellie got up and started out, but Jack added one more thing.

"You OK working with Alvarez?"

She jerked around and stared at him. "What?"

"Jesse Alvarez. Are you OK working with him?"

Ellie felt the flush spread across her face. Her heart raced with panic. "Sure," she squeaked.

Jack gazed at her over the rims of his glasses. His eyes were narrowed into tiny slits. He finally nodded. "Just checking."

She couldn't get out of his office fast enough, her heart thumping wildly in her chest. How much did he know and how did he know it? To her knowledge, there weren't any policies about dating a co-worker. Again, if there had been an intra-office memo about it, she missed it. It was probably back there in the fax pile. But she wouldn't exactly call their one-night stand a date. She was fairly certain she wouldn't lose her job over it, but how embarrassing if others knew. Especially if one of the others was your boss. Be sure your sins will find you out—how many times had her father preached that message before his sins found him.

Furious, she marched into the AV room and planted herself between Jesse and a monitor, her hands jammed on her hips. He looked around her at the flickering images, paused the machine, then looked up at her. "What's up?"

"What's up is Jack just asked me if I could work with you." She angrily crossed her arms and pulled her mouth into a tight knot. "Why would he ask me that, Jesse?" she asked through clenched teeth.

Jesse opened his mouth to speak, but nothing came out. Instead, his mouth contorted into various wordless shapes. He opened his hands wide, like he was getting ready to explain something but again, said nothing.

"Please, tell me you didn't tell him about..." She couldn't bring herself to say the word "us." They never had been an "us." Besides, he was the one who never called back.

"Using the Feds' scanner? Of course I told him about it. You know, the whole budget thing you mentioned."

Ellie narrowed her eyes and glared at him. "That's all you told him?"

"I told him I thought it could be useful in your investigation." He spoke slowly, like a prisoner carefully gauging his words before divulging too much information. "Was there something I was *supposed* to tell him?"

Ellie wasn't completely sure she believed him. Other than her own guilty conscience and a good dose of paranoia, she had no reason to not believe him. She marched out of the room and headed to the hospital.

On the way, she called Brady Mitchell and arranged to meet them in the Emergency Room. She didn't want to drag the parents through the army of press crowding the main lobby. She realized when she pulled into the parking lot, she'd probably made a mistake.

News vans with colorful logos and satellite antennas jabbing at an overcast sky lined the patient pick-up and drop-off lane. The reporters crowded around the double doors in clusters, their watchful eyes zeroing in on everyone who came or went. Ellie took a deep breath and pushed her way through, motioning for the admitting nurse to buzz her back into the treatment area. Safe behind the electronic door, she stuck her head in the admissions booth. "I'm expecting a detective from Avery County. When he gets here can you page me?"

"He's here. Exam room two."

Ellie nodded, found room two, and peeked behind the curtain. Mitchell was standing beside the examining table while the parents were seated in two metal chairs. "Detective Mitchell?" Ellie pushed the curtain aside and offered the detective her hand. "Detective Saunders."

Mitchell looked about a month shy of his thirty-year mark chasing bad guys. The lines etched deep into his face and gray hair were the tell-tale battle scars of a man who had seen it all. He had a flat face with sagging jowls that reminded Ellie of a bulldog. And she'd bet money he *was* a bulldog.

He introduced the parents as Richard and Tina Chambers. They looked to be in their mid-twenties, teetering on the poverty level, and very tired. There was a difference between numb and tired, and these parents fell into the latter. He was wearing navy work pants with wrinkles as deep as the lines on Mitchell's face and a light blue work shirt with an oil stain on the front tail. "Bekley's Wholesale Seafood" was monogrammed on a white fish sewn onto the upper left chest. His blond hair looked about an inch or two longer than a good buzz cut was supposed to be, creating scattered porcupine-like spikes all over his head.

She wasn't faring much better. Her bleached blonde hair hung straight, falling on her shoulders like dirty mop strings while her face was long and narrow with sunken cheeks void of color. Her amber eyes reflected a perpetual state of confusion, or boredom. She was wearing dark brown corduroy pants accessorized by tiny balls of gray lint and a plain yellow sweatshirt whose sleeves had been shortened in the dryer.

The mother's eyes darted back and forth between Mitchell and Ellie, while the father studied a callus between his thumb and index finger.

"Ritchie," Mr. Chambers said in a voice barely audible.

"Pardon?" Ellie cocked her head to hopefully hear him better.

"I go by Ritchie." He finally looked up, met Ellie's eyes then returned his attention to the callus.

Ellie looked at Mitchell. He slightly moved his tired shoulders, raised his brows.

"Is he OK?" Tina asked. She looked back and forth between Mitchell and Ellie, not sure who would answer. "Dusty. Our son."

Ellie smiled slightly. "His name's Dusty?"

Tina bobbed her head up and down. "Is he OK?"

"If our Johnny Doe is your son, then yes, he appears to be fine."

"We're paying a babysitter and need to get back. Can we see him now?"

Ellie glanced at Mitchell then at Tina. "I'll be glad to take you up in just a minute but I need to speak with Detective Mitchell first."

She motioned for Mitchell to join her in the hallway, smiled at Tina then drew the curtain. She stepped a few feet away from the room, hoping the Chambers were safely out of earshot. She wondered if it would be wrong to pray that Tina and Richie Chambers were *not* little Johnny Doe's parents?

"You have got to be kidding me?" She whispered to Mitchell as he joined her. "They have to hurry this up because they're paying a babysitter?"

"Mom don't work; dad makes nine bucks an hour. They've got a one-year-old, a three-year-old and an eight-year-old back at home." He shrugged then popped a piece of chewing gum in his mouth. "I checked out Bekley's Wholesale Seafood. The dad's route is up through Tennessee. The driver that handles this area is a guy by the name of Jerome Kenton."

"Have you talked to him?"

"He's running Charlotte today. He'll be back in your area tomorrow. I figured either you could grab a few minutes with him tomorrow or I can pay him a visit at the loading dock."

Ellie nodded. "I'll talk to him tomorrow. What about the parents? What's your take on them?" She stared at the curtain, angry at the complacency behind it.

Mitchell shrugged again. "If stupidity's a crime, then they should probably be arrested. But I don't really see 'em doing anything harmful to the kid."

"Not even in the heat of anger? Maybe a spanking that went too far?"

Mitchell shook his head. "Like I said, they're not the brightest bulbs in the chandelier, but they're not criminals."

Ellie ran her hand through her hair. "Well, let's get this show on the road. We don't want to run up that babysitting tab."

"He's named after Dusty Rhoades."

Ellie stared at him, her brows raised.

"Dusty Rhoades. The wrestler," he said.

"They named their son after a wrestler?"

Mitchell smiled. Ellie sighed and followed him back into the room.

"Y'all ready?" Mitchell asked.

Tina pulled herself out of the chair like she had been planted there with weights. Maybe she had. Maybe this wasn't the way she had envisioned her life to turn out. Maybe she loved her kids desperately and cried at Christmas and birthdays when there wasn't enough money to go around. But would she cry if there was one less mouth to feed?

Ritchie tagged along behind as if disjointed from the whole experience.

Ellie led them through the treatment area and to the elevators. "The media should be confined to the lobby and entrances, but you never know. Some of them may have wormed their way up to the fourth floor. If you're approached, just turn your head away and if you say anything at all, just say, 'no comment,'" she said, as they stood there waiting.

Tina stared with her empty eyes then turned back to the elevator door and watched and waited. Ritchie studied his callus again. Mitchell shrugged.

The ride to the fourth floor was so silent, Ellie wondered if the Chambers understood that they were going to see if a found child was their missing son. She wondered if they even cared.

"He'll be in a playroom where you can observe him without him seeing you." The elevator stopped, and Ellie held the door as the Chambers and Mitchell stepped off.

A small group of reporters were clustered around the nurses' station, their attention zeroed in on the same perky nurse Ellie had spoken with earlier. "It's truly a miracle," she said, her voice as animated as her hands flaying about.

Ellie wanted to scream at the nurse and tell her to shut-up, to scurry the reporters away from hearing anything more about miracles and little Johnny Doe. But if she interrupted, the vultures would turn their attention to her and to the possible parents of the miracle child. She opted to hurry the Chambers and Mitchell away from the scene, herding them down the left hallway and toward the playroom.

"What was that all about?" Tina asked. It was the first time she had showed an interest in anything other than getting back home.

"A sick child was apparently healed." She figured that was all they needed to know at the moment. If Johnny Doe turned out to be their son, they'd hear the rest of the story soon enough. If he wasn't their son, they could return home, pay the babysitter, and watch the story of Johnny Doe on the evening news.

Ellie peered through the window of the playroom. Johnny Doe, wearing the blue Spiderman sweat suit, and Leon were building a skyscraper out of red and green Legos. Johnny Doe erupted in a fit of laughter apparently over something Leon had said. He grabbed his belly and swayed back and forth in his pint-sized chair while Leon had a goofy "what I'd say?" look on his face. Another child, a little girl with a purple cast covering her leg, was playing a board game with a nurse and glanced over at the dynamic duo, then went back to her game.

Ellie watched Johnny Doe for a moment then stepped aside and allowed Tina and Ritchie to step up to the window. "Remember, he can't see you."

Ritchie glanced up then went back to picking at his callus. Tina shook her head. "That's not him." There was no emotion in her voice. No disappointment. Nothing. She turned away and stared at Ellie. "Can we go now?"

"You're sure that's not him?" Mitchell asked. "We can have him turn more toward the window so you can get a better look."

Again, she shook her head. "It's not him. Dusty's hair's shorter. Can we go now?"

Ellie couldn't tell if the Chambers' detachment stemmed from the shock of having your child go missing, or if they just didn't care. She had seen people more upset over a pair of lost gloves. She wished them all the luck in the world finding their son, Dusty. But was almost thankful her little Johnny Doe wasn't the child they were looking for.

8

Gray clouds rolled from the west like a soft flannel blanket being fluffed for a waiting bed. Forecasters were calling for a light dusting of snow, which meant they would probably get a couple of inches. Ellie cranked up the heat in the car and drove to the alley where little Johnny Doe had been found.

She parked in front of the fish market and headed inside to see Dwayne Andrews. Shorty McCorkle and a younger man she assumed to be Andrews had their noses jammed into the backside of one of the freezers.

The younger man looked her up and down while McCorkle pushed the fur rim of his toboggan away from his face. "You're back."

"What can I say? I love the smell." She pressed a finger between her upper lip and nose as the foul odor from the thawing fish invaded her sinuses.

"This is the cop I was telling you about," McCorkle said as he jabbed an elbow in the young man's side.

"Detective Saunders, Burkesboro PD." Ellie offered him her hand.

"Dwayne Andrews." He jerked off a glove and pumped Ellie's hand hard. He was gangly with a hook nose and butter-colored hair that hung over the edges of his gold-rimmed glasses. "Shorty told me you were wanting to ask me some questions about that little kid."

"Yes. I was wondering if I could talk with you a minute about it."

"Sure, sure. I didn't see much, but I'll be glad to help all I can."

Shorty offered the use of the so-called office then cussed at the malfunctioning thermostat. Ellie followed Andrews to the partitioned office where the fish odor wasn't quite as strong. Andrews offered Ellie a seat in Shorty's worn leather chair then pulled up a white resin lawn chair splotched gray with mummified bird poop.

"Why don't you tell me what you saw?" Ellie asked, sinking so far into the leather, she wondered how she was going to get out of the thing.

"I was loading some mackerel in the front freezer and heard all these sirens. That's not real unusual for this neighborhood, but there was a lot of 'em—sirens, I mean. Usually it's just one. The police, maybe an ambulance now and then, but I don't think I've ever heard so many at one time. It got me a little concerned. I mean, I was thinking it must be something big like nine-eleven or something."

"Did you go outside?"

He nodded quickly. "Yeah, yeah. I stepped outside to see what was going on, and that's when I saw it."

"Saw what?" Ellie opened her notepad, pen poised.

"All the police cars. There were ten. No wait—I think it was eleven, and two fire trucks. Well, they weren't fire trucks, so-to-say, they were, you know, the emergency response trucks, the red ones with—"

"What about earlier in the afternoon? Did you see or hear anything out of the ordinary then?" She knew what happened after the emergency personnel arrived.

What happened before was what she was interested in.

"Yeah, when I was coming in I saw this black guy in the parking lot. He got in a green Honda. I think it was an Accord. He pulled out of the parking lot behind Marisol's then crossed over to Salem Street."

Ellie nodded. "What time was this?"

"A little after three."

"Can you describe him?"

"He was big, like a body-builder type, and his head was shaved. I didn't see his face, though."

"Do you remember what he was wearing?"

"Gray pants and a black leather jacket. The pants were those fancy, athletic kind. You know, with zippers at the ankles."

"What about his complexion? Was he dark-skinned, light-skinned?"

"Light."

"And you didn't see which direction he came from?"

Andrews shook his head. "No. He was already in the parking lot when I pulled in."

"Have you ever seen him around before?"

Again, he shook his head.

"OK, you've been a big help, Dwayne. If you think of anything else, give me a call." She handed him a card. He studied every letter on the card like he was studying for a test then slipped it in his nylon and Velcro wallet.

When they returned to the front of the warehouse, Shorty was still working on the freezer, and his temper was flaring hot. He banged on the side of the unit with the handle of a screwdriver, cursing through clenched teeth. "Worthless piece of...." He blew air out his nose and smacked at the fur tickling his face. "Did you find out anything?" He threw Ellie a glance then kicked the freezer with his midget-sized foot.

"Dwayne was very helpful. He said there was a man in the parking lot Tuesday when he got here. A man wearing athletic pants and black leather jacket. Do you remember seeing anyone fitting that description? A customer maybe?"

He thought about it a moment then shook his head. "He didn't come in here."

"When customers park, do they use the back parking lot?"

He shook his head again. "Most time they park on the street. I don't think they even know we have a parking lot."

"Who uses the parking lot?"

Andrews chimed in. "Just us and some of Marisol's customers. When the building next door was open, they used it some."

"The abandoned building?"

Andrews nodded.

"How long has it been empty?"

Andrews and Shorty looked at each other and both shrugged. "Six months," Shorty said. "Give or take."

"Do you know who owns it?"

"I don't know who owns it but it's managed, if you want to call it that, by Foothills Realty."

"What type of business was there before it closed?"

"Print shop. Before that a TV repair shop and before that some kind of little office." The freezer hissed, and Shorty cursed again then sighed. "Look, I don't mind helping you out but I've got to get this thing fixed before I lose a grand of flounder."

Ellie smiled and nodded. "Sure. No problem. Bekley's Wholesale Seafood, when will they be delivering again?"

"Tomorrow morning. They usually pull in around nine."

Ellie left Shorty and Dwayne to their freezer and rotting flounder and went across the street to Kellum's Insurance Agency. Signs on the inside of the plate-glass window declared "The Lowest Rates Around!!" and "We can Insure Anyone!!" Ellie wondered if they insured a green Honda Accord.

The office was sparsely furnished with two metal chairs in a small waiting area, separated by a dying plant. A large U-shaped desk was planted in the middle of the room. Phone cords, fax lines, and computer cables were stretched across the room and taped to the grungy carpet with large swatches of silver duct tape. An insurance agency couldn't very well have someone tripping over a cord in their own office.

The secretary boxed in the center of the U looked to be in her early twenties and thankful she wasn't working at a fast food joint. Her too-tight blouse stretched across a pooching belly. Gaping buttons fought a life or death battle to keep everything in. Her hair was three shades of blonde, fashionably straight, and parted in the middle, exposing black roots.

"Can I help you?" She asked, her voice reflecting the late hour of the day.

Ellie showed her badge and introduced herself. "I was here earlier, and Mr. Kellum said you were out running errands. Mind if I ask you a couple of questions?"

The poor girl looked like a proverbial deer caught

in headlights. "Sure," she said in a small voice, probably frantically wondering if she had paid those traffic tickets.

"And your name is?"

"Candice. Candice Summers."

"Hi, Candice. I'm investigating the beating of a small child who was found Tuesday in the alley across the street. Do you remember seeing anything out of the ordinary?"

Candice shook her head. "I left at four Tuesday, so I didn't know anything about it until yesterday morning."

"What about earlier Tuesday when you were here? Did you see anything then? Maybe something that didn't look quite right?"

She shook her head again. "I don't pay much attention to stuff out there. When we get kinda slow in here, I try and study some. Stan don't mind."

"You're still in school?"

"I'm taking some classes at the community college. That's why I left early Tuesday. I have a class that starts at five." She kneaded her hands together, her eyes still wide and scared.

Ellie smiled to hopefully put the girl at ease. "There was a man seen Tuesday around three in the parking lot behind the fish market. He was a black man with a light complexion, shaved head, and a muscular build. He was driving a green Honda Accord. Do you remember seeing anyone fitting that description?"

Candice gnawed on her bottom lip and concentrated hard on the description. After a moment, she shrugged as if she were apologizing. "It don't sound familiar."

"What about the car? Think one of your clients

might drive a green Honda?"

"I don't know right off the bat, but I can do a search and see."

"Would you? That would help a lot."

"Sure." Candice turned to her keyboard and typed in the make and model. "You don't know the year?" She asked while the system searched the agency's database.

"No year. Just that it was a green Accord."

Candice studied the monitor. "Here it is. We have four Accords. Here's a green one, too." She turned the monitor so Ellie could see and pointed it out on the screen.

"Can you tell who it's registered to?"

Candice moved the cursor over the link then double-clicked. "Reginald Booker. 4816 Apartment E, Stanford Street."

Ellie wrote down the name and address. "Thanks, Candice. You've been a big help."

"You don't think he was involved, do you?" She seemed as shocked as a parent defending their child to an angry principal.

"I just want to talk to him to see if he remembers seeing anything." Ellie smiled and closed her notepad.

Outside, the clouds were spitting snow and a thin white blanket covered the walkway. Ellie called Jesse on his cell phone, angry with herself for knowing the number without having to look it up. "Hey. Can you run a check for me?"

"Let me switch screens. What's your password?"

"What?"

"Your password."

Ellie huffed then gave it to him. "Don't you have a desk anymore?"

"Yeah, but I like yours better. They stuck me and Ricky Delwood down in the basement, and have you ever smelled Ricky Delwood?"

Ellie rolled her eyes. "No. I've never smelled Ricky Delwood."

"Trust me. You don't want to. What's the name?"

"Reginald Booker, 4816 Stanford—"

"Whoa, whoa, whoa. What are you doing looking up Reggie Booker?"

"Apparently, he drives a green Honda Accord, and a green Honda Accord was seen in the area Tuesday."

"There's a lot of green Honda Accords out there, Ellie. It doesn't mean it was Reggie Booker's."

Ellie pursed her lips, her anger slowly creeping upward. "Someone matching his description was seen in the area getting into the green Honda Accord. Is that enough info?"

"Reggie's not your man."

Ellie tapped her foot in a slow, deliberate manner. "And you know this how?"

"Reggie and I go way back. He's not a nice guy, but he's not the kind to kill a kid."

She swept at a patch of snow with the toe of her shoe. "We may not even be talking about the same guy. What does he look like?"

"Big. Built like a linebacker."

"Shaved head?"

"Last time I saw him, he had the dreadlock thing going on. Looked kinda stupid on a guy his size."

"Maybe that's why he shaved. You didn't like his haircut."

Jesse laughed. "Reggie Booker doesn't exactly care what I like. Be careful around him. He takes no

88

prisoners."

"Thanks for the concern, but I think I can handle this. He was seen in the area. No matter how big and bad he is, he may have seen something."

"When are you going to talk to him?"

Ellie grinned and shook her head. The worm was trying to weasel his way in again, anyway. "I don't need your help on this, Jesse."

"I wasn't offering it. I was just asking for an estimated time so I'll know what to tell the guys when you turn up missing."

Ellie stared at a mangy looking dog across the street while trying to swallow the venomous words she was tempted to say. The dog stared back at her then sauntered off toward Shorty's rancid fish. "Bye, Jesse." Ellie started to close her phone, but Jesse wasn't quite finished with the conversation.

"What time did you say you were going to talk to him?" he asked. "Seriously. For my own knowledge. It's part of the case, right?"

Ellie sighed. "I don't know. I've got to go talk to Alvin B. Kepler, the third, attorney at law, then—"

"Alvin Kepler is Booker's attorney."

"You sure?"

"Yep."

"Well that could explain why he was in the neighborhood Tuesday."

"Kepler won't tell you squat."

Ellie stared at the sky and let the snow cool her rising temper. She spoke through clenched teeth. "After I talk to Kepler, I'm going in Marisol's and talk to a guy named Mickey Mak—"

"Mickey Mouse?"

Ellie shot a blast of air out her nose, pulled the

phone away from her ear and glared at it. *Is there anyone you don't know?*

"What's Mickey got to do with it?"

"He called it in to 9-1-1. Do I need to be careful around him, too?"

Jesse laughed again. "No, Mickey's harmless."

He cleared his throat. "Seriously, though, are you going in Marisol's?"

"I've been in Marisol's before, Jesse. Who appointed *you* my guardian?" Why was he so interested now? He'd avoided her for months.

"I was just going to tell you to be careful on that floor. I'd hate for you to slip and fall on a peanut hull."

Ellie slammed her phone closed and stuffed it in her pocket. She wondered if it was too late to change her mind and tell Jack she had reconsidered. There was no way in the world she could work with Jesse.

She headed in to Kepler's office which consisted of three rooms: a reception area, a cluttered conference room, and Kepler's office, all with cheap, salvage store furniture and threadbare carpet. Mismatched discount store artwork hung lopsided on nicotine-yellowed walls. A bell with a red bow was hung over the door and jangled each time the door was opened.

The bell slammed against the glass door as Ellie pushed it open, and seconds later, Kepler strutted into the reception area. The secretary, if he had one, had already left for the day.

"Oh, it's you again. What can I do for you?" He stepped around Ellie and bolted the door. She wasn't sure if he was locking her in or locking others out.

"I wanted to ask you a couple more questions."

Kepler looked at his bulky watch. "I can spare you ten. I like to get to the gym before the crowd hits." He puffed out his chest and hiked up his pants.

Everything about Kepler reeked cheap, from his haircut to his suit and faded tie. He was just a shade taller than Shorty, with a barrel-chest and stubby fingers that looked like sausage links. A mole the size of a dime clung to his jaw near his ear and at first glance, made you think some type of insect was ready to invade the orifice.

He glanced at his watch again. "Clock's ticking."

"Reginald Booker. Is he a client of yours?"

"Sweetheart, you know I can't tell you that. Attorney-client privileges." He coupled a *tsk-tsk* sound with a wink.

"OK, let's back up. There was a black man, muscular build, seen in the area Tuesday. Do you remember seeing anyone that fits that description?"

"The majority of my clients fit that description."

"Were any of them in the neighborhood Tuesday?"

He stared at her a minute then sighed. "It was a busy day. I had a lot of people in and out."

"Anyone fitting Booker's description?"

He grinned, shook his head, and pointed a fat finger at her. "You're slick. You know I can't give you the names of my clients. And no judge in his right mind is going to grant you a court order for it, either."

Kepler was right. It was aggravating but there was little she could do about it other than play on his heart. If he had one. "A child was brutally beaten and left for dead. It takes a very sick person to do that to a child."

Kepler nodded. "I agree with you one hundred percent. Look, between you and me, most of my clients are petty crooks. Shoplifting, bad checks, minor drug offensives. They're not pillars of the community, but they're not killers, either. If you're still interested in this guy, I'd suggest you drop by Ripped Fitness Club between five and six. You might find a few guys fitting your description." He unbolted the door and looked at his watch.

"My ten's up?"

"Your ten's up."

"And this Ripped gym would be located where?"

Kepler sighed. "Langston Avenue. You're going to show up, aren't you?"

"Probably."

He slightly nodded and chewed the inside of his mouth. He opened the door and made a sweeping motion with his arm like he was sweeping Ellie out with the trash. "I guess I'll see you there, then."

Kepler bolted the door behind her, waved his chubby fingers then dropped the lopsided blind with its several broken slats.

Ellie headed across the street to Marisol's. She brushed the snow from her hair and glanced around, squinting against the dim light.

Marisol was at the bar filling frosted mugs from the tap. She noticed Ellie and bobbed her head toward the lone pool table in an open alcove joining the main room. Four men were hovered around the table racking a new game.

"Lost?" One of the men asked as he eyed Ellie. Sweat gathered and glistened on a swastika tattoo on the side of his shaved head. A braided beard touched his chest.

Another man walked behind her, his pool stick clasped to his side. He was tall and lanky with a mouth full of rotting teeth. "Sure brightens the place up a bit, doesn't she?" His rancid breath was warm against the back of Ellie's neck.

The third man pointed his pool stick like a sword, stretching it across the table, the tip resting on the top button of Ellie's blouse. "They call me Rat. What do they call you, pretty lady?"

Rat, Mickey Mouse...what other vermin called Marisol's home?

Rat pressed the end of the pool stick against her flesh. Ellie silently told herself to remain calm. She feared the rodent would hear her heart thundering in her chest.

"You don't have a name?" Rat asked, nudging the top of her blouse aside.

Ellie grasped the end of the pool stick and pushed it away then brushed the tail of her blazer to the side, exposing the Glock hanging on her hip. "Detective Ellie Saunders, Burkesboro Police."

Rat raised his hands in surrender. "Hey, we're cool. We were just playing around. No harm meant."

Ellie eyed each one of them, her heart slowly returning to a normal rate. "Good. Which one of you is Mickey?"

The men glanced at one another. Then Rat and the guy with the shaved head went back to their game. Among several of the little quirks she had, the one thing that irritated Ellie more than anything was being ignored. It was downright disrespectful. "OK, Marisol said Mickey was back here shooting pool. Now I know you're Rat, so which one of you three is the mouse?"

The guy with the shaved head started laughing. "I almost like her."

"Mickey Mouse!" Jesse brushed past Ellie, grabbed a pool stick, lined up the cue ball then broke the rack. The balls clattered against one another as the seven-ball rolled into the left corner pocket. "What do you say, Mickey? Long time no see." Jesse took another shot, rolling the five-ball into the right corner pocket.

"Hey, Jesse," one of the men said, resignation resonating in his voice. He was as big around as he was tall, with carrot-colored hair and a baby face splotched with freckles.

"Detective Saunders wants to ask you a couple questions about that kid they found in the alley Tuesday. You don't mind helping Detective Saunders out, do you Mickey?"

Mickey shook his head.

"That's what I thought. You're a real stand-up guy, Mickey." Jesse dropped another ball then straightened up and motioned for the other three guys to move on.

A part of Ellie fumed, but part of her was so relieved she could've kissed Jesse Alvarez at that very moment.

Jesse stuffed the pool stick back in the wall rack. "So, tell us what you saw, Mickey." Jesse propped himself on the edge of the pool table.

There he went with the "us" thing again. But this time, Ellie wasn't so sure she resented it.

"I didn't see anything." Mickey said, staring wide-eyed at Jesse.

"Mickey, Mickey, Mickey. You called it in, man. And you expect us to believe you didn't see anything?"

"I didn't call anything in."

"The call was traced back to your phone, Mickey," Ellie said.

"I wasn't on it long enough for a trace."

Jesse chuckled. "What she meant was the *caller ID* came back to you. But now that you've admitted calling it in, tell us what you saw."

Mickey scrunched his face and looked like one of those little pug dogs. "I'm telling you, I didn't see anything."

Jesse rolled the eight-ball around the table with the palm of his hand. "Been hanging out at Buckaroos lately?"

Mickey's eyes flew wide. He scoped out who was within earshot then leaned into the table. "Come on, Jesse," he whispered. "You wouldn't—"

"Tell us what you saw, Mickey."

He glanced around the corner then settled his gaze on the table. "I went out to take a leak."

"Why didn't you just use the bathroom in here?" Ellie asked.

Jesse leaned over to her. "You've obviously never been to the bathrooms here. So you were outside in the alley and what did you see?"

"I was standing there doing my business, you know…looking around the alley, when I saw him."

"Did you check to see if he was alive?" Ellie asked.

He shook his head. "I got a little closer and could see he wasn't breathing."

"Did you touch anything? Move anything out of the way? Food wrappers, anything like that?"

He shook his head again. "I didn't touch anything. I mean, he was lying there in plain view. You didn't have to move anything to see him."

"Do many of Marisol's customers come from the parking lot through the alley?"

"Most use the other side. Phil Cooper slipped on some trash last year, cracked his head on the brick, and ever since, most people walk around."

"Whatd'ya do after you saw him?" Jesse asked.

"I came back in the bar and had a few beers."

"You didn't tell anyone?" Ellie raised her brows and stared at Mickey.

Mickey shrugged. "I didn't want to get involved, you know?"

Ellie sighed. "So how long before you called 9-1-1?"

"I don't know, maybe thirty minutes. I started feeling kinda bad, you know, thinking maybe the kid was still alive and maybe he needed help."

"Pretty good observation, Mickey." Jesse rolled the eight-ball into the far pocket and shook his head.

Mickey turned to Ellie. "Like I said, I started feeling pretty bad and went back outside. I looked in the alley to make sure he was still there and then I called 9-1-1."

Jesse burst out laughing. "Where were you expecting him to go?"

Mickey rolled his eyes then turned back to Ellie. "Like I said, I didn't really want to get involved."

"Several officers canvassed the area Tuesday night. Why didn't you come forward and admit you were the one who called 9-1-1?" Ellie asked.

Mickey looked at Ellie then at Jesse and smiled. "I didn't want to have to answer a bunch of questions."

Jesse pulled a piece of paper from his pocket, unfolded it, and slid it across the table. It was a photocopied picture of a black man, shaved head, and a jagged scar under his left eye. Ellie assumed it was Reginald Booker. "Ever see him before?" Jesse asked.

Mickey studied the picture a moment then nodded. "Yeah. He was in the parking lot Tuesday when I got here. I thought it was kinda odd, you know, a black dude in here. I mean, they ain't skinheads but pretty close to it." He glanced around at his companions in the bar then stared at Jesse.

"So tell me what you know about his guy." Jesse said.

Mickey bobbed his big head around like he was totally confused. "Nothing. Only time I've ever seen him was the other day in the parking lot."

"Between the time when you got here and the first time you went out to the alley, did you notice anything out of the ordinary?" Ellie asked.

"Just that guy in the parking lot." He motioned toward the picture of Booker. "You think he's involved?"

Ellie shrugged. "It's still early in the investigation. Did you notice any strange cars in the parking lot?"

Mickey shook his head. "Just that one—the one your dude was driving. I remember thinking it was kinda weird seeing that big hulk climb into that little car."

"And you didn't see any other cars you didn't recognize?"

"Like I said, it was pretty early in the afternoon. There weren't that many cars out there."

"You've been a big help, Mickey. I appreciate it." Ellie slid one of her cards across the table to him but Jesse intercepted and pocketed it.

"We'll call you if we have any more questions," Jesse said and smiled. "I know how to find you. Keep it clean, Mickey." He rose and stuffed the picture of Reginald Booker into his pocket.

Outside, Ellie grabbed Jesse's arm and spun him around, her temper flaring. "Why'd you take my card? What if he thinks of something?"

"One—he's not going to volunteer information.

You want more information, you're going to have to call him. And two—you really want those *not quite skinheads* to have your contact information?"

Ellie rolled her eyes. "Burkesboro PD? It's not like they can't look it up in the phone book."

"Hate to burst your bubble, sweetheart, but they're not *that* interested. Looking it up in the phone book would require some degree of effort. Haven't I taught you anything?"

Ellie was stunned. "I've been working with you six hours!"

Jesse smiled. "And they've been six very good hours, haven't they?"

9

Ellie was still trying to figure out what had just happened. She couldn't decide if she was livid or amused. Regardless, Jesse Alvarez sure had a way of confusing her emotions. And the bad part was, after she'd had time to settle down and think it through, he was right.

"Reggie Booker ain't your man." Jesse rubbed his hands together to warm them from the cold. He blew puffs of warm air into his fists.

Ellie jacked up the heat in the car and held her own hands in front of the vents. "Why do you say that?"

"Not his style. Reggie's a mid-level drug dealer, and he may take out a couple teeth of someone who owes him, but beating the crap out of kids isn't his style."

"Maybe a deal went bad, and he grabbed the kid for payback." Ellie turned on the wipers and watched as the blades pushed the snow from side to side.

Jesse shook his head. "To people like Reggie Booker, kids are a nuisance. He wouldn't want to be bothered with one."

"All the more reason to kill him."

Jesse sighed. "I'll dig around some and see if any of his customers are missing a kid."

"Good. Now, if you'll get out of my car, I can run by the hospital and check on Johnny Doe before I go to the gym. Kepler said Booker would be there around five."

Jesse looked at her, his coal black eyes wide. "You're going to question him at the gym?"

"Yes," she said in a hesitant voice.

"Uh, no. You don't want to question him at the gym. He's in his element at the gym. He'll walk all over you like a rug."

Ellie pursed her lips tight. "I can handle it, Jesse. I handled those skinheads in Marisol's, didn't I?"

Jesse chuckled. "You were about to become one of their girlfriends whether you liked it or not."

Ellie's jaw dropped in anger. "I had it under control! All you did was point out which one was Mickey."

Jesse sighed. "Fine. If that's what you want to think. But you still don't need to be questioning Reggie Booker at the gym." He turned in the seat and faced her. "Look, he's in his comfort zone at the gym. Not to mention he's buds with every guy in there. You think they're going to defend *you* if something gets out of hand?"

Ellie glared out the windshield at the wipers slapping against the glass. Admitting Jesse was right made her blood congeal in frozen clumps. But there was no sense getting herself killed because she was too proud to admit he was right. "Then what do you suggest?" She didn't try to hide the anger in her voice.

"Have a uniform pick him up and bring him downtown."

"And you think he's going to come willingly?" She glanced at him, rolled her eyes, then turned back to watching the wipers slide across the snow.

"If he doesn't, they can pat him down. Nab him

for a probation violation."

She glared at him. "What violation?"

"He'll be packing. Carries a piece with him everywhere he goes."

Ellie rolled her eyes again. "Wonderful."

As Jesse started to get out, a white van with a News Seven logo turned onto the street and crept through the thin layer of snow. The satellite antenna swayed slightly like a tentative sword swiping at the flurries. It parked in front of Marisol's, nose-to-nose with Ellie's Taurus.

"Oh this is great." Ellie watched Derek Cobe climb out of the van and survey the area for his live shot. A cameraman and an engineer joined him. Cobe's nose twitched with disgust.

He peered through the snow patches on the windshield, recognized Ellie, and smiled.

Cobe approached the car and knocked on the driver's window. Reluctantly, Ellie rolled it down. "Hey, Ellie. Got yourself a doozy of a story, don't you."

"We call it an investigation. That alley's going to get awfully crowded." Ellie pointed to News Central Three's dark blue van slowing to a stop behind Derek's van.

"Crap." Derek motioned to his cameraman and engineer then sprinted toward the alley with his crew in tow.

Ellie brushed away the snow that had collected on the inside of the door and rolled up the window. Another news van slowly passed and parked across the street in front of Kepler's office. "Go. Get out of here." Ellie shoved Jesse against the passenger door.

"You don't have to get violent." Surprise registered in his voice and raised the tone a full octave.

"Yes, I do. I've got to get out of here before I become a sound bite."

"I'm going, I'm going. I'll see you back at the office."

He had barely slammed the door when Ellie threw the car into reverse, backed up enough to get clearance between the Taurus and Cobe's van, and then jammed it in drive and sped off. Cobe and the rest of the piranhas could find a sound bite elsewhere. Dwayne Andrews alone would keep them busy for hours. She laughed, thinking about the reception the news crews would get from Mickey and the gang in Marisol's.

****

The news crews that weren't lurking around the alley were at the hospital. Sara Jeffries jammed herself into a packed elevator and rode up to the fourth floor with Ellie.

"Any change in his condition?" Sara asked, peeking between an elderly man and a nurse in blue scrubs.

The nurse stared at Sara. "Pardon?"

Ellie watched the second floor then the third floor button light up, counting the seconds before the fourth turned bright yellow and she could escape. Sweat beaded on her forehead. She rubbed her hands on her pants to dry the moisture collecting on her palms.

"The Lazarus boy. I was asking Detective Saunders if there had been a change in his condition." Sara peered around the elderly man. "Detective Saunders?"

The fourth floor button turned yellow and the carriage jolted to a stop. Sara stepped out first and waited for Ellie. Ellie thought about stepping out but allowed the doors to close and rode up to the fifth floor. She had told Sissy she'd be back later in the afternoon, and now was as good a time as any.

She didn't see her aunt in the hallway and hoped she wasn't in Peggy's room. Ellie wasn't ready to deal with seeing Peggy whether she was dying or not. Peggy may not have held the razor blade that sliced through Ellie's mother's wrists, but in Ellie's mind, Peggy was the reason behind it.

Ellie trudged back to the nurses' station and stood there debating whether to ask for Peggy's room number.

A nurse looked up from a monitor, smiled, and asked if she could help.

The words just wouldn't come. Ellie slowly shook her head and started to back away.

"Well, you did make it back, didn't you?" she heard Aunt Sissy say from behind her.

Ellie spun around and nearly collided with her father. He grabbed her and locked her in a hard embrace. "I'm so glad you came."

Ellie blinked back tears and melted into her father's arms. It had been years since she had felt those arms around her, felt their strength. This time though, the strength wasn't there. It had been replaced with trembling uncertainty.

As she pulled away, her father brushed tears from his cheeks. His lips trembled as he tried to smile.

Ellie had seen her father cry before but never over sadness. She remembered often seeing tears streaming down his face, arms raised toward heaven, as he stood in the pulpit proclaiming God's love.

He didn't cry at her mother's funeral, saying "she

was finally at peace." Why was he crying now? Was Peggy's impending death more devastating than the death of Ellie's mother?

"I can't stay but just a minute. I'm working a case that's pretty involved."

Her father nodded, knowingly.

"The little boy?" Sissy asked. "There's television crews all over the place. We walked down to the coffee shop, and they were even in there."

Ellie hoped the reporters were getting coffee and not looking for a willing mouthpiece. "Yeah, unfortunately the story's generating a lot of publicity."

"Is it true the little boy came back from the dead?" Sissy took a sip of her coffee, peering over the rim at Ellie.

Ellie shrugged. "There has to be a medical explanation."

Her father had regained his steadfast composure, and smiled. "The answer's not always in the test results, you know? Maybe God has a purpose for this child."

He smiled again, and Ellie felt the warmth wrap around her like a soft blanket. Back when he was a reverend by title, Ferrin Saunders wasn't the splashy, fist-pounding, fire-and-brimstone type preacher. He never swung the Bible like some swing a sword. Instead, he told of God's love in soft words and a gentle nature.

"Yeah, well, I hope God's purpose for this child isn't to make some news reporter rich and famous." Ellie half smiled, and her father chuckled.

"We may not know in our lifetimes what this child's purpose is, but I can guarantee you there is one." He winked at her and wrapped an arm around her waist. "Go on and tend to your work. I'm curious to see how this one turns out."

Ellie reached up and kissed him on the cheek, silently thanking him for giving her the escape. She'd see Peggy when she was ready, and it might be in the room down the hall or it might be stretched out in a casket. Either way, it would be Ellie's decision, and her father seemed to understand that.

Ellie gave Aunt Sissy a hug then started toward the elevator. She stopped and turned back. "Y'all aren't driving back and forth every night are you?" The hospital was a good hour's drive from home, an hour and a half in the snow.

Her father and Sissy looked at one another and shrugged.

"Look, my house isn't that big, but I do have a spare bedroom and a shower. You're welcome to stay if you'd like."

Sissy grinned sheepishly and winked at her. "That would be nice."

"I'm not sure what time I'll get in, but go on in and make yourselves at home. I'll call Mr. Robins next door and have him unlock the door for you."

In the elevator, Ellie punched the button for the fourth floor and wondered what in the heck she had just done.

Sara Jeffries was interviewing a nurse who seemed reluctant to talk. Ellie slipped past the nurses' station and headed down the hallway to Johnny Doe's room. He was sitting on the side of the bed with the table pulled up to him, munching hungrily on chicken nuggets. A nurse sat beside him, reading *Horton Hears a Who* out loud.

"Hey." Johnny Doe smiled and dipped his nugget

in a dollop of ketchup.

"Hey yourself. That looks *good*." Ellie scanned the dinner tray and fought the urge to scrunch up her nose in disgust. Rubbery nuggets, soggy fries, and shiny green peas weren't her idea of a good supper.

"Leon came and played with me for a long time. We played Legos in the playroom." He dunked a fry in the ketchup. The green peas remained untouched, and Ellie doubted that would change.

Ellie caught the nurse's gaze move past her and turned to see Sara Jeffries in the doorway.

Sara jerked a small digital camera from her bag but before she could even get the camera turned on, Ellie had spun around and pushed her out of the doorway.

"What are you doing?" Ellie snapped as she slammed the door closed. "He's a child. He doesn't need his face plastered all over every newspaper in the country."

"His picture's already out there, Ellie," Sara huffed through gritted teeth. She stuffed the camera back in her bag.

"Not a picture of him sitting on a hospital bed. If I catch you anywhere near this room again, I'll arrest you."

Sara rolled her eyes then glared at Ellie. "From what I hear the chief wants it out there. How's he going to take it when one of his own blocks our attempts to help find his parents?"

Ellie took a deep breath to keep from spouting off something that would probably get her fired. "If the chief wants you to take a picture of him in his hospital bed, I'll have him call you. Until then, he's off-limits," she said after a moment.

Marc Deveraux joined the two and introduced himself to Sara.

She jumped right in, seizing the opportunity. "Can you give me an update on his condition?"

Deveraux smiled but shook his head. "I'm sorry. I really am, but I can't release that information."

Sara stood gazing at the hunky doctor, her tongue nearly lolling out of her mouth, and Ellie wondered if Sara realized Deveraux had just killed her story.

"Look, I know you're just doing your job. And I wish I could help, but until our legal department gives us an OK to discuss his condition, we can't." Deveraux smiled that gorgeous smile.

"Are they looking into it?" Her eyelashes actually fluttered.

Deveraux nodded. "There're a lot of issues involved. But as soon as I get a go-ahead, I'll give you a call."

Sara scrambled in her bag for a business card. "Oh, I really would appreciate that." She scribbled a number on the back of the card then handed it to him. "That's my personal cell. You can always reach me on that one."

Ellie fully expected Sara to wink and probably would've knocked her silly if she had.

Deveraux slipped the card in his pocket. "I'll call you as soon as I hear something."

"What about a picture?"

"Sara! I told you no pictures," Ellie yelled.

Deveraux took a step in, putting his shoulder between them like a referee. "Once our legal department says OK, you'll get the first picture."

Sara peered over his shoulder and glared at Ellie. "Thank you." She offered her hand to Deveraux then traipsed off toward the elevator.

"Are you really going to let her take a picture of him?" Ellie's voice was higher than usual.

"Let's go to my office. I need to talk to you about the test results." He started down the hallway with Ellie in tow.

"You're going to let her take a picture of him, aren't you?"

Deveraux grinned. "You're persistent aren't you?"

"I just don't want to see him plastered across every newspaper and television set in the country."

"He's probably going to be sooner or later. We might as well control who has access."

"Yeah, but Sara Jeffries?"

Deveraux held the door open to his office and ushered Ellie in. "It's a dying breed, newspapers. I have a soft spot for them."

The office was decorated in cartoon characters and Tulane University memorabilia with a couple of framed photographs of Deveraux and different people in various places doing various things. Skiing, white-water rafting, on top of a mountain. There were several pictures of him—surrounded by smiling children in frames date stamped and labeled Darfur and Croatia.

Ellie was amazed at the smiles on the children's faces. Despite the ugliness of the Sudan and the horrific conditions they were forced to live in, they managed to smile. Kids were so resilient. Take Johnny Doe— despite being beaten and left for dead, the kid still found reason to smile. "How long were you in the Sudan?"

"Fourteen months, two weeks and three days."

Ellie turned around and looked him. "Wow. Sounds like you were anxious to leave."

"Just the opposite. I would have loved to stay, but they thought it was too dangerous." He sat down behind his desk and stared at the picture on the bookshelf. "It's an amazing place."

Ellie raised her brows and sat down in a chair in front of his desk. *Amazing* wasn't a term she heard often in association with Darfur. "I've never heard it called amazing before."

Deveraux smiled. "The people are very special."

"I guess they were very thankful to have a doctor around."

Deveraux shook his head. "I wasn't there as a doctor. I was there as a missionary."

Ellie was wide-eyed and at a loss for words. Missionary? She remembered her daddy's church sponsoring missionaries all over the world. She remembered the church sending care packages of toiletries and over-the-counter medicines and small first-aid kits to their missionaries in countries she had never heard of.

"I guess the parents that were here at three weren't his parents?"

Ellie shook her head, partly to answer his question and partly to push away the images of her father, the church, the whole missionary thing. "No. They weren't his parents. Thank God."

Deveraux tossed his head back and laughed. "I think you're getting a little possessive of our little guy."

Ellie tried not to grin but failed. "What did Doctor Mertzer find out?" she asked finally.

"Mentally, he appears to be around the four to five year range but there are some things he's very bright and animated about and then others he appears developmentally hindered."

Ellie stared at him, her confusion obviously evident on her face.

"For instance, he likes playing trucks with Leon. He really enjoyed playing with the Legos. He enjoys watching Sesame Street. These activities are somewhat juvenile, almost pre-school age."

"So you're saying he may not be as old as we think he is?"

"It's possible. Or he could be developmentally challenged. Most children by the age of two, or three at the latest, can tell you at least their first name, sometimes their last. By the time they're four or five, most of them know their parents' names. The same thing with age. Some two year olds can tell you how old they are. He knows neither."

"Do you think he's blocking it out? Maybe it's something he doesn't *want* to remember."

Deveraux shook his head. "It's possible but not likely. Children this age may block out something like continual abuse or some other traumatizing event, but seldom would they block out their name."

"What about amnesia? Maybe he suffered blunt force trauma."

"Remember when he told you he liked Spiderman? That indicates he has some collective memory."

Ellie sank down in the chair and sighed. "Physically, is there a test that can determine how old is he? I know the medical examiner can determine a person's age by the length of their bones, but is there a test that you can do?"

Deveraux nodded. "I've already ordered it. Also, there's something else you might be interested in." He opened Johnny Doe's medical folder and removed a computer printout. "The tissue sample that we took this morning—it came back abnormal."

10

Ellie's mind reeled with a myriad of questions. Was it cancer? Or some other dreadful disease? Maybe there was an abnormality with his DNA? Would that show in a tissue sample?

"Abnormal how?" She finally asked. She stepped into the service elevator with Deveraux and watched him push the button for the basement.

"Dr. Jenkins will be able to explain it better."

"You must have some thoughts on it."

Deveraux smiled. "Given the extent of his injuries when he was brought in, personally, I think it's a miracle he's alive."

Of course, a former missionary would think of it as a miracle. But a doctor? "I thought he was dead."

Deveraux looked at her and smiled again. "A miracle."

Ellie huffed. "OK, forget the miracles. From a medical viewpoint, what's your opinion?"

The door opened in front of the morgue and Deveraux held the elevator door for Ellie. The faint sound of fun in the sun and surfing wafted from the morgue. "My opinion is it's a miracle. Ask another doctor and they may give you medical mumbo-jumbo. Is that what you're looking for? Medical jargon?"

Whether it was lack of sleep or general frustration, Ellie was beginning to take offense at the good doctor's attitude. "I'm used to dealing with facts. Cold, hard facts. The fact is the boy was dead or near dead, and now he's alive, and yes, I'd like someone to tell me how that's medically possible."

"The cold, hard fact may be that there is no explanation." Deveraux keyed in a code and the morgue door swung open. "Surfing USA" blasted from Leon's CD player at concert-level decibels. Leon was near the office, dancing with a mop.

Ellie and Deveraux were able to scoot through the morgue to the adjoining medical examiner's office and lab without Leon noticing. At least that was one thing Ellie was thankful for; she didn't think her back could take another of Leon's dips.

White light bounced off the stainless steel table and equipment, casting an ominous glow over the room. Ellie wondered if people with near-death experiences could be mistaken about the great white light they often claimed to have seen—maybe it wasn't Heaven beckoning them as they thought. Perhaps it was just the glowing white lights of an examining room they had seen.

Dr. Doyle Jenkins was elbow-deep in someone's abdominal cavity and acknowledged Ellie and Deveraux with a nod of his balding head.

Jenkins was about ten years shy of retirement and often as grumpy as Leon was happy. He wore a short, neatly trimmed beard without the complimentary mustache, making his face look as long as a football field.

"Marc, Ellie. Be with you in just a second." He removed a body part and dropped it on a scale.

Ellie's nose twitched with the array of smells permeating the room. Everything from chemicals to body fluids mingled in a sickly odor that could send the squeamish hurling their lunch in the nearest trash can. Although the urge was often there, Ellie refused to hurl. She had money riding on it; ten dollars in the office pool said she wouldn't. There was fifty dollars in the pool that said she would.

Jenkins stepped away from the corpse on the table and removed blood-covered gloves. He motioned for them to follow him over to the desk area. "Your little Johnny Doe is quite the mystery."

"Dr. Deveraux said there was an abnormality in the tissue sample."

Jenkins turned a microscope toward Ellie. "Take a peek."

She peered through the lens and stared at two very different sections. Even her untrained eye could tell there was a noticeable difference in the two samples but she had no clue what the differences meant.

"The one on the left is normal healthy tissue," Jenkins said. "The one on the right is Johnny Doe's."

The healthy tissue was pink, reminding her of fresh salmon; Johnny Doe's sample looked like the freezer-burnt pork chops she kept pushing to the back of her freezer.

Ellie raised her head and looked at Jenkins. "Hypothermia?"

"Possibly. There's evidence the intracellular fluids were frozen at some point."

"But wouldn't there be evidence of frostbite?"

Jenkins bobbed his head back and forth. "More than likely. But, from all accounts, and from what I've been told, the child appears perfectly normal. No injuries, no indications of any trauma."

"Could this be from an old injury? Maybe an

accident that happened prior to this incident?"

Jenkins shook his head. "With this kind of cellular damage, there would definitely be noticeable damage on the outside. Amputations, dead muscles, bone damage. A body part just wouldn't recover from what appears to be a case of frostbite this severe."

"But the hypothermia could explain how he was mistakenly pronounced dead, right?" Ellie looked at Deveraux expecting him to start spouting off about miracles again.

"There're documented cases of near-death severe hypothermic patients making a full recovery, but Johnny Doe wasn't hypothermic when he was brought in," Deveraux said. "And, it still doesn't explain how the injuries disappeared." He smiled.

As handsome as he was, Marc Deveraux was becoming rather annoying. She turned back to Jenkins. "Was it cold enough Tuesday for someone to suffer hypothermia?"

Jenkins again shook his head. "Not around here. Last night, perhaps. But I believe he was found in the early evening?"

Ellie nodded. "Around five."

"I'm not a meteorologist, but I don't think it dropped below freezing until later in the evening."

It didn't really matter what the temperature was outside; the kid was found *dumped* in the alley. Maybe it was freezing where he was before he was dumped? Like in a refrigerated truck delivering seafood. Ellie was going to have to endure Shorty McCorkle's fish market one more time.

"In the meantime…" Jenkins said. He walked over to the counter and opened a manila folder. Ellie and Deveraux followed. "From everything I can gather—

the size and number of teeth, and an X-ray of his wrist—Johnny Doe looks to be around six years old."

Ellie glanced at Deveraux. If Jenkins was right, then Deveraux was right, too. She was no expert in child development, but like Deveraux had said, most normal six-year-olds could tell you their name and age. If Johnny Doe did know, why wasn't he telling them? Could a six-year-old be ingenuous enough to purposely conceal his identity? If so, why would he want to? What had happened in this poor kid's life to make him want to forget who he was?

"Wish I could be more help," Jenkins said. The sound of his voice jarred Ellie from her thoughts.

"Oh, no, you've been a lot of help. I appreciate it."

Jenkins pulled on another pair of gloves and returned to the bloated corpse while Ellie and Deveraux scooted through the morgue, bypassing Leon. In the elevator, Ellie leaned against the back wall and sighed heavily. "Now what?" she asked as Deveraux punched the button for the fourth floor. The elevator lurched upward, leaving Ellie's stomach in the basement.

"We get Doctor Mertzer to reevaluate him. Now that we have an approximate physical age, she can better evaluate his cognitive development."

"Why would a six-year-old *not* know his name?"

Deveraux shrugged. "There could be a number of reasons. If, in fact, he is six, he falls between the preoperational and concrete operational cognitive development stages so we need to look at both stages."

Ellie stared at him through the glaze clouding her vision. "And in laymen's terms, that means…"

"Children between the ages of four and six fall into what's known as the intuitive phase of preoperational cognitive development; between the ages of six and eleven, they fall into the operational stage, meaning they're capable of understanding more concrete aspects."

"That still doesn't explain why he doesn't know his name. Or how old he is."

"No, but there's a chromosome abnormality that might."

The elevator stopped and opened. Deveraux escorted Ellie back to his office.

"What type of abnormality?" She sat in the chair facing his desk.

"The Fragile X syndrome. It affects boys more than girls. It's the most common cause of autism." He took a seat at his desk and rifled through a stack of phone messages.

"You think he's autistic?"

Deveraux gnawed on the inside of his lip, his brows lowered, then finally shook his head. "My guess is no. But it could be such a mild case, it's hard to distinguish by outward observation."

Ellie's cell phone rang. She pulled it from the pocket of her jacket and saw her own desk number. She flipped open her phone. "What, Jesse?"

"Thought you'd like to know the uniforms just picked up Reggie Booker. They're bringing him in now."

"OK. I'll be there in a few minutes." She closed the phone and slipped it back into her pocket. No sooner than she had, it rang again. She jerked it from her pocket and flipped it open. "What?"

"Bye."

"Bye, Jesse."

"And by the way, you're welcome."

Ellie stuffed the phone into her pocket and smiled at Deveraux. "The office. We've actually got a witness to interview." She stood to leave and gave him a tiny wave.

He nodded. "Good."

She stuck her head back through the open door. "About this Fragile X thing, you're going to order the tests?"

Deveraux smiled. "I'll call you when we get the results."

****

Reggie Booker was just a tad smaller than a moose. Ellie would bet one bicep was bigger around than her entire body. She glared at him from the outside of the one-way window in the interview room. He didn't look very pleased to be there. A cop in uniform stood in the far corner of the room, one hand casually perched on his holster as if he were just resting it there.

"Are we going to play good cop, bad cop?" Ellie asked Jesse. "If we do, I want to be the good cop."

Jesse laughed. "We'll see how it plays out."

As much as it pained her to admit it, she'd have to give Jesse credit for saving her butt on this one. She shuddered at the thought of approaching Booker at the gym, surrounded by the entire herd of moose.

"You ready?" Jesse asked, his hand already on the door.

"Remember, I'm the good cop." Ellie took a deep breath and nodded, then followed Jesse into the room.

"Reggie, how are you man?" Jesse tossed a folder on the long table then turned a chair around backwards and sat down.

Booker simply glared at him then Ellie. She wanted to scream "I'm the good cop!" but stood frozen near the door.

"I don't think you've ever met Detective Saunders. She's good people so treat her nice."

She started to offer him her hand but was scared he'd body-slam her, so she just slightly smiled.

Booker looked at Ellie, his gaze travelling slowly from the top of her head to her feet. Her skin crawled at the invasion.

"Why don't you have a seat, Mr. Booker. We have a few questions we'd like to ask you." She was standing a few feet away from him, silently calculating his height. The top of her would probably come up to about his mid-chest. She couldn't imagine this bulk of a man climbing in and out of a Honda Accord.

"Sit down, Reggie," Jesse said.

He finally pulled his gaze from Ellie and glared at Jesse. "What do you want, Alvarez?" His voice was bottom-of-the-barrel deep, reminding her of someone using a voice distorter.

"First, I want you to sit down, then I want you to tell me what you were doing in the alley behind Marisol's on Tuesday."

Booker rolled his eyes then finally took a seat across from Jesse. "And what are you going to do for me?"

"Possibly keep you from pulling more time for that piece you were carrying."

Booker studied his manicured cuticles, his face as empty as an uninspired artist's canvas. He raised his eyes and stared at Jesse then shrugged his massive shoulders. "Charge won't stick. Improper search."

Jesse smiled. "You're a convicted felon. Packing a

piece...hmm. Well, if you're willing to take your chances. Looks like we're done here." Jesse stood, scooped up the folder and headed toward the door.

Ellie's gaze darted back and forth between Jesse and Booker. She hoped Jesse was just playing hardball. She wasn't about to give up that easily and the thought of doing this interview alone came close to terrifying her.

"Go ahead and book him," Jesse instructed the uniformed officer.

Ellie was on the verge of panic. Besides the fish delivery guy, Booker was the only lead she had. Granted, it wasn't a strong one, but it was something. "OK, look, Reggie, we don't care about the gun—"

"Excuse me?" Jesse said.

"All I care about is whether or not you saw anything in that alley."

Reggie cut his eyes at Jesse then stared hard at Ellie.

Jesse took Ellie by the arm and tugged her toward the door. "Can I speak with you outside, please?"

Ellie pulled away and moved in front of Booker, safely separated by the table. "All I want to know, Reggie, is if you saw anything. A little boy was nearly beaten to death and left to die in that alley. We know you were in the area Tuesday."

Booker leaned back in the chair and folded his massive arms across his chest. "I don't mess with kids. You know that, Alvarez." He glanced at Jesse then returned his steely gaze to Ellie.

"Yeah, I know. You're a real honorable guy," Jesse said, moving beside Ellie. "She didn't ask you if you put him there. She asked you if you saw anything." He sat back down and pulled a chair out for Ellie.

She sat down beside him, feeling a little safer. She didn't know why. Jesse stood only an inch or two taller than she, and on a bloated day, she probably outweighed him by a couple of pounds.

Ellie pulled Johnny Doe's picture from the folder and slid it across the table to Booker. "This is the child that was found in the alley. Have you ever seen him before?"

To her surprise, Booker actually looked at the picture. "Somebody messed that kid up."

"Yeah, they did. What do you know about it?" Jesse asked.

Booker slid the picture back to Ellie and shook his head. He picked at his fingernails. "I haven't ever seen him before."

Ellie pushed the picture back at him. "We know you were in the area around three. The kid was found around five."

"I didn't see anything. Why don't you find someone who was there around five that you can harass?"

"Harass? Is that what you think we're doing?" Jesse made a *tsk-tsk* sound then cut his eyes up at Booker. "Reggie, honestly, do you think we're harassing you?"

Booker stared at him then went back to picking at his fingernails.

"All we're asking is if you saw anything out of the ordinary," Ellie said.

Booker huffed then spread his monstrous hands open wide. "What do you want me to say? Yeah, I saw someone hanging around with a kid under their coat? I'm telling you I didn't see anything."

"Why'd you park behind Marisol's?"

"It's the only parking lot in the area."

Jesse busted out laughing, and Booker's eyes narrowed. Ellie's throat tightened.

"It's not like you have to fight for a parking space in that area of town," Jesse said, the laugh fading into a chuckle. "Most people just park on the street."

"What were you doing in the area, anyway?" Ellie asked.

"I was being a good citizen and paying my car insurance." He smiled. A front tooth shined with gold.

"Why not just pull up in front of the building? Makes me think there was a reason you wanted to walk through that alley." Jesse said.

Booker sighed and leaned back in the chair. He grinned. "Alvarez, you are one funny dude. I didn't park in front of the building because I didn't want to run into Kepler."

Alfred B. Kepler, Attorney at Law. Ellie almost laughed, but the fear of Booker flying over the table and strangling her made her think twice.

"Why were you avoiding Kepler? You owe him money?" Jesse asked.

Booker stuffed his fat tongue in his cheek and gazed around the room. If avoiding Kepler was Booker's reason for parking in the alley, Ellie figured it was as good as any. "How long were you in the area? Total time," Ellie asked.

He shrugged then shook his head side to side. "Fifteen, twenty minutes."

"And you didn't see anything suspicious around the alley?"

"Nothing. Only thing I saw was that skinny kid that works at the fish market. He was pulling up when I was leaving."

That matched what Dwayne Andrews had told her. "And you actually walked *through* the alley on your way to the insurance agency?"

He stared at her a moment as if she were the stupidest broad ever to be birthed. "Naw, I walked all the way 'round the buildings," he snipped, his head moving in a sing-song motion.

"The lady asked if you walked through the alley. You can tell her in a nice way that 'yes' you walked through the alley, or you can tell her 'no, ma'am, I did not walk through that alley.'"

He cut laser eyes at Jesse, his lips curled in a bull-dog snarl. "You're a piece of work, Alvarez."

Ellie knew for a fact Jesse had been called much worse. "Did you walk through the alley, Reggie?"

"Of course, I walked through the alley. And I'm telling you, I didn't see any kid."

Jesse smiled like an excited kid. "Why didn't you just say that to begin with? That's all we wanted to know."

Booker rolled his eyes then smirked. He glared at Jesse. "True what they're saying on the street about you?"

"I don't know. What are they saying on the street?"

Booker's laugh started deep and low then rose in volume and tone like a submarine slowly coming to the surface. "They say you got busted down 'cause you was sampling the evidence. You ain't nothing but a two-bit street junkie, Alvarez."

Although Booker had piqued her curiosity, Ellie was staying clear of this conversation.

Jesse grinned that sly grin of his and slowly shook his head.

Booker snorted. "Can I go now?"

Jesse motioned toward the door. "Go on and get out of here before I remember that gun violation. Officer Thomas will see you out."

Booker stood, pulling himself inch by inch out of the chair, slowly rising to his full monstrous height. He purposely brushed the back of Ellie's chair as he passed, his fingers lightly touching her hair, sending a cold shiver tingling up her spine. She waited until she was certain Booker was long gone before letting out a long sigh and dropping her head to the table.

"Now aren't you glad you didn't try to interview him at the gym?"

She lifted her head and glared at Jesse. "I think he's the biggest man I've ever seen."

"He's just as mean as he is big, too, darling." He kissed the top of her head, and to her surprise, she didn't want to knock him silly.

She rose and stretched, arching her back like a cat. "Regardless of how big or mean he is, he didn't give us anything we can use."

"Yeah, he did. He gave us a good timeline. If he was in the alley at three, and the kid was found around five, we've got a two-hour time frame."

"But how do we know for sure the kid *wasn't* in the alley at three? Booker's not exactly a reputable witness."

Jesse shook his head. "He ain't an upstanding citizen, but he was telling the truth. He doesn't do kids."

"But what if it was what I said earlier? A drug deal gone bad, and he snatches the kid for payback."

"I think you're barking up the wrong tree, sweetheart. Even if he had snatched a kid, he's not going to beat him to death. There is *some* honor among thugs."

Ellie was so tired, she couldn't think straight. Fragile X syndrome, Reggie Booker, and trash-filled alleys were beginning to run together. Her mind just couldn't think any longer about the sicko that would beat a child and leave him for dead. She wanted to think simple thoughts with simple answers like what she was going to have for dinner or why Jesse always turned his chair around backwards like he was the sheriff in some old western movie. She propped her chin in her hand and stared at him. "Why do you turn your chair around backwards?"

"You're tired, aren't you?" The corner of his mouth turned upward in a slight smile.

She slowly nodded. "You didn't answer my question."

"Self-defense. You can get out of it a whole lot easier, and faster."

She considered it for a moment then sighed. "That almost makes sense. I just thought it was because you're so cocky."

"Well, that too."

11

Ellie yanked off her clothes, pulled on an old Carolina Panthers sweatshirt and a pair of flannel pajama pants then collapsed on the bed. Time and energy had evaporated, leaving her feeling like the case should be measured in weeks rather than hours.

She slowly rose and slipped on a pair of fuzzy socks then padded into the kitchen. Dinner would be either leftover Moo Goo Gai Pan from China House or two slices of leftover pepperoni pizza from Paulie's Pizza. Settling for a glass of tea, she headed to the living room. She sat cross-legged on the floor in front of the chunky coffee table she bought at a yard sale last spring. It was light pine, heavy, with thick legs and time-worn corners, and matched absolutely nothing in her house, but she liked it so much, it was part of her fire escape plan. She imagined herself frantically dragging the thing through the house to the back porch—providing, of course, the fire was located in the front part of the house. If the fire was in the back, no problem; she'd just open the front door and shove the table and her one box of childhood memorabilia into the yard. A pair of initials encased in a rudely drawn heart was carved into one of the corners of the old table. Ellie sometimes sat at night and studied the carving, imagining who the lovers were. Were they still together? Were they still a couple or was their proclaimed undying love just a summer fling?

She looked over the phone messages Jack had given her earlier then glanced at her notepad she had transcribed from her voicemail. There must have been fifty numbers between the two, and that didn't include the new messages she had yet to transcribe. She opened her cell phone and called the first number.

Teresa Batten answered on the first ring.

"This is Detective Saunders with the Burkesboro Police Department. I'm returning a call regarding a missing child."

"Yeah, I saw the story on the news about that little boy." She spit the words out as if they were flames rising up through her throat. "My son disappeared eight years ago. He had blond hair and—"

"How old was your son when he disappeared, Ms. Batten?"

"Six. His father took him. Said I was unfit."

Ellie's heart went out to the woman, but her son didn't seem to be the only thing missing. The woman seemed to be lacking simple math skills as well. "Ms. Batten, I'm assuming your son would be about fourteen years old now, right?"

The woman didn't answer immediately. Ellie imagined her mentally calculating the years. Parents of missing children often ignored time, holding a missing child in a perpetual age freeze. Ellie imagined Teresa Batten still thought of her son as a six-year-old. When she finally spoke again, Ellie could hear the resignation in her voice. "He'll be fourteen his next birthday."

"I'm sorry, Ms. Batten. The child we found is much younger." Before she hung up, Ellie told her she was sorry about her son and gave her the number to the National Center for Missing and Exploited Children.

The second call was parents whose daughter went missing a year ago. The third call was parents who said their son was abducted by aliens, and the aliens must have sent him back.

"A rowdy little fella," the father said.

If she hadn't been so tired, Ellie would have busted out laughing.

She had gotten through ten of the messages when a loud knock at the door stopped her heart and caused her to spill her tea. "Crap," she yelled as she jumped to her feet, the cold liquid seeping through her flannel pants. There was another knock, louder this time.

"Hold on just a second," she yelled as she ran into the kitchen and grabbed a dish towel. She dabbed the wetness from her pants then wiped up the spill. "I'm coming, I'm coming."

She opened the door with a fake smile then wanted to slam it in Jesse Alvarez's face. He pushed by her and dropped a pizza box and a two-liter soda on the coffee table. "Figured you'd need some help returning all those phone messages. I brought food." He smiled. If he weren't so annoying, he really would be a doll.

Ellie jammed her hands on her hips. "Don't you have some sex offender to track down?"

He shrugged. "You got paper plates? Or napkins will work."

Ellie shook her head then went into the kitchen and grabbed a roll of paper towels and two glasses of ice. She should just pile his pizza and soda back in his hands and head him out the door. But she was hungry and figured he owed her for barging in on her case.

When she came back into the living room, he was on the sofa rifling through the pink message slips with one hand while holding a slice of pizza with the other. Thin crust pepperoni and mushrooms—her favorite. How did he know that?

"You've got some duplicates." He laid the messages back on the table and devoured half a slice of pizza in one bite.

"What?" She tore off two paper towels and handed him one then poured them each a glass of soda.

"Duplicates. Same person, same number. We should call them first."

"I was calling in the order they came in. I figured the first callers were the ones most excited about seeing Johnny Doe on the news." She sat on the floor at the coffee table, across from the wet spot, and took a piece of pizza.

"But if someone called more than once, they're frantic for information. Let's pull out the duplicates and check the times. Maybe some of these duplicates *were* the first callers."

She wasn't going to argue with him. Besides, it did sound reasonable.

"So what's new with the kid?" Jesse asked. He took a long swig of his drink.

"Dr. Jenkins found some abnormalities in the tissue sample. But still nothing conclusive." She picked a piece of pepperoni off her slice of pizza and popped it in her mouth, and then filled Jesse in on what Jenkins had told her.

"So the tissue samples could indicate hypothermia, and hypothermia could explain his resurrection—" he said.

"Don't call it a resurrection." She pointed her finger at him and glared with lowered brows.

Jesse laughed. "Why not?"

She sighed heavily. She didn't know why not; it just didn't seem proper. "I don't know. Just don't call it a resurrection."

"Fine. The hypothermia could explain his *coming back to life*, then."

"It could. And the fact he was found in an alley beside a fish market that uses refrigerated trucks makes it even more possible." She angled her glass toward his and tapped the rims of the glasses together then smiled.

"You haven't solved it yet, Sherlock."

"Yeah, but at least we may have some of the medical questions answered."

"What about the bruises and cuts that disappeared?"

Ellie stared at him for a hard minute then finished her pizza. "We're still working on that. Dr. Deveraux's convinced it's a miracle."

"And you're not?" He started on his second piece of pizza.

She slowly shook her head. "I don't know what to believe. I saw the bruises, Jesse. I have pictures of them. They were real."

Jesse grinned. "You're thinking too much like a seasoned detective, sweetcakes."

She raised one brow while lowering the other. "I don't know if I should be offended or take that as a compliment."

"A little of both. Despite what most evidence will tell you, everything's not black and white. Sometimes there's just no logical explanation."

Ellie burst out laughing. "Don't tell me Jesse Alvarez is jumping on the miracle bandwagon, too."

"I was raised Catholic. We're big on miracles." He winked then handed Ellie another slice of pizza.

When she finished, she tore off a couple sheets of paper from her notepad and handed them and a pen to Jesse. "If we get a hit, send them to the station to see Mike Allistar. They can identify him through the picture. I'm not having a whole line of people gawking at him through a hospital playroom."

Jesse settled into the sofa and began calling. They had finished several calls each when the yellow glow of headlights swung across the living room.

"*Oh, no.* I forgot all about Dad and Aunt Sissy," Ellie said as she pulled herself off the floor. She went to the front door and opened it, welcoming her new visitors. She'd never had so much company in her little house.

"Hey, Daddy, Aunt Sissy." She kissed her aunt on the cheek.

"Hey, sweetie," her dad said as he gave her a hug.

"I hope we're not intruding," Aunt Sissy said, casting a sideways glance at Jesse.

Ellie shook her head and laughed. "No. You're not intruding at all." She introduced everyone then offered something to drink. "I can heat some water for coffee, or I've got a fresh pitcher of iced tea."

"Tea would be fine," her dad and Sissy nodded in agreement.

"Why don't you help me in the kitchen, Jesse." Ellie hoped he understood it wasn't a question.

In the kitchen, she took down two mismatched glasses from the cabinet and handed them to Jesse. "My dad used to be a preacher," she whispered. "So watch your language and don't mention anything about…us."

"Us?" He raised his brows and watched her shake ice cubes from a plastic tray. "What *us*?"

She blew a heavy breath and glared at him. "You know what I'm talking about. That…night."

It took him a moment but then his eyes widened. He nodded then smirked. "What are you afraid I'm going to say to him? 'So, Ellie's dad, I hooked up with your daughter, but I wish I never had, so I'm not really a bad dude. I just play one on TV?'"

She shushed him then glared in the direction of the living room. "Please. Just mind your manners, OK?" She filled the glasses with tea then took a deep breath and headed into the living room.

What did he mean by he wished he never had?

****

Ellie carried a pillow and set of sheets into the living room and dropped them on the sofa. Her dad was in the shower, Jesse was gone doing whatever Jesse did at night, and Aunt Sissy was in the spare bedroom getting ready for bed. Ellie returned to her bedroom and grabbed an extra quilt from the chest then carried it to the living room. She stuck her face deep into the floral patchwork and sucked in the sweet smell of cedar. Every now and then, she'd swear she could smell her mother's perfume imbedded deep within the fabric.

Aunt Sissy was back in the living room tucking the fitted sheet around the cushions of the sofa. She was wearing a black tank top with the Harley Davidson emblem stretched across her chest and a pair of flannel lounging pants. "You've still got that old quilt? I'd figured the thing would have dry-rotted by now."

Ellie smiled. "I drag it out every now and then. Aren't you going to be cold? It gets a little drafty in here in the wee hours of the morning."

"You've never had a hot flash, have you?"

Ellie laughed a tired laugh. "All right. But don't say I didn't warn you."

"So tell me about Jesse."

"What?" Ellie's mouth fell open.

"Don't play all innocent." Sissy smiled. She took the quilt and spread it across the sofa. "There's some major chemistry going on between you two."

Ellie plopped onto the sofa and propped her feet on the coffee table. Sissy sat beside her and stared at her, waiting for an answer.

Ellie looked away and laughed. "Stop staring like that. I told you earlier, he's helping me with the case." She could still feel Sissy's questioning gaze.

"Uh-huh. Guess it doesn't hurt that he's absolutely gorgeous, does it?"

"He's gorgeous? I haven't noticed."

They chuckled like school girls. But why was it he never called back? And, why had he all of a sudden pushed his way back into her life? Maybe it *was* all about the case. "Jesse and I work together," she said to Sissy. "That's the extent of the relationship."

Sissy gazed at her unbelievingly.

Ellie looked away, hiding from the knowing gaze.

12

Ellie parked in front of the fish market and walked through the alley around to the back loading dock. It was right at 9:00, and there was no sign of a Bekley's delivery truck. As she ducked back into the alley to escape the wind, her cell phone rang. The caller ID showed her own desk extension.

"Good morning, Jesse."

"Morning, sweetcakes. Tell me about Richie and Tina Chambers."

Ellie stepped over fast food containers and broken beer bottles as she headed back to the warmth of her car. "Why? You got something on them?"

"Tina called this morning and wants to talk to you."

Ellie stopped and drew in a deep breath. "He's not their son, Jesse. They probably saw the news coverage and now they're thinking they missed their chance to be on the cover of some tabloid."

"That's not a very nice thing to say."

"No, but it's probably true. I'll call her when I get back to the office," she said and sighed. "Anything else?"

"Nope. Just returning these calls we didn't get to last night. By the way, Aunt Sissy invited us up to the cabin for a weekend."

"What?" Anger pushed the blood to her head, giving her an immediate headache. "First, she's not *your* aunt so don't call her *Aunt* Sissy, and second, there is no *us*, remember?"

"Chill out. I thought it was a nice gesture."

Her head was pounding. "When did she say this? I *was* there the whole time last night, and I sure don't remember any such invitation."

"She called this morning to tell me how much of a pleasure it was to meet me last night. I told her likewise."

"She called *you*? She must have just called my extension, and since you're loitering at my desk—"

"Actually, she had me paged."

Her head felt like it was going to explode. All she needed was Aunt Sissy involved in her personal life. What there was of it.

The sound of airbrakes and a diesel engine hissed through the alley and around the corner.

"I've got to go. The delivery guy's here."

"OK. We'll talk about it later when—"

Ellie slammed her phone closed and slipped it into her pocket. They would not talk about it later. And she was going to give Aunt Sissy a piece of her mind, too.

A refrigerated delivery truck sporting a blue and green logo of a fish bent into a circle was backing up to the loading dock. The fish looked like it was chasing its tail. Arching over and under the circular fish were the words "Bekley's Wholesale Seafood."

"I see you're back," Shorty McCorkle yelled from the dock. He was wearing his poofy gloves and heavy parka with the fur-lined hat.

"Good morning." Ellie said as she raised herself onto the dock, feeling the rough concrete picking at the seat of her linen trousers. More evidence to support her fight with Jack about the dress code.

"Steps are around on the other end," Shorty said, motioning toward the other side of the dock.

"Thank you." Embarrassed, Ellie smiled and dusted off her bottom.

"Any new leads on the kid?"

"We have several we're following. Have you heard anything new?"

McCorkle shook his head, sending the fur around his face into a frenzied dance. Ellie offered a casual nod then crossed the dock to the driver's side of the truck. A moment or two later, the door opened; the driver got out slowly and even more slowly made his way up the few steps.

"Are you Jerome Kenton?" Ellie asked.

The man glanced at her and nodded. Even that looked painful. Purplish green bruises crossed the bridge of his nose and spread out toward his cheekbones. He looked to be mid-thirties, with shallow lines bordering his lackluster eyes. Average size with drooping shoulders, his confused expression looked like it was permanent. Carrot-colored hair poked from underneath the sides of his Bekley's ball cap.

Each movement seemed to bring a new pain and a new grimace. He moved like a slug toward McCorkle.

"I'm Detective Ellie Saunders with the Burkesboro Police Department. I'd like to ask you a couple questions."

He flashed a surprised glance then quickly looked back at McCorkle. "You're going to have to unload today, Shorty. I'm still pretty banged up." He spoke with a thick accent that wasn't local, similar to Dr. Deveraux's strange cadence.

"Sure, sure. No problem." McCorkle waited for Kenton to unlock the door then rolled it halfway up before his height gave out. He grunted and moaned as he tried to stretch his too-short body just a little bit more. Kenton reached up and finished the job, the pain evident in his scrunched-up face.

"You wanted to ask me some questions?" he said, turning to Ellie.

She stepped out of McCorkle's way. McCorkle carried three large boxes past her and disappeared through the open door of the warehouse. "How'd you get the bruises?" She vaguely pointed at her own nose.

"I was in a wreck, the other night."

"Sorry. We're you in the truck?" She looked at the delivery truck then back at Kenton. "Looks like you got the worst of it." She tried to smile, hoping to put him a little more at ease.

Kenton shook his head. "My old lady and I were coming home the other night and a deer ran out in front of us."

"Ouch. Lot of damage?" She leaned against the outside wall of the warehouse, relaxed, out of McCorkle's way.

He nodded. "Totaled."

"Big ouch." She raised her brows for emphasis. "I saw a big ol' buck the other day lying on the side of 401. Wonder if that was him?"

Kenton shook his head again. "This was on Valley Road, up in Avery County."

Ellie chuckled. "I guess there is more than one deer out there, isn't there? I hope your wife wasn't injured too badly?" She wasn't sure if he was actually married to his *old lady* but didn't feel comfortable using the term herself.

He shrugged. "Broke her wrist. You wanted to ask me some questions?" He shifted his weight from one foot to the other.

"Yeah. You made a delivery here on Tuesday. Do you remember seeing anything odd or out of the ordinary? Maybe someone hanging around in the parking lot that you didn't recognize?"

Kenton shook his head. "I'm not really up here enough to know who belongs and who doesn't."

"So you didn't see anyone?"

Kenton gnawed on his bottom lip. "No, can't say that I did. Sorry." He shifted his weight again. "Did something happen?"

"Actually, yeah. A child was found Tuesday evening badly beaten and dumped in the alley."

Kenton glanced toward the alley and slowly shook his head. "People these days. You have to wonder about 'em."

That was an understatement. "Did you drive this truck Tuesday?"

He stared at her a moment before answering then nodded. "I always drive this truck. You don't think someone did something to it while I was here, do you?"

Ellie cocked her head to the side, unsure of what exactly he meant. It was an odd question. "Do you?"

He shrugged. "I haven't noticed anything."

Ellie walked over and peered inside the back of the truck. Metal shelves bolted to the walls held various sizes of cardboard boxes neatly stacked one on top of the other and secured with bungee cords. Besides being painfully cold inside, it was unusually *clean*.

She turned back to face Kenton. "Where'd you stop before coming here?"

"Today or Tuesday?"

"Does it differ from day to day?"

He bobbed his head. "A little. I've got some stops I make on Tuesday or Thursday, but not both. And then some, like Shorty, I make both days."

"On Tuesday, where'd you stop before Shorty?"

He scratched at his head, sliding his fingers beneath the ball cap. "Garner's Fish Fry. A little restaurant in Dentonville."

"And nothing out of the ordinary happened there?"

Again, he shook his head then smiled. "I'm not college educated or anything, but I probably would have noticed if someone had put a little dead boy in the back there. I mean, maybe not at first, but when I got here to Shorty's, I probably would have seen it."

Ellie stared at him. "I never said he was dead."

Kenton's already pale face turned white. He studied Ellie for a moment. "Sorry. I thought they said on the news that he was dead."

Ellie smiled. "Just goes to show you can't always believe what you hear on the news."

****

Ellie jacked the heat up in the car, flipped open her cell then punched in the extension at her desk. After the third ring, she heard her own voice instructing the caller to leave a detailed message. Where was Jesse? The one time she *needed* to talk to him, he wasn't at her desk. Her heart was beating so fast, she could feel it pulsating in her throat. A flash of anger gripped her as she realized she *wanted* to talk to him.

She wanted to know everything Jesse could dig up on Jerome Kenton, and she wanted to know it *now*. She punched in Jesse's cell number, praying he'd answer. "Come on," she mumbled.

After what seemed like a thousand rings, he finally answered. "Hey, sweetcakes."

"Jerome Kenton knows something. He referred to him as the little *dead* boy and was just a little shocked when I told him the kid wasn't dead."

"Maybe he hasn't seen the news lately. I don't watch it every day."

"You're missing the point. His whole demeanor changed when he found out the kid was alive."

"Didn't yours when you found out he was alive?"

Her excitement evaporated not like a slow deflating tire, but like a total blowout while going a hundred miles per hour.

It was snowing again. Ellie turned the wipers on low and watched as they gently wiped away the cold evidence. She pushed her hand through her hair, digging her nails deep down to her scalp. "S'OK. You're right." She had so many thoughts banging around inside her head she couldn't get a good grasp on any of them. But one did finally spring forward and slammed her so hard she felt her breath catch. "Jesse, what if he is involved, and now that he knows the kid's alive... Tell Jack I want twenty-four-hour security on the kid's room. No one goes in that room unless they're cleared by me."

"OK, OK. Calm down."

"After you do that, I want everything you can dig up on Jerome Kenton. Send his driver's license picture to my cell phone. How long will it take you to get it to me?"

"Not long."

"Good. I'm heading back to the hospital now, and

I'd like to have it when I get there."

She heard him huff. "When'd you get so bossy?"

13

The snow had increased in intensity, and a thin white dusting coated the hospital parking lot. Ellie parked between two news vans near the emergency room entrance. At least they weren't doing live remotes. She waved to Peter Bryson as she passed through on her way up to the fourth floor. Her blood boiled when she stepped off the elevator and saw Sara Jeffries loitering around the nurses' station, chitchatting with one of the nurses. Luckily, Ellie passed without being noticed. She smiled to herself, wondering if Jeffries was losing interest in the story or if she wasn't as observant as she should be. Either way, it was fine with Ellie.

Her cell phone dinged just outside Johnny Doe's room, indicating she had an email. At least Jesse did have good timing. She knocked lightly on Johnny Doe's door then eased it open. He was at the window with Deveraux, working a puzzle spread out on a small table.

"Hey, Ellie," the boy said, a brilliant smile spreading across his tiny face. He was dressed in the red Spiderman sweatshirt.

"How you doing?" She joined them at the table and ruffled his hair.

"We're going to glue it together when we finish, and it'll make a picture." He motioned proudly to his newest work of art. From what she could tell, it was going to be a Golden Retriever puppy in a field of bright yellow daisies.

"Oh, that's *beautiful*."

"Leon came to see me real early this morning. He's coming back later, and we're goin' to the playroom." He added another piece to the puzzle.

"That sounds like fun." Ellie quietly opened her cell phone and downloaded the picture Jesse had sent. It was Jerome Kenton, all right. "Hey, Johnny, I've got a picture, too, and I was wondering if you'd take a look at it. You want to see it?"

He looked at her with an excited smile. "Yeah!"

Deveraux, however, gave her a less than approving glance. Ellie attempted to set his mind at ease. "It's a picture of someone, and I want to know if you've ever seen him before, OK?"

Deveraux's expression was still cautious, and Ellie wondered what in the world he thought she was going to show the kid. The before and after pictures of himself?

Johnny had all but crawled into her lap, anxious to see the picture. Ellie turned it toward him, angling it so he could get a good look. "Have you ever seen this man before?"

She had barely got the question out when Johnny shook his head, the smile wiped from his face as quickly as wipers batting away the snow. He quickly moved away from her and returned to the puzzle. A noticeable anxiousness replaced his enthusiasm. He picked up a piece and turned it over and over in his hand, his eyes searching the puzzle for where to put it.

He laid it down and looked at Deveraux. "Is it time for Leon to come?"

Deveraux glanced at Ellie then back to Johnny and

gently smiled. "Not yet, buddy. He'll be here after lunch, OK?"

Johnny nodded then slowly pushed the puzzle out of the way. "Can I watch TV now?"

"Sure."

As he climbed up in the bed, Deveraux punched the remote and the television clicked on. Johnny sat cross-legged, staring expressionless up at the cartoons skittering across the screen.

"Johnny, are you sure you've never seen this man before?" Ellie asked, moving beside the bed. She moved the phone in front of him but he wouldn't look at it. Instead he looked away, purposely avoiding even the slightest glimpse. "Johnny, it's real important. If you've—"

He jerked his whole body away from the phone and focused on the wall, as if staring at something only he could see.

Deveraux reached over and snapped Ellie's phone closed. "Hey, you know what? I think I'll go call Leon and see if he can come a little early. Would you like that?"

Johnny nodded quickly but didn't turn away from the wall. Deveraux grabbed Ellie by the elbow and led her outside the room.

"I'm sorry. I—"

"Save it." He asked one of the nurses on the floor to stay with Johnny for a few minutes then marched down the hall toward his office with Ellie in tow.

"Marc...can I call you Marc? This is the first good lead we've had, and I, for one, think it's kind of important that we find out who beat him half dead and left him to die in that stinking alley." Ellie pulled her arm away from his grasp.

"It is important." He opened the door of his office and motioned her in. "But so is his emotional stability. Sit."

Ellie felt like a school girl in the principal's office. And she resented it something fierce. "I'll stand. And I won't apologize for doing my job."

"Neither will I." Deveraux moved behind his desk and plopped down in the soft leather chair.

"Marc, you saw his reaction. He recognized the picture."

"No—" he held up one finger, pointed sternly at Ellie. "The picture looked familiar to him, yes. But you don't know if it's the same man or just someone with similar features."

"Regardless, right now this man is the only human being alive that we can connect to this child. And, speaking of this man, I've asked for twenty-four-hour security on Johnny's room. I don't want anyone in that room who's not cleared by me."

Deveraux stared at her as if she had sprouted an extra head. He propped his elbows on his desk, his palms pressed together as if he were praying. "What happened to not wanting to traumatize him?"

"I'm not *traumatizing* him. I'm protecting him."

"Really? Are you sure you're protecting him, or making a name for yourself with this case? You're too focused on the case to see how you're traumatizing this kid. You think having some stranger hanging around outside his door every minute isn't going to scare him? And you think showing him that picture *didn't* traumatize him?"

"You think I *want* to traumatize him?" Ellie hissed. She paced in front of the desk. How dare he think she would ever purposely hurt this or any other child.

"How can you even think such a thing?"

"You saw his reaction, Ellie, and you kept pressing him. You got what you needed as soon as he saw the picture."

"But you didn't give me time to find out how he knew him."

"It wouldn't have mattered at that point. He'd already shut down."

"So now what? I'm just supposed to let it go? I'm not supposed to question him again? I can't do that, Marc."

Marc sighed and leaned back in his chair. "I'll have Doctor Mertzer work with him. *After* he's settled down."

"She's not going to know the questions I need answers to."

He slid a memo pad and pen across the desk. "Write them down."

"At least let me be there when she questions him."

"You can watch from the one-way mirror."

"But—"

"You can *watch* from the one-way mirror," he said again.

Reluctantly, Ellie accepted the pad and pen and sat in the chair across from the desk. Instead of the logo of some pharmaceutical company splashed across the top of the pad, there was a faint picture of Jesus holding a child; the words *"Blessed are the pure at heart for they shall see God"* inscribed beneath it. Ellie jotted down a line of questions then slid the pad back across the desk.

Deveraux glanced down at the paper. "Look, I know you're in a hurry, and I respect that. But we can't push him. It's going to take more than one session to get these answers."

Begrudgingly, Ellie nodded. "What about the other tests? That X-factor test. Anything new on that?"

Deveraux shook his head. "Fragile X. Came back normal. He has a slight indication of a possible marker but it's not really enough to classify as a chromosome abnormality."

"So what does that mean? He's not autistic?"

Again, Marc shook his head. "From all indications, no."

Ellie thought about it for a moment. "I guess then, that's good. But it still doesn't explain why he doesn't even know his name."

"Well, yes and no. There're no physical abnormalities that would cause a mental deficiency. But he's obviously developmentally delayed."

Ellie lowered her brows, questioning what Marc was saying. "Environment?"

He nodded. "Very likely."

She tried to control the sudden rage boiling in the pit of her stomach. Churning and twisting like a vile poison. "Neglect," she mumbled, the word rancid on her tongue.

Whatever connection Jerome Kenton had to this child, she was going to find out. And Kenton may not like the way it was going to end.

Neither of them spoke for a moment. "Do you mind if I ask you a question?" Ellie asked.

He shook his head. "As long as you don't bully me."

Ellie flushed with embarrassment. Jerome Kenton flashed through her mind. "Oh, you haven't seen me bully."

He chuckled. "What's the question?"

"You speak with a hint of an accent I can't place.

The man in the picture speaks in the same dialect."

He lowered his brows and glared at her. "So you think we're related?"

Ellie's eyes widened. "No! That's not what I meant. I just thought if I knew where you were from, it might give me some insight into where *he's* from."

Deveraux nodded. "Cajun country."

"New Orleans?"

"Home of the Mardi Gras itself."

Ellie pondered the information for a moment. "His accent is thicker than yours."

"Then he hasn't been away as long as I have. Like most natives to any given area, Cajuns generally stick close to home. Until Katrina. A lot of them went back; a lot of them didn't."

"And you're one that didn't?"

He shrugged. "I was long gone before the hurricane." There was a certain sadness in his eyes, and Ellie wondered what he'd left behind.

"Why'd you leave? If you don't mind me asking."

He grinned and the sparkle returned to his eyes. "I found God."

Ellie didn't say anything for a moment, deciding to let his statement rest on its own before asking anything else. Finally, she asked in a quiet voice, "You couldn't worship God in New Orleans?"

He smiled, reflectively. "Have you ever read the story of Sodom and Gomorrah?"

She remembered it well from her days in Sunday school. The story of the town so filled with sin, God burnt it to the ground. She wondered what sin Jerome Kenton had in his life.

"Excuse me," a dark-haired nurse said as she poked her head into the office.

"Yeah, come on in. We were just finishing up," Deveraux said.

"I'm glad you're still here," she said to Ellie. "Johnny Doe asked me to give this to you. He said he drew it just for you." She handed Ellie a piece of folded paper, torn from his drawing pad.

Ellie opened the paper and stared at the drawing. Slowly but surely, the pieces of the puzzle were starting to fit together. Although drawn and colored by a child's hand, it didn't take an art expert, or a child psychologist, to recognize the symbols in the picture. A crudely drawn road, a box-shaped car, and a bloodied deer.

****

Ellie punched in Jesse's cell number so fast she didn't notice she had no signal. "Crap," she said out loud, startling the woman standing beside her in the elevator. She smiled at the woman apologetically then hurried out as soon as the doors opened. Once outside, standing in the hard-falling snow, she tried again.

He answered on the second ring, but before he could even say hello, Ellie started rambling. "What did you find out about Kenton? The kid recognized him and then even drew me a picture describing the same wreck Kenton told me about. I don't know exactly what the connection is but—"

"Slow down, slow down! What do you mean you don't know what the connection is?"

She wiped a smattering of snow from her lashes. "I don't know if Kenton's his father, or the guy that dumped him, or maybe both. But there *is* a connection."

"He didn't tell you how he knew him?"

Ellie let out a despairing sigh. "I didn't exactly get that far with him."

"What happened?"

"It's a long story." She didn't feel inclined at the moment to get too deep into the argument with Deveraux.

"Hmm. OK, meet me at Caper's. I'll buy your lunch. You can tell me about it then."

She glanced at her watch. "It's ten thirty."

"Then I'll buy you brunch."

"I'm not even hungry."

"Work with me, Ellie."

She supposed she could use another cup of coffee. "OK. But I'm going to run up and see my dad for a minute while I'm here then I'll be on my way. Give me half an hour, and I'll meet you there."

"OK, so we're back to lunch."

She tried hard not to smile. "Whatever. Thirty minutes." She clicked off her phone then hurried back into the hospital and up to the fifth floor.

She hoped Peggy hadn't...like, died or anything. That would sure throw a damper on her enthusiasm. She turned down the hallway where Peggy's room was but didn't see her dad or Aunt Sissy. *Great. They're in the room.* She stood outside the closed door for a moment, gathering her courage, then lightly knocked.

"Come in," Aunt Sissy said, her voice muted through the door.

Ellie gently pushed open the door. She threw a quick glance at Peggy and was relieved beyond measure when she saw her stepmother was sound asleep. Medically induced or otherwise, it really didn't matter. Ellie didn't have to talk to her, and that's what mattered. Her father was in a recliner beside the bed and rose to greet her. He looked so tired, like he didn't sleep well, although he'd told Ellie he had. Aunt Sissy was sitting in a chair near the window reading one of those romance novels she loved so much. She closed it and set it aside then stood to offer Ellie a hug.

"I have a bone to pick with you," Ellie whispered in her aunt's ear.

Aunt Sissy pretended to look surprised then grinned mischievously.

"How's the little boy?" her father asked in a low voice.

Ellie bobbed her head up and down. "We're making some headway."

"Good. I've been praying for him."

Ellie couldn't help herself from glancing at Peggy. Her father's wife so sick, so near death, and he still found time, and strength, to pray for others. Even for a little boy he didn't even know.

She felt tears welling in her eyes and quickly looked away from the dying woman in the bed. "Are y'all going to stay again tonight? You're welcome, to you know."

"We appreciate it, but we don't want to impose."

"Dad, you're not imposing. Besides, it's snowing pretty hard, and you don't need to be on the roads driving deeper into the mountains."

He glanced out the window and twisted his lips into a tight grimace. "It is coming down pretty good now, isn't it?"

Peggy gasped a noisy breath then settled back into oblivion. Ellie's father moved to the bed and lovingly stroked her small gray tufts of hair. Ellie's heart wrenched, and she batted back the tears that threatened to spill onto her cheeks. She never saw him stroke her mother's hair like that. She never saw him hovering at *her* bedside, spilling tears onto the sheets. But in all fairness, her mother never gave him the opportunity.

Ellie shook the images of blood and razor blades and wailing sirens from her head and sucked in a deep breath. "Well, it's settled then. I'll see y'all tonight at home." She forced a smile, gave her dad a quick hug then started to hug her aunt but Sissy took her by the hand instead.

"I'll walk you out."

Outside the room, Aunt Sissy continued to hold Ellie's hand as they walked slowly toward the elevators. "Now what was that bone you wanted to pick with me?"

"Whatever, in your right mind, made you call Jesse this morning and invite us to the cabin?" She stopped walking and turned to face her aunt. She pulled her hand away and folded her arms tight across her chest, jaw set, ready for the face-off.

"Us?" Sissy scrunched her brows, a look of confusion darkening her eyes.

Ellie huffed. "Yes. He said you called and invited us to come up for a weekend. Called him specifically. You didn't bother to run it by me first, did you?"

Sissy's lips slowly spread into a tight smile. "There was no need to run it by you first. You weren't invited. Obviously, he missed that part."

Ellie's mouth fell open, allowing a slight gasp to escape. "Aunt Sissy! He's young enough to be your grandson." She turned away and paced back and forth up and down the hallway. She didn't know what was going to be worse: telling Jesse he had misunderstood the invitation or telling him her crazy aunt had the hots for him.

"What's the big deal?" Sissy asked, innocently. "Am I stepping on your toes? You made it clear last night you had no interest."

"No, I said we had a *working* relationship." Ellie stared at her aunt, unbelieving. "Aunt Sissy—he's thirty years old!" She fought to keep her voice down. "If I'm not mistaken, you celebrated your seventieth birthday over the summer. You don't find anything *weird* about that?"

"I'm game if he's game."

Ellie shuddered at the mental image that flashed through her brain. Sissy lowered her brows and glared at Ellie for a long moment.

"I don't think age is your problem—" Sissy said.

"Oh, it's a part of it all right."

"No, I think your problem is you got your toes stepped on. I told you last night you two had chemistry, but *no,* you were adamant it was a *working* relationship. You can't have it both ways, sweetheart."

Ellie spun around in a circle, not believing she was having this conversation. "I really don't need you to play matchmaker, Aunt Sissy. I'm perfectly capable of ruining my own life."

Sissy busted out laughing. "That's your problem, Ellie. You have no joy. Where's the joy in your life?"

"OK, this conversation is over." Ellie marched toward the elevator and slammed her hand against the down button. Why was it every time she needed to make a quick escape the darn elevator stopped at every floor?

"We'll continue tonight over a cup of hot chocolate," Sissy yelled from down the hall.

Ellie turned her head and glared at her crazy aunt. Sissy waved and smiled as Ellie escaped into the elevator. She leaned against the back wall, closed her eyes, and took a long deep breath.

14

The parking lot of Caper's was beginning to fill with the early lunch crowd. Ellie wasn't used to eating lunch this early, but she wasn't one to pass up a free meal, even if it was with Jesse. She parked beside Jesse's car and went inside. He was in a back booth and waved her over. She wondered what was wrong with the stools at the counter. Being in a back booth with Jesse Alvarez seemed a little too…personal.

It didn't help that at that moment he looked like the stuff fantasies are made of. He was wearing a navy V-neck sweater with a white t-shirt peeking out from the V, a five o'clock shadow outlining his perfect jaw line. His coal-colored eyes shone like black onyx. She took a deep breath and slid into the booth.

"How's Peggy?"

She looked at him a moment, her brows lowered. "Peggy who?"

"Peggy—your step mom."

Ellie felt her breath catch. "She is *not* my step mom. She is nothing more than my father's wife. And besides, how do you know about Peggy?"

"Aunt Sissy told me all about her, and you…and your dad."

Although it was freezing outside and there was a cold blanket of snow on the ground, her rising anger made her insides boil. The only thing that saved Jesse from her leaping across the booth and choking him to death was the waitress walking up at that moment to take their drink order.

"Tea. With lemon," Ellie snapped, still fuming.

Jesse ordered the same and smiled at the waitress then hesitantly turned the smile on Ellie.

Not a chance. Not this time. He'd crossed the line.

"We do *not* discuss my father's wife. Is that understood?"

Jesse twisted a paper napkin between his fingers. "Aunt Sissy said you had issues."

Ellie leaned across the booth and gritted her teeth. "I do not have issues."

He raised his hands in defeat. "I'm just saying."

The waitress returned with their drinks and stood by waiting for their order. Ellie sighed heavily and leaned back in the seat. "BLT with mayo and cheese."

Jesse smiled at the waitress. "The same." She scribbled on her pad then trotted off toward the kitchen. Jesse leaned into the booth, his arms folded in front of him. "Don't be mad at Aunt Sissy."

Ellie guffawed. The list of *issues* she had with Aunt Sissy at the moment was growing. "I just don't appreciate my personal life being the topic of someone else's conversation."

Jesse slowly nodded. "Fair enough."

Ellie eyed him suspiciously. "That's it? Just 'fair enough,' and I'm supposed to believe you and Aunt Sissy will stop trying to figure out everything that's wrong with me?"

He furrowed his brows and frowned then slowly nodded again. "When you're ready to talk about it, you'll talk about it. Tell me about Kenton."

Ellie sank down into the vinyl seat and glared at Jesse. "*Just like that*—you're going stop talking about me behind my back?"

He chuckled then took a drink of his tea. "We're not in high school. No one is talking about you behind your back. Boy, are you paranoid."

"You and Aunt Sissy sure seem to have a lot of conversations involving me that I'm not a part of."

Jesse laid his forehead on the table and lightly thumped it against the wood. "We won't talk about you anymore." He groaned. It came out as a mumble. He lifted his head and stared at her, then smiled that glorious smile. "Tell me about Kenton."

She'd lost her enthusiasm about the new lead about the same time her crazy aunt insinuated she wanted to do unspeakable things to Jesse. She leaned into the table and propped her chin in her hand. "Johnny Doe recognized him."

"How do you know? How do you know it wasn't someone he thought he knew?"

"The kid totally shut down. He couldn't get away from the picture fast enough." Ellie took a drink of her tea and continued. "When I was interviewing Kenton, I noticed he was pretty banged up so I asked him what had happened to him. He said he and his wife were in a wreck Tuesday night, that a deer ran out in front of them and they ended up totaling the car. Before I left the hospital, a nurse brought me this picture Johnny Doe drew. He told her to give it to me." She dug the folded picture from her jacket pocket, opened it, then slid it across the table toward Jesse.

He stared at it hard, his lips pursed with concentration. After a long moment, he looked up at Ellie. "That seems to be a definite connection."

"Did you find anything on him?"

He shook his head. "Nothing that piqued my

interest. He's from New Orleans, been at Bekley's about four years."

"I figured he was from New Orleans. He speaks with the same accent as Dr. Deveraux." She could tell by Jesse's expression the name was foreign to him. "He's the chief of pediatrics. I asked him about his accent, and he referred to it as Cajun country. I told him Kenton's accent was a lot stronger than his, and he said Kenton probably hadn't been away as long as he had."

The waitress brought their sandwiches, and Ellie dove in before the lady had time to set Jesse's plate down. The crispy bacon eased her anger with Jesse.

"And Kenton being from New Orleans is important how?" He was still munching on his chips and hadn't even touched his sandwich.

Ellie shook her head, swallowed a mouthful. "I don't know. Maybe he was uprooted by Katrina. And just never went back." She shrugged her shoulders. She didn't know if Kenton's Cajun roots had anything at all to do with little Johnny Doe, but she knew there *was* a connection between Kenton and the kid.

"Sorry, sweetie, but I still don't get what Kenton possibly being from New Orleans and the kid have in common. Is the kid from New Orleans?"

Ellie thought about it for a moment then shook her head. "I don't think so. He's got a little bit of an accent, but it's not the same as Kenton's and Dr. Deveraux's. It's more of a regular Southern accent."

Jesse finally took a bite of his sandwich then made a face. "Who puts cheese on a BLT?" He opened the sandwich and pulled off the piece of cheese.

"You're the one who ordered it."

He turned his nose up and frowned. "I'll dig

further into Kenton's background, and you press the kid."

Ellie laughed out loud. "Yeah, wish me luck with that. Deveraux had me write a list of questions for the child psychologist to ask him. He doesn't want me questioning him again."

"What'd you do to him?" He looked at her with a blank expression.

"The picture of Kenton really upset the kid. Deveraux thinks I *traumatized* him."

"Did you?"

"No. If I did, I certainly didn't mean to." She had accepted the fact Johnny Doe had an unpleasant reaction to Kenton's picture, but how else was she supposed to make any headway on this case? She wasn't being given a lot to work with.

Jesse took another bite of his sandwich and chewed slowly. Ellie could almost see the wheels in his head turning. Finally, he swallowed then lifted a finger pointed at Ellie. "But, the kid drew *you* a picture of the deer and the car. He was connecting with you, *not* the child psychologist."

Ellie thought about what Jesse had said then leaned back in the booth. "Deveraux can't argue with that."

"If Deveraux's being uncooperative, we can—"

Ellie was quick to shake her head. "No, it's not that. He's just protective of the kid. Which, honestly, I am, too. I cringe every time I see a reporter lurking in the hallway."

"Yeah, but you're not looking for a headline. You're actually trying to help the kid."

Ellie sighed. "Deveraux did tell me all of Johnny's tests came back negative. There's no physical reason for him to be developmentally delayed, so it's more than likely environmental."

"But is he really *delayed*, or is he just not telling what we need to know?"

Ellie rolled her shoulders to release the mounting tension. Johnny Doe, Jerome Kenton, Jesse. They were each causing her a great deal of stress. "I don't know. You know he hasn't once asked for his mom or dad? I don't know that much about kids, but it seems like a kid his age would be asking for his mommy and daddy. The only time he's even mentioned them was when I interviewed him in the morgue."

Jesse lifted an eyebrow. "What'd he say?"

"I asked him if he remembered what he was doing before he woke up in the morgue, and he said he was talking to his daddy. When I asked what they were talking about, he changed the subject, and Doctor Terry wouldn't let me push him. It was clear he didn't want to talk about it anymore."

Jesse leaned into the table, his lips puckered with deep thought. "Then it's possible his dad was the last one to see him before *someone* beat the crap out of him. And if daddy's the one who beat the crap out of him...maybe he doesn't want to get him in trouble."

Ellie's heart quickened. She leaned into the table, just inches away from Jesse. "Or maybe someone *didn't* beat the crap out of him. Maybe he was in a *horrible wreck*."

Jesse's eyes narrowed. Ellie could feel his warm breath on her face.

"But why dump him? Why not call for an ambulance?" he said.

Her heart beat so fast it throbbed in her throat. "I've got to find out Kenton's connection to this kid."

****

Ellie burst out of the elevator on the pediatric floor, sprinting toward Deveraux's office. The door was open but the office was empty. She found one of the nurses and asked where he was.

The nurse glanced at her watch. "He's probably at lunch. You might find him in the cafeteria."

Ellie thanked her then turned and ran toward the stairs. She shoved the heavy door open then flew down the concrete steps to the first floor. She hurried to the cafeteria and found Deveraux at a table by himself, eating a too-healthy looking salad. *Figures,* she thought.

"I know what you're going to say, but I *have* to talk to Johnny," she blurted out as she slid into a chair across from him. She dug the picture out of her pocket and slid it across the table so he could see it. "He's reaching out to *me*. Not Doctor Mertzer."

Deveraux stared at the picture then started to speak, but Ellie cut him off. "This picture has meaning. It's directly connected to the man in the picture I showed him earlier."

Deveraux slightly shook his head. "The picture you showed him traumatized him. I can't have—"

"And afterward, he drew this picture. For *me*, Marc. He's telling me there is a connection."

Again, Deveraux shook his head. "Then it's up to *you* to find the connection."

Ellie's excitement threatened to turn to anger. "I can't find the connection without his help. He drew the picture, Marc. He wants to help. He *wants* to tell me what happened."

"And what if he shuts down again?"

"Each time I've questioned him, I've learned a little bit more. Piece by piece. If that's how I have to get the information, I'm willing to take it like that, at his pace." She jabbed her finger at the picture between them on the table. "This is a major piece. This is a breakthrough, Marc. I can't *not* move on it."

Deveraux sighed heavily then pushed his salad aside. "I want Doctor Mertzer present."

Ellie bit her bottom lip. She wasn't sure she should push any harder. Johnny was comfortable talking about everything under the sun with any number of people in the room, but when it came to what happened to him, Ellie knew she was the lone person with that honor. "What if I talk to him in the playroom with you and Doctor Mertzer watching from the one-way mirror?"

Deveraux lowered his brows and glared at her. "We've already discussed this."

Ellie nodded. "But that was before he drew the picture. I'm not asking to take him off somewhere alone. You and Dr. Mertzer will be twenty feet away. Y'all can swoop in and rescue him at any time. Please, Marc. I know you want to find who did this to him as much as I do."

Deveraux blew a defeated breath. "I'll set it up. But I'm warning you—the first time I see him so much as flinch, I'm coming in there."

Ellie nodded her agreement. "Fair enough." She leaned into the table, perched on the edge of the plastic chair. Adrenaline was surging through her veins and she didn't want to lose the momentum. "Can you set it up now?"

"She's scheduled to see him later this afternoon.

I'll let you know what time."

Ellie pulled her cell phone from her pocket and held it out in front of him. "Could she come now?"

He stared at the phone a moment then took it, shaking his head. "You're very pushy." He punched in a number then drummed his fingers on the table while he waited. A few seconds later, she answered. "Liz— it's Marc. There's been a new development in the Johnny Doe case. Detective Saunders would like to question him in the playroom, and I'd like for you to be on hand to observe." He slightly nodded his head, said "uh-huh" a couple of times, grinned once. "As soon as possible." He nodded again. "Yeah, I think she can live with that. See you then." He closed the phone and handed it back to Ellie. "She'll meet us at the playroom in thirty minutes. She's eating lunch." He glanced at his salad then smiled sarcastically at Ellie.

Ellie flushed and grinned sheepishly. "Thanks. You don't know how much I really do appreciate this." Ellie leaned further into the table. "In your professional opinion, could the injuries he came in with be consistent with injuries received in an automobile accident?"

Deveraux looked again at his salad then finally pushed it aside and sighed. "It's hard to say. Remember, I didn't actually see the injuries."

Ellie spoke quietly, afraid Sara Jefferies and her recorder might be lurking behind the condiment rack. "But you saw the pictures."

"You think this all might be explained by a car wreck?"

She sighed heavily and slowly pushed her fingers through her hair. "I don't know. Even if he was involved in a wreck, it doesn't explain how he got in that alley. Someone had to put him there."

"What if whoever did it, did it out of love or remorse? Not out of meanness."

Ellie raised her brows and stared at him. "They beat the crap out of him out of love? Sorry, doc, I'm not buying that."

"Let me explain. What if what ever happened to him *was* an accident. And whoever-it-was took him to the alley because they didn't know what else to do."

Ellie shook her head. "He was dumped. If someone had felt the least bit of pity for him, they would have covered him with something. An old newspaper, a trash bag, anything they might have had on hand. And there was plenty of stuff lying around him to have covered him with. Besides, if they cared anything at all, why didn't they bring him to the hospital to get him help?"

Deveraux thought about it for a moment then nodded his understanding. "We don't always know what makes people do the things they do. It's not up to us to judge, anyway."

Ellie's mouth turned upward in an evil grin. "You're right—it's up to a jury of their peers."

Deveraux smiled. "That's not exactly what I meant, but I suppose you're right to a certain degree. But"—he lifted a finger and pointed it at her—"even *they* don't have the final judgment."

****

Ellie paced back and forth outside the playroom like a nervous cat, waiting for Dr. Mertzer to join them. Johnny was already in the room with Leon, smashing tiny cars into stacked blocks, laughing hysterically at their destruction. Ellie glanced at her watch and wanted to point out to Deveraux that Dr. Mertzer was five minutes late. But since they were doing her a favor, she thought perhaps she'd better not.

"She'll be here," Deveraux said and smiled.

Ellie nodded slightly and leaned against the glass, staring at the little boy on the other side. What was he going to tell her? How far would she get before he shut down again?

"Marc, sorry I'm late. Got tied up on a phone call."

Ellie spun around to get her first look at Dr. Mertzer. She was a squatty woman with short chestnut-colored hair and glasses too big for her face. She was wearing an ankle length skirt and a boxy sweater, layers of colorful beads hanging around her thick neck.

Ellie wasn't sure why she had expected a tall, leggy blonde in a power-suit with waxed brows and shiny lips, but the real Dr. Mertzer looked a lot more kid-friendly than the imagined one.

Deveraux introduced her to Ellie. "Why don't you show Doctor Mertzer the picture he drew for you?"

Ellie pulled the picture from her pocket and carefully unfolded it then handed it to Mertzer. "I had showed him a picture of a man we think may be connected to him, and that man was recently involved in a car accident involving a deer."

Mertzer studied the drawing, slowly nodding her head as Ellie spoke. "And the picture of the man you showed him frightened him?"

"I don't know if it *frightened* him, but there was a definite reaction."

"He shut down," Deveraux said. Ellie threw him a sideways glance, objecting to his choice of words.

"And he drew this after you showed him the picture?" Mertzer asked.

"Yes. Doctor Deveraux and I had left the room and a short while later a nurse brought it to me and said he wanted to give it to me."

Mertzer handed the picture back to Ellie. "Concentrate on the drawing first. See if you can get him to discuss the meaning behind it. He's obviously more comfortable talking about the accident than his relationship to the man in your picture, and if there is a connection, you'll still get your answers."

"And if he starts shutting down, you shut up." Deveraux glowered at her with very threatening eyes.

Ellie returned the threat with a smirk then headed into the playroom.

"Hello, gorgeous!" Leon shouted and sprang up from the miniature chair, grabbed Ellie and spun her around in one of his impromptu dances.

Johnny laughed so hard his blue eyes watered.

"You like that, huh?" Leon said, laughing at Johnny.

Could he possibly like it a little less before I get dizzy? Ellie bowed out of a third spin then ruffled the little boy's hair. "Hey, kiddo," she said, nearly breathless.

"Did you come to play with us, too?"

"Well, actually I came to play with *you*, because Leon has to go back to work. Don't you, Leon?"

Leon looked at her a moment, a puzzled look on his face. But then Leon always had a puzzled look on his face, so Ellie smiled and clarified. "I need some alone time with my favorite little guy. You don't mind, do you, Leon?" She bobbed her head toward the door.

Leon had an *ah-ha* moment and followed with a high five with Johnny. "Yep, my break time's over, so

I'll see you again this evening, sport."

A twinge of disappointment shadowed the child's face, driving a searing dagger straight through Ellie's heart. She wondered how much disappointment this child had had in his life. And knowing she contributed to any amount of it broke her heart. She took a deep, slow breath. She had a job to do, and the sooner she found out who this child was and what had happened to him, the sooner he could begin to heal from the wounds no one could see.

She lowered herself into one of the tiny chairs. She could have choked on her own knees. She wondered how Leon managed to sit in the things. She picked up one of the small cars and turned it over and over in her hand. "So you and Leon were playing cars. Bet that was fun, huh?"

Johnny grinned a grin that totally divided his face into two different plains. "It was awesome! We built these castles with these blocks—see—and then rammed the cars into them like this." He demonstrated the process and cackled at the flying blocks. Ellie ducked to avoid getting whopped in the face by a large red block.

"Too funny," she said as she straightened up.

"I got a bunch that time. Count them."

Ellie started counting the blocks then stopped. "There's too many here to count by myself. You help me."

He counted out three blocks then quickly stopped and handed her a green Mustang. "Your turn."

"You have to tell me what comes after three first." She smiled and held up one block, holding it above the pile of three.

He honestly tried, studying the block as if he were

cramming for an exam.

"Four," she mouthed silently.

"Four!" he shouted, smiling widely.

"Very good!" She dropped the block and held her hand up for a high five.

He slapped her hand then she took her turn and rammed the Mustang into a tower, causing a couple of the blocks to topple over.

Grinning, Johnny shook his head. "You're still learnin'. Whoever knocks down the most blocks wins."

"Oh. I see." She grabbed the Mustang and slammed it into the remaining tower. "Better?"

He bobbed his head. "A little. It's my turn now. Help me build another castle first." He gathered the blocks and started the project. When they had several layers of colorful blocks locked into place, he picked a black Corvette and took out a corner of the foundation with one try. He sprang up from his chair, clapping, hooting, and hollering. "Did you see that?"

"I saw! You are very good at this."

"Your turn now." He handed her the green Mustang.

Ellie pursed her lips. "Let's see, the object of the game is to knock down the most blocks, right?"

Johnny nodded. Ellie put the little car back in line with the others and started to take a heavy-duty pickup truck, but Johnny grabbed it first. "We don't use this one," he said quietly, his face suddenly serious. He shoved the truck to the side and handed her the Mustang.

"Oh. OK. The Mustang it is, then." She rammed the little car into the same general location where Johnny had hit jackpot. A couple of blocks fell and Johnny shook his head again then swept the blocks over to Ellie's side of the table. "Why can't we use the truck?" she asked.

"We just can't. I don't like playing with it."

Maybe the little box-shaped car in his drawing wasn't a car at all. "I thought, from the picture you drew me, you liked trucks."

He shook his head then smashed the Corvette into the tower. But he wasn't laughing. He quietly swept his blocks onto his side of the table. "Your turn."

"That was a truck in the picture, *wasn't* it? And a...dog, maybe? Do you like dogs?"

He nodded quickly.

"So do I. I used to have a big 'ol brown dog named Callie. Have you ever had a dog?"

"It wasn't a dog. It was a deer." They weren't taking turns anymore. He rammed his car into what remained of the faltering tower.

"I didn't see any people in the truck you drew for me. Were you in the truck in the picture?"

In one clean swipe, he cleared the table of the remaining blocks. Ellie jumped, startled at the sudden intensity of his action. She held her breath, glancing toward the window, waiting for Deveraux and Dr. Mertzer to come rushing into the room. *Come on. Don't shut down on me, Johnny. Not yet.*

"You were in the truck when it wrecked, weren't you?"

His eyes glittered with tears. "We hit a deer. We killed it."

Ellie took the child into her arms and gently pushed his head onto her shoulder. "Shh. It's OK. It wasn't your fault. Accidents happen." Who was *we*? Who was in that truck with him? She had a good idea it was Jerome Kenton.

Ellie sat the child on her lap and brushed away a spattering of tears. "Johnny—who was in the truck with you? Was it your mom and dad?"

She felt his little body tense. She didn't want to push him, to traumatize him more than he had already been, but she needed answers to help him. "Johnny, tell me who was in the truck with you."

He bolted from her lap, shaking free of her grasp. He moved away from her, moving to the other side of the room. She glanced at the window. *Just one more minute. Please, one more minute.* She moved after him, pressing him for an answer. "Johnny, were your mom and dad in the truck with you?"

He coward in the corner, shaking his head violently then burst out crying. "They aren't my mom and dad!"

Ellie tried to calm her pounding heart. "Was it the man in the picture?"

Deveraux and Dr. Mertzer burst through the door and rushed over to the corner but Ellie moved in and swooped the child up in her arms. She wrapped her arms tight around him as he sobbed onto her shoulder. She glanced at Deveraux. His usually warm eyes were blazing with anger. Ellie turned away, hating herself for putting the child through this.

"Was the man in the picture in the truck with you? Johnny, please, you have to tell me. Was it the man in the picture?"

Through the sobs, she felt the slightest bit of a nod. She finally let out a long, slow breath then quietly held up her hand to let Deveraux know it was over. She carried Johnny over to a rocking chair in the opposite corner and sat, coddling the child with as much comfort as she could offer.

Ellie remembered...

She tromped through the snow covering their long driveway and up the steep incline toward the parsonage. She heard the school bus pull away but didn't turn around to wave to her friends. Or the ones she used to call friends. If they had been real friends, they wouldn't have whispered and laughed at the rumors swirling around town about her dad and the church secretary, Peggy Clayton. She didn't even know what half the rumors meant. All she knew was her father wasn't preaching anymore, her mom cried all the time, and she just wanted to crawl in a hole and never come out. She choked back tears each time the kids at school pointed their fingers at her, their hands cupped around their mouths so she wouldn't hear as they spread the horrible gossip.

She stomped the snow off her boots then went inside the house through the back door, stopping in the laundry room to remove her boot. She wiggled out of her heavy parka, stuffed her gloves in the pockets and hung it on the knob behind the door. The house smelled like warm brownies. Ellie stood in the laundry room a minute taking in the smell, wondering if what was supposed to be a pleasant smell brought other kids the same fear it brought her. She swallowed hard then joined her father in his office.

It was a small office, off the big dining room with the heavy drapes and rickety-old cabinet that held her mother's china. It was drafty and cold and she couldn't remember ever eating in the room. Her father's office, though, was small and warm and clustered with piles of books and various Bibles and pictures of Jesus dying on the cross. The pictures gave her the heeby-jeebies. Not that she didn't appreciate His sacrifice; she did. It was just seeing it on every wall.

She gave her dad a quick peck on the cheek. He wrapped an arm around her waist. "Hey beautiful," he said and returned her simple kiss. "How was school?"

Ellie shrugged, wondering if she should tell him the truth. He looked like he had his own problems to deal with.

"I got an A on my English test," she said.

"Great! I knew you could do it." He squeezed her waist then kissed her again. "Your mom…made some…goodies. They're in the kitchen." He forced a smile but the sorrow in his eyes gave away the sadness.

Ellie wondered what all her mother had made this time. Brownies, cookies, cakes, pies—enough to feed the whole town twice. She'd take these spells when she wanted to prove she was a good wife and cook and bake into a maddening frenzy. The kitchen would look like a bomb had exploded, leaving a dusting of white flour over every surface. Pots and pans of every shape and size with sticky residues of chocolate and fruit and cream-colored batter were scattered all over the kitchen, some teetering on top of others.

Her mother would measure and stir and mix and bake until exhausted, leaving Ellie and her father to deal with the aftermath. They would clean up silently, neither wanting to acknowledge the sound of her mother wailing from the back bedroom. The crying would go on for hours, eventually petering down to a few moans then her mother would fall off to sleep and wake up the next morning as if nothing had happened.

Ellie stood at the door of her father's office for a moment before going to the kitchen. She had to get her nerve up, wondering what kind of mess her mother had left her to clean up this time.

But something was different this time. The house was silent. Ellie peeked into the kitchen and wasn't surprised to see the piles of dirty baking dishes. She stood perfectly still a moment and listened for the sobs but they never came. Quietly, she moved down the long hallway to her parent's bedroom. There was no sound at all. Ellie gently pushed the door open, expecting to see her mother curled up on the bed crying softly into her pillow. But she wasn't there. Slowly, Ellie walked into the bedroom, each step more guarded than the last. "Mom?" she said in a tiny voice.

She moved a couple steps toward the bathroom in her parent's room and stopped. The door was closed but she could see the blood seeping underneath it, seeping into the white carpet, staining it bright pink. She opened the door and wanted to scream but no sound would come out. She had never seen so much blood in her entire life. She was eleven years old and watching her mother die.

The next few hours, she felt like the birds that gathered on the back fence. Watching, just watching. She wondered where Ellie had gone. Had she floated off somewhere far away? But she was here—she had to be. She could feel the rough texture of the wallpaper in her parent's bedroom poking through her sweater as she pressed her back against the wall, hoping she could just fade into it. She could hear her father's screams, she could hear him crying "No, no…no," over and over again. She could see him slipping in the puddles of blood on the bathroom floor then cradling her mother's lifeless body in his arms. She could see her mother's arms, limp, no longer spewing the blood she needed to live. She could see the glint of the shiny razor gleaming like a precious gemstone. She could feel the coldness of the steel gurney as it brushed her arm when the paramedics hurried into the room.

Then suddenly she felt warmth, felt comfort, as Aunt Sissy pulled her out of the way and away from the death. Sissy grabbed her up in her arms, carried her into the living room, and sat in her mother's rocking chair, cradling her in her arms like Ellie had seen women cradle the babies in the nursery at church. She knew she was probably a little too big to be rocked like a baby but it felt good. It was comforting.

15

Ellie was so drained, her body ached. Mentally, emotionally, and physically. She didn't even bother with a flight or two of the stairs leading to her desk, opting instead for the elevator for the complete task. Forget firming her legs. She'd do that tomorrow.

She stopped at her desk for a moment and stared at Jesse.

He glanced at her, his eyes suddenly serious. "You look like crap."

She was too tired to defend herself. Even to Jesse.

"You found out something, didn't you?"

She nodded once. It was a slight movement, and if someone weren't looking for it, they would have missed it. She walked back to Jack's office with Jesse following at her heels. She didn't wait for an invitation and instead went in and sank into one of the chairs in front of his desk. He looked up at her over the rims of his glasses. Jesse propped himself in the doorway.

Ellie rolled the words around in her mouth like she was chewing a tough piece of meat. She never thought she'd be the one asking this of Jack, especially with this case. "I want to go to the national media."

Jack leaned back in his chair and propped his hands behind his head. "No new leads?"

Ellie shook her head. "Just the opposite." She filled him in on the new developments and Jerome Kenton and how they were connected. "I don't know if the child was kidnapped or if Kenton was a neighbor, an uncle, or a family friend who might have been babysitting that day. I do know Kenton's not his father so his real parents are out there somewhere."

"Didn't he say he remembered talking to his dad before he woke up in the morgue," Jesse reminded her.

"Maybe his dad was the third person in the truck?" Jack asked.

Ellie shook her head. "Kenton told me he and his 'old lady' were involved in the wreck."

Jack leaned into his desk, folding his arms in front of him. "Let me talk to the chief. I'm sure he'll be fine with it, but don't want to jump the gun. Let me get his blessing first."

Back at her desk, Ellie buried her face in her hands. She took a couple of deep, slow breaths.

"You OK?" Jesse asked. He had claimed the chair in front of her desk and sat, staring at her, a look of genuine concern on his face.

She nodded. "I had to push him further than I wanted. Whatever memories he has, they aren't good ones." She thought of her own memories and how she wished she had kept them buried instead of reliving them again in that playroom. Maybe one day she would share them with Jesse. But today wasn't that day.

"Tina Chambers called again. I think you might want to call her back. She said she thought she recognized the boy."

Ellie perked up. "Did she say anything else?"

Jesse shook his head. "She didn't want to talk to anyone but you."

Ellie frowned, wondering what suddenly brought that bond on. "Have you got her number?" She scanned her desk for the pink phone message.

Jesse slid her notepad in front of her. "It's on your doodle pad."

"I don't have a doodle pad." She looked down at the pad full of swirls and curls and block letters and funny animal faces.

Jesse grinned sheepishly. "Sorry."

Ellie found the number buried within the intricate artwork and punched it in. It felt like ages since she had sat in *her* chair, at *her* desk.

Tina Chambers picked up on the second ring.

"Hi, Tina. This is Detective Saunders with the Burkesboro Police Department. Detective Alvarez said you might have some information for me."

A television blared in the background, barely drowning out a screaming toddler. "I think I recognize that little boy we saw the other day. He's...hold on a minute. Dusty, stop that this minute. I've seen him with this couple, the guy works with Richie and-- Dusty, stop it. Can you hold just one second?" She didn't wait for Ellie to answer and instead went into a screaming tizzy against Dusty. Dead silence followed. Ellie was growing just a tad concerned when the silence began to stretch on then Tina came back on the line. "Sorry—look, I don't know the guy's name. Richie would know it, though. He'll be home—Dusty!—he'll be home around three if you want to talk to him."

"What's your address, Tina?"

Tina gave it to her, in between screaming at various kids, then hung up. Well, at least Tina and Richie Chambers had obviously found *their* kid. Ellie scribbled the address on her "doodle pad" then looked at her watch. She glared at Jesse. "You want to take a ride?"

Jesse shrugged. "I love a road trip."

Jack walked up and tossed Jesse an envelope. "It's official. Sign 'em and put the original on my desk. Keep the copy for your record."

Ellie furrowed her brows, not liking being left out of something. "What's official?"

"His transfer. Chief's out of town but Deputy Chief Grostemeyer said if you think the national media will do us any good, go for it."

"His transfer? Jesse's transferring? To what department?"

Jesse waved at her. "Hello...I'm right here."

"Jesse's the newest member of the Criminal Investigation Department. You two seem to work so well together, I thought you could use a good partner."

Ellie nearly choked.

"Call Sara Jeffries and set up an interview. She can get it on a national feed."

Sara Jeffries? Ellie was still reeling from news of her new partner. And now Jack was throwing Sara Jeffries into the mêlée? "Jack—you know I'm not good with interviews. Don't you think it would be better if you, as head of the department, spoke to her?"

"Get your new partner to do it." Jack smiled then turned and headed back into his office.

Her new *partner*. Jesse Alvarez. Interviewing with Sara Jeffries. Over her dead body.

"So, you ready to hit the road?" Jesse asked, evidently oblivious to Ellie's glowering eyes. "Where are we going?" He turned the doodle pad around so he could read the address. "That's in Avery County."

Maybe we don't have to go national. Maybe Tina Chambers will give us enough information we can put it all together right in our own backyard.

She tore the page with the address off the doodle pad then grabbed a clean notepad from her drawer. "I'm driving."

Outside, the sky was one giant gray cloud hovering low, dumping a good amount of snow on the ground. The snow was accumulating on the roads, separated by tire paths. Ellie programmed the Chambers' address in the GPS then as she was backing up, hit the gas too hard and spun her tires in the parking lot.

"You sure you don't want me to drive?" Jesse said as he snapped his seatbelt into place.

Ellie glared at him. "I can drive in the snow, thank you. Besides, what do you know about driving in snow—aren't you, like, from Mexico, or something?"

"Actually, I'm from Missouri. And we have plenty of snow there." He smiled at her.

"Missouri?"

"And so were my parents, and grandparents, and great-grandparents. I think my great-great-grandparents came from Texas, so yeah, they probably came across the border a couple hundred years ago."

"How'd you end up in North Carolina?" Ellie asked with genuine interest. It always fascinated her how people could pick up and move from one place to another. She'd lived within a two-hour drive of her home place her entire life.

"How'd I end up in North Carolina? Why do most guys leave home?"

"Outstanding warrants?"

He busted out laughing. "A girl. My high school sweetheart went to Appalachian State, so I came too."

Ellie felt the back wheels slide just a little and thought for a fleeting moment she might take Jesse up on his offer to drive. "How much snow are we supposed to get?"

"National Weather Service said it was a pretty big storm. Probably the last one of the season. Spring's just around the corner, sweetcakes."

"That's comforting. At least it gives us something to hope for."

"There's always hope when there's nothing else." He smiled.

Ellie huffed and tightened her grip on the wheel. She was relieved when she saw snowplows lined along the road. At least the trip back wouldn't be as nerve-wracking.

"So, tell me about your session with the kid," Jesse said. He'd settled into the passenger seat and looked quite comfortable.

"It was...draining." She couldn't have found a more perfect word if she'd looked in a dictionary. "I know Jerome Kenton was in the truck with him, but he's not his father. And Johnny was *real* upset they had killed the deer."

"And how do the Chambers fit into all this?"

"They came in because they thought Johnny might have been their missing son, Dusty. Who they named after some wrestler."

"Dusty Rhoades. One of the greatest wrestlers of all time."

Ellie glared at him. "Well, apparently, they found *Dusty* because she was screaming at him the whole time I was talking to her. The husband, Richie, works with Jerome Kenton. Tina said she thought she remembered seeing the kid with Kenton."

Jesse nodded. "So, like you said earlier, Kenton could be an uncle or just a neighbor."

"Possibly." Her death grip on the steering wheel made her shoulders ache. She didn't have to glance at her knuckles to know they were as white as the snow plastering against the windshield. Why were the snowplows just sitting alongside the roads? Why weren't they already moving to get this stuff cleared?

The rear tires jerked slightly to the right, birthing a knot as big as a full-term baby in the pit of her stomach.

"You sure you don't want me to drive?"

"No," she snapped. *I can do this. I can do this.* Like the little engine that could, she'd just keep right on going like they were going...and hopefully they'd be there before spring. She took a deep breath and forced herself to relax. "So...tell me about the transfer." Anything to keep her mind off the road.

"I transferred."

Well, that went well. "Why did you transfer? Why my department?"

"It's not *your* department. I was in this department when you were still in uniform writing tickets."

"Oh, *please.* That's the trouble with you vice guys. You're elitist. You think you deserve the red carpet every time you walk into a room."

She waited for him to respond. When he didn't, she continued her rant. "Oh, that's right. You're not in vice anymore. You were *reassigned.*" She would have glanced at him but was terrified to take her eyes off the snow-covered road.

"I *wasn't* reassigned. I *asked* to be moved."

She wondered if what Reggie Booker had said was true? "The lifestyle started hitting too close to home?"

"Just the opposite. The job wasn't conducive to *my* lifestyle. Would you pull over, please?"

"What?" Had she ticked him off enough to make him want to get out of the car?

"Pull over."

"Look, I'm sorry. I didn't mean to step on your toes. Whatever the reason was, it's none of my business."

"Ellie, just pull over. There's no traffic so you're not going to slide into anyone."

She threw him a quick glance. Was he serious? Did he really think she was going to leave him stranded on the side of the road?

"Ellie—just ease the car to the side of the road."

"Jesse, I said I was sorry. I didn't realize you were so touchy about it. And I'm *not* going to leave you on the side of the road."

"Touchy about what?"

She glanced over at him again. "About why you left vice."

"What?" He chuckled. "What are you talking about?"

"I thought you were upset about what I'd said."

"So, you thought I was just going to stand on the side of road? In the freezing snow?"

"Then why'd you want me to pull over?"

He burst out laughing. "So we can change drivers. At the rate you're going, Johnny Doe's going to graduate high school before we get back."

16

The Chambers and their litter of kids lived in a tired-looking single-wide mobile home in need of a good power wash and fresh paint on the peeling window shutters. The front yard looked like a toy graveyard with bicycle handlebars and the carcasses of various action figures poking up through the snow. Ellie kicked a layer of snow off the rickety wooden steps leading to the front door. She wondered if she should open the frame of the screen door to knock or just knock where the glass used to be. She looked at Jesse, who shrugged. Before she decided what to do, the door jerked open. Tina, with a baby on her hip, greeted them.

"Hey, come on in." She wiped the baby's nose with her shirt-tail.

Ellie carefully climbed the steps then held the door for Jesse. Tina eyed Jesse suspiciously until Ellie introduced him. "Detective Alvarez is helping me with the case."

"Oh, yeah. I talked to you on the phone." Tina slowly nodded then put the baby down beside one of the other kids sitting cross-legged in front of the television. "Dylan, watch your brother for a minute. These people need to talk to me and your daddy."

Dylan glanced at the baby then turned back to the television. Another child was stretched out on the threadbare sofa, playing a handheld video game. The child looked remarkably like Johnny Doe. Ellie assumed he was the one called "Dusty." A toddler with a sagging diaper and stained t-shirt banged a toy car on the coffee table, adding more scratches and dents to the already beat-up table.

"Richie's in here in the kitchen," Tina said and motioned for Ellie and Jesse to follow.

They didn't have to travel far. The kitchen and living room were separated only by a curved counter. Richie, in his Bekley's Seafood uniform, was sitting at a small oval table in the tiny kitchen.

"Y'all have a seat. I've got to get these fish sticks in the oven," Tina said.

Jesse stepped to the side so she could open the oven door, and then sat down across from Richie. Ellie took the seat in front of the window and immediately regretted her placement at the table. The cold air from outside pushed its way through the glass, making her fight off a shiver.

"I'm glad y'all found Dusty," Ellie said and smiled.

Richie shook his head. "That boy. I'm telling you..." And that was all he said. He just continued to shake his head.

When Tina joined them at the table, Ellie pulled her notepad from her jacket pocket and opened it to a clean page. "Tina, you told me on the phone that you thought you had seen Johnny Doe with someone Richie works with."

"Jerome Kenton," Richie said. "Guy's kinda weird."

"Weird how?" Ellie asked.

Richie shrugged. "You know, don't have a lot to say."

And this coming from a guy Ellie had heard speak a total of about ten words.

"Richie saw him the other day at the regional drivers' meeting, and when he came home, he said he thought he remembered seeing the little boy with him and his wife at the company picnic back in the fall. And then, I remembered, too."

"When was this drivers' meeting?"

"Day before yesterday," Richie said. "He was all banged up and said he'd been in a wreck."

"Did he say if anyone was with him when he wrecked?"

Richie shook his head.

"And you met his wife at the company picnic?"

Richie nodded, and like any good tag-team, Tina jumped in. "She's even weirder than he is."

"Weird how?" It wasn't exactly a concrete word.

"She was really protective of the little boy. I mean, like—*really* protective."

"Could you elaborate?"

"She wouldn't let him play with any of the other kids. Said he had some kind of immune disease."

Ellie and Jesse glanced at one another. In all the tests Johnny Doe had been put through, there had never been any mention of an autoimmune deficiency. "And you're sure the child you saw in the hospital is the same child that was at the picnic?" Ellie asked.

Both Tina and Richie nodded. "I remember him because he looked a lot like Dusty," Tina said.

"But you didn't recognize him at the hospital..." Ellie said.

The toddler in the sagging diaper and stained t-shirt waddled into the kitchen and started banging the toy car against Jesse's leg.

"Damien, stop that," Tina scolded.

The kid toddled off and came back a minute later with another car and handed it to Jesse. He continued using Jesse's thigh as a drag strip. Jesse joined in the fun, stretching his leg out to give the kid a longer straight-away.

Tina sighed. "The kid *did* look like Dusty, but we were so mad we didn't even think about it being the kid from the picnic."

"Mad at who?" Ellie figured the question didn't have a lot to do with her case, but she was curious. For Dusty's sake.

Tina jerked her head toward the living room while Richie shook his head back and forth like a slobber-slinging dog. "Dusty," Tina said. "He is always runnin' off somewhere. Going to his grandma's through those woods. Playing at the creek. He had gone off with one of Mama's neighbors' kids and didn't tell her or me. That kid is one more handful. We don't have any problems out of any of 'em but that one." She glanced at Damien still playing cars on Jesse's leg, and for the first time, Ellie saw a hint of maternal love in Tina's expression rather than contempt.

Ellie turned the conversation back to Johnny Doe. "Did she say how old he was?"

"Six," Tina answered.

Finally! She had a confirmed age. If, in fact, they were talking about the same kid.

"Did she ever mention his name?"

"They called him JJ," Tina said. "I guess for Jerome Junior."

"Some dads like naming their sons after themselves," Richie added then rolled his eyes in Tina's direction.

"And some people like giving kids original names," Tina snapped back.

Ellie wanted to remind her she had named at least one of her sons after a wrestler but thought now wasn't the time. "Did she say what grade he was in or what school he went to?"

Tina shook her head. "She said she couldn't send him to school because of his immune disease."

Ellie scribbled some notes in her notepad then asked, "Did Jerome or his wife ever specifically refer to JJ as their son?"

They both nodded. "Jerome referred to him as 'my boy,'" Richie said.

"How much contact do you have with Jerome at work?" Ellie asked.

He twisted his mouth like he had to really think about it. "We have a regional drivers' meeting twice a month. Other than that, I never see him."

"And the company picnic was the first time you met his wife?"

He nodded.

"How'd they act at the picnic?"

Tina and Richie looked at each other and both shrugged. "She kinda kept to herself," Tina said. "Like I said, she wouldn't let the little boy play with any of the other kids, so they just kinda sat there at one of the tables."

"And what was Jerome doing?"

"Just hanging out. He played horseshoes," Richie said.

A fight broke out in the living room. "Boys!" Tina screamed as Richie stomped off toward the action.

In the chaos, the baby started wailing. Tina grabbed him up and bobbed him up and down on her knee while Richie was threatening to kill the next kid who moved.

"The fish sticks! Here, can you hold him a minute." She quickly handed the baby off to Jesse as she tended to their dinner.

Jesse stared at the baby and the baby stared back. Jesse started making goofy faces, and the baby smiled then chuckled.

Ellie was captivated at the sight of Jesse with a child on his lap. He looked so natural, like he was born to be a father. She pushed those thoughts out of her mind.

Richie came back and assumed his position at the table. "Sorry. They get a little crazy sometimes."

"Understandable," Ellie said and smiled. She jumped right back in with the questions. "How long has Jerome been with Bekley's?"

Richie shrugged. "Three or four years, maybe?"

"And he didn't say anything during the driver's meeting about anyone being with him the other night when he wrecked?" Like perhaps his son had been killed or was missing? Events like that usually spread through companies faster than the flu.

Richie shook his head again. "He didn't say if anyone was with him or not. He did joke about being a bachelor again 'cause his wife was going back to Louisiana to visit her aunt for a couple weeks."

****

"Remind me again why we're at the hospital," Jesse said as he carefully navigated the Taurus around the snow-covered parking lot.

"I want to see how he's doing. And, I want to test

something. Park over there at the ER." She pointed toward the emergency room entrance, and Jesse sighed.

"I'm not exactly *new* to the job, you know."

Ellie cut him a sideways glance. She was still curious about this whole transfer thing.

Jesse parked beside a patrol car but left the engine idling. "Any idea how long you're going to be?"

"How long *I'm* going to be? You're going with me."

"I'm just the chauffeur, sweetcakes."

Ellie glared at him. She unlatched her seatbelt and opened the door. "You have to come. You're part of the test, partner." It was so easy to say, it almost frightened her. Behind her, she heard the engine shut off and the door slam then his footsteps crunching through the snow. He was grumbling something she couldn't quite make out.

"How do you know doctor what's-his-name will even let you see him again so soon?" Jesse had caught up to her and tapped the snow off his boots.

"His name's Doctor Deveraux, and he'll let me see him." Probably not alone, but he shouldn't argue about a brief visit in Johnny's room. Hopefully, he'd be gone for the evening, anyway.

A blast of warm air hit her in the face as they made their way into the entrance hall of the ER. The warmth was almost suffocating, and Ellie quickly shook out of her coat. She flashed her badge at the nurse at the registration desk, and they were buzzed through.

The ER was a flurry of activity with patients on stretchers parked in the hallway along the walls.

"Pretty busy tonight, huh?" Ellie said to one of the nurses as she sprinted by.

The nurse shook her head. "Snow. People 'round here just can't drive in it."

Jesse chuckled and Ellie glared at him.

Life was a little quieter upstairs on the pediatric floor as nurses made their final rounds and tucked the little ones into bed for the evening. The door to Johnny Doe's room was open, and Ellie poked her head in. "Hey, there," she said in a cautious voice. She was a little unsure how he'd respond to her after their last session together.

He sat at the table near the window working on a puzzle and smiled broadly at Ellie. Her heart fluttered with satisfying warmth.

"Hey," he said shyly.

She walked into the room quietly, aware of the *click-clack* of her heels against the cold tile. Johnny stared at Jesse, unsure of the new person in his room. Ellie sat in an empty chair at the table. "Wow, you got a lot done this afternoon," she said, looking at the nearly completed puzzle.

Johnny gave Jesse a final glance then turned back to his puzzle. "Leon's goin' to bring me a new one tomorrow."

Ellie picked up a piece of the puzzle and put it in place. "I brought a friend with me. Is that OK? I've been telling him a lot about you, and he really wanted to meet you."

He glanced at Jesse again and nodded. Jesse offered the child his hand. "I'm Jesse."

Johnny shook Jesse's outstretched hand and offered a slight smile in return.

"His name's Jesse Alvarez, junior. Some people call him JJ."

Both Jesse and Johnny looked at Ellie then Johnny

quickly went back to working on his puzzle. "Why do they call him JJ?"

Ellie picked up another piece of the puzzle and turned it over and over again in her hand. "JJ is his nickname. A lot of people name their sons junior, after the dad, but then they call them something else, like Jesse, or JJ...or Jerome."

Johnny pushed his chair away from the table then got up and went to Ellie and crawled up in her lap. Taken aback, Ellie carefully wrapped her arms around the child. "That's stupid," he said in a small voice.

"What's stupid?"

"Why would you name someone one thing but call them something else?"

"Yeah, it doesn't make much sense, does it?" She ran her hand gently over his hair. "Sometimes adults do stupid things, I guess."

Jesse sat in the chair Johnny had been sitting in. "I like your puzzle," he said and smiled.

Johnny burrowed deeper into Ellie's lap. Ellie continued to stroke his hair. "Johnny, did the man in the picture call you JJ, too, like Jesse?"

Johnny turned away and stared out the window then slightly nodded. "But that's not my name."

Ellie's heart quickened as her breath caught deep in the middle of her chest. She stared at Jesse for a moment. God knew in her heart she didn't want to upset this child any more than she already had during the course of the day, but she was so close....

"Johnny, what *is* your name?"

He stared out the window for a long while without saying anything. Snow was falling hard and glistened like sparkling crystal in the white-yellow glow of the mammoth lights in the parking lot below.

"Will you tell me your name? I know it's not Johnny." She rested her chin on the top of his blond hair.

"My daddy called me Landon," he whispered after a long moment.

Ellie felt like a slowly deflating balloon. Sheer exhaustion wrapped itself around her bones and squeezed every ounce of energy from her being. She took a long, deep breath. "Landon. I like that name," she said softly. After a moment, she asked, "do you know your last name?"

He shook his head.

"Do you know what your dad's name is?"

Again, he shook his head. "No, but I knew who he was as soon as I saw him."

Ellie stared out the window at the swirling snow, trying to put the pieces together. He knew who his father was as soon as he saw him? How long had it been since he had seen him? Maybe they were dealing with an absentee parent? And how was Jerome Kenton connected?

The child seemed relaxed enough. There was no tension in his little body, and he seemed willing to talk at his own pace. Ellie slightly pulled away from him and turned him in her lap so she could see his face. "Landon, remember you told me you were talking to your daddy in the room where Leon works, and that was all you remembered before you woke up?"

He slightly shook his head. "We weren't in a room. We were on a road."

Ellie glanced at Jesse. "Oh, that's right. You said y'all were walking down a road. Do you remember what kind of road it was? Were there trees on the road or buildings?"

Landon shook his head again. "There wasn't anything—it was just a road. Real bright and shiny. Like in that movie."

"What movie?"

"The one with that girl and little dog, and there was a big lion and a man made of hay. And there was a witch, too."

"You mean Dorothy and Toto?" Jesse asked.

"Yeah, that one." He smiled brightly. "The road was like that one."

The yellow brick road? Wonderful. Just wonderful. And she supposed there were munchkins, too.

Ellie glanced up and saw Deveraux standing in the doorway. The expression on his face indicated he wasn't overly pleased. Didn't the guy ever go home? Ellie slightly raised her hand, silently begging him to back off. She mouthed the words, "he's OK."

Deveraux frowned then came in and sat on the corner of the bed. Landon turned and looked at him then smiled a huge smile.

"Hey Johnny. It's about bedtime for you, isn't it, sport?"

Landon slid off Ellie's lap and crawled up beside Deveraux in the bed. "My name's not Johnny. My name's *Landon*."

Deveraux looked at Ellie, surprise registering deep in his eyes. "Landon. That's a pretty cool name."

"He was just telling me about walking with his dad along a real pretty road, right before the accident," Ellie said, her brows raised, hoping Deveraux wouldn't put the kibosh on their talk.

Landon quickly shook his head. "No, we were walking down the road *after* the accident. Not before."

After the accident? Was his dad the one who dumped him in the alley? But he said his dad was with him in the morgue...if he was with him in the morgue, why didn't *he* bring him to the hospital? Why dump him like a piece of trash?

"Landon," Ellie said, "Did your dad talk about anything else while you were walking?"

Sadness shadowed his blue eyes as he looked away. "He said he missed me."

17

"I reviewed every second of every security tape they gave you, and no one entered that morgue," said Jesse. "No one that wasn't supposed to be there, anyway."

Deveraux was sitting at his desk, his chin propped on his folded hands. Ellie plopped into the extra chair in his office, leaving Jesse to stand. She had introduced them in the hallway outside Landon's room, and she wasn't sure which one seemed less impressed with the other. Maybe they were both just tired?

"And you're one-hundred percent certain no one was with him in the ER?" Ellie asked Deveraux. She already knew the answer. They'd only been over it a hundred times already.

Deveraux shook his head. "I've reviewed the files a thousand times myself. The paramedics brought him in as a DOA. They did everything by protocol."

"You didn't come with the body?" Jesse asked, turning toward Ellie.

She shook her head. "Jack said there wasn't any need. He was dead at the scene; they just couldn't pronounce it."

But he wasn't dead. He was very much alive. The little dead boy, bloodied and battered, called Johnny Doe was alive and well and tucked safely in a warm bed down the hall. And his eyes were the bluest she'd ever seen, and his hair as white as the snow, and his name was Landon.

Ellie sighed. She was so tired she couldn't even think straight. "How was he this afternoon?" She almost hesitated to ask, wanting badly to avoid the lecture she knew would come about how she had traumatized him even more.

Deveraux slightly shrugged. "Actually, a lot better than I had expected. He didn't talk about what happened in the playroom, but he didn't shut down either."

"In all the tests you've run on him, did you ever come up with anything indicating an immune deficiency?" Jesse asked.

Ellie knew she had brought him along for a reason. Not only was he driving for her, right now, he was thinking for her, too.

Deveraux lowered his brows and shook his head. "His immune system's completely normal. Why?"

"According to a possible witness who may have seen him with the man in the picture I showed him, they said the man's wife wouldn't let him play with other kids because he had an immune deficiency."

"That was one of the first tests we ran. It would explain some of his developmental issues, though."

"Such as?" Jesse asked.

Deveraux leaned back in his chair. "If children aren't properly socialized at an early age, they'll often fall behind their peers in mental and social development. All the tests we've run show nothing abnormal, so basically, that leaves an environmental cause."

"But—he does know his name. So we're making progress, right?" Ellie asked.

Deveraux shrugged again. "A two-year old knows

their name. What I question is, why now? What was it that triggered that memory?"

Ellie explained how she used Jesse and the nickname to see if or how he'd react to hearing the name "JJ."

"And his reaction was to tell you his real name," Deveraux said. He twisted his lips, deep in thought. "But he didn't have the same reaction when we were calling him Johnny."

"But," Jesse said, "He said his *dad* called him Landon. Maybe he was called something else—like JJ— by people other than his parents? People, for some reason, that he doesn't want to associate that name with."

"But the memory of his dad is a happy memory," Ellie said. "And it's the last memory he had before the accident. And we know Jerome Kenton was involved in the accident, and he definitely has a strong reaction to Kenton. So how can it be both?"

"He didn't say his dad was with him *during* the accident," Deveraux said. "He said he was with him *after*." A slight grin played on his lips, and Ellie wondered what the heck that was about.

They were going around in circles. And she was tired and getting dizzy. "We've already established there was no way his father was with him after the accident. At least not here in the hospital. We're missing something, and apparently it's connected to the morgue."

Deveraux was smiling now, not just grinning. "There doesn't always have to be a logical explanation."

Ellie cocked a brow and glared at him. Certainly he was beyond tired and talking out of his head. "The opposite of logical is illogical. So you're saying the explanation is *illogical*?"

"To the non-believer." Deveraux's eyes brightened as if he'd just been given a shot of pure adrenaline.

"An afterlife experience," Jesse said, his voice rising with excitement. "Of course! He said he was walking with his dad—"

"Along a beautiful shiny road," Deveraux finished.

"Like a road paved in gold. The yellow brick road," Jesse said.

Ellie stared back and forth at each of them like they had completely lost their minds. "You're joking...right?"

"This child's seen Heaven." Deveraux was looking at Jesse now in some sort of weird camaraderie that obviously didn't include Ellie.

Sure, she was a believer. She just wasn't so sure she believed *this* theory. "OK, let's all come back down to earth for a minute."

"How else can you explain him talking with a man that doesn't exist on *any* surveillance tape?" Jesse asked. "He said he was talking with his dad after the accident. After the accident, he was clinically dead. Right, doc?"

Deveraux nodded excitedly. "Exactly. The thought crossed my mind earlier because there was just no scientific explanation for why this child is alive."

"The Lazarus Syndrome," Ellie said, remembering her earlier conversation with Dr. Terry.

"To very extreme measures, but yes," Deveraux said.

All of this was getting a little too freaky. Ellie sank further into the chair and scrubbed her hands across her face, hopefully washing away the confusion and exhaustion. "OK, so what you're both saying is this child had an out-of-body experience, hooked up with his dad in heaven, and then, through some Divine Intervention, somehow came back to life."

"Yes," Deveraux and Jesse answered in unison.

Ellie burst out laughing. She laughed until her eyes were wet with tears. She got up and paced around Deveraux's office, catching glimpses of his pictures in foreign countries as a missionary, the plaques on his wall with biblical sayings and prayers. And Jesse! Where had all that come from? What happened to the Jesse she took home with her that night so long ago? She sure wouldn't expect to see *that* Jesse in church on Sunday.

"OK. We're assuming a lot here," she said. "One, that the kid's father is dead, and two, that he's in heaven."

"The first one's not difficult to confirm," said Jesse.

Ellie spun around and glared at him, fighting back another gut-wrenching laugh. "We don't even know who his father *is*. We don't even know who *this* kid is!"

Jesse stared back at her with an intensity she wasn't used to, not from him. "We know his name is Landon. We know he's six years old. We know there's a possibility his father's dead. And, somehow, Jerome Kenton's connected."

****

Ellie sank into the passenger seat, cupped her hands together, and blew warm air into them. What had she done with her gloves? "You really believe all that...stuff?" Her teeth were chattering.

"You don't?" Jesse adjusted the air vents, forcing the heat to blow toward their faces.

"I believe in heaven, yeah. But I'm not sure about all that 'just here for a visit' stuff."

Jesse laughed. "You're funny."

He lightly tapped the brakes as they neared the intersection of Main and Danville Road. There was little traffic on the roads as most sane people had taken the weather forecasters' advice about staying in. Although the light was red, Jesse eased through the intersection, not sacrificing the forward momentum for small legalities. At the next intersection, he carefully turned left and kept the car in the deep tracks heading out of town.

"Where are you going?" They were now heading in the opposite direction of the office.

"I'm taking you home. Unless you have somewhere else you'd like to go first. But you'd probably be hard-pressed to find anything open now."

She watched the wipers slap at the snow. It was difficult to see the front end of the car through the thick flurries. She'd never been through white-out conditions, but she imagined this was pretty close. "And how are you supposed to get home?" She didn't even know where Jesse Alvarez lived, and she wasn't overly excited about driving home on roads she wasn't familiar with.

"Maybe I should have said I'm *dropping* you off at home. I don't think you'll be needing your car tonight."

"Maybe you should have asked first if I'm on call." She smiled sarcastically. Whether she could drive in the snow or not, if she was on call, Jack expected her to show up if needed.

"Gotcha covered, partner. But you'll have to call me. My pager hasn't been re-programmed yet."

Partner. She still wasn't sure how she felt about the whole thing. Mike Allistar would probably be retiring come summer, and they'd need the extra hand. But why had Jesse come back to CID? There was a small part of her that was a little flattered, thinking maybe, just maybe, he came back because of her. And that thought in itself confused her...and scared her. Realistically, though, what other department was there for him to go to? He was a good cop and a great investigator—he'd moved out of a patrol car years ago. Why he'd returned to CID wasn't the real issue that piqued her interest. Why'd he leave vice? That was the real question.

Surrounded by the warm blowing air and the comfort and safety of her *partner's* excellent snow driving skills, her eyes fluttered as she fought to stay awake. She sure didn't want to doze off now, especially now. Not with thoughts of Jesse swirling through her brain. He'd invaded enough of her life already. She sure didn't want him invading her dreams, too. "So. What's on tap for tomorrow?" she asked, forcing herself awake. "Are we supposed to check the guest list with Saint Peter?"

Jesse smiled. "Good idea, but I probably wouldn't recommend it. Some people don't come back, you know."

Ellie slightly nodded and smiled half-heartedly. "So, we really don't have any way to *confirm* the heaven story."

"Just believe. Just believe."

Ellie rolled her eyes. She didn't know what she believed anymore. "Well, I'm sure the DA's office would like something a little more concrete."

"That's why God blessed us with technology. We have databases for everything. I'll key all this new information into the registry and could almost guarantee will get some hits."

"What new information? All we have is his name may be Landon."

"White male, aged six, first name Landon, father deceased. We'll get a hit."

"Father *may* be deceased," she said, still unsure of all this *heaven* stuff.

Jesse *tsked*. "O ye of little faith."

Faith. Her faith in the Man upstairs had taken a major hit the day they buried her mother. Her faith in mankind had all but dissolved the day she saw her first murder victim.

She sighed heavily. The last thing she wanted right now was a sermon. Especially from Jesse. "I *do* have faith in some technology," she said. "I think we have enough for a warrant to search Jerome Kenton's home, especially his personal truck and even the delivery truck."

"The delivery truck's probably not going to do any good. Even if we found blood, it's probably contaminated with fish blood. Unless we found hair fibers, any other evidence probably wouldn't hold up in court."

"Maybe we will find hair fibers. O ye of little faith."

Jesse grinned for a moment then frowned and shook his head. "Given everything we've got, sorry, but I don't think it's enough for a warrant, sweetcakes. It's enough to bring him in for questioning, or at least pay him and his wife a visit at home."

"Richie Chambers said Kenton was talking about his wife going back to New Orleans for a while," Ellie reminded him. She doubted Jack would dig deep enough in the budget to pay airfare for a trip to New Orleans for an interview. Interviewing Mrs. Kenton may pose a problem.

Jesse carefully turned onto Ellie's dead-end road. The little country lane looked like a velvety picture on the front of a Christmas card. There were no streetlights, and tonight there was no need. The snow blanketing the few yards illuminated the area with a beautiful white glow. Massive pine branches drooped under the weight of the powdery snow as gray-white smoke rose from chimneys. The smell of burning wood was strong and homey, bringing with it the knowledge of warmth and comfort.

Ellie's heart sank when she saw her little house. Her father's car was in the driveway with a thin layer of snow accumulating in the tire tracks. They'd been here awhile. There was only one reason her father would have left the hospital hours ago.

Ellie unlatched her seatbelt and was out of the car before Jesse had parked. She moved as fast as she could through the snow and along the slippery walkway and hurried through the front door. Aunt Sissy was at the small kitchen table sipping from one of the chipped coffee mugs. Their eyes met and Sissy smiled. "Helped myself to some tea. Hope you don't mind."

Ellie stared at her a moment, judging her look. Her eyes were clear and bright, no redness. Her expression was ordinary, same ol' Aunt Sissy. "Of course I don't mind. Where's Daddy?"

Sissy cocked her head toward the bathroom. "In

the shower. Peggy was resting comfortably, so we left before the roads got any worse."

Ellie let out the breath she'd been holding since seeing the car in the driveway. Every muscle in her body relaxed to the point she was scared she'd melt like a snowman. She tossed her coat on the sofa. "Hot tea. That sounds good."

"The water should still be hot."

Ellie was fixing herself a cup of tea when she heard the front door close.

"Everything OK?" Jesse called from the living room.

"Well hello, gorgeous," Sissy said. She got up, went into the living room and gave him a deep hug. A little deeper and longer than Ellie thought necessary, but she was too exhausted to go there.

"You two look rather tired." Sissy took Jesse's coat and hung it over one of the kitchen chairs. Ellie hoped that wasn't an indication he was planning on staying awhile. Her bed was calling, and she didn't know if she trusted leaving Sissy alone with him. No telling what they'd end up talking about.

"You want some hot tea? Ellie, fix him a cup of tea, please. Warm him up a little bit."

Yeah, you'd like to warm him up, wouldn't you?

Ellie filled the teakettle with more water and put it back on the stove to boil.

"How's Peggy?" Jesse asked. He sat in one of the kitchen chairs. Begrudgingly, Ellie set the cup she had fixed for herself in front of Jesse.

Who was he to be asking about her family members? Not that she really considered Peggy a family member.

Sissy slowly shook her head. "'Bout the same. The

pain meds are keeping her knocked out most of the time. Probably won't be much longer."

Ellie wondered if it would be totally uncool to pray for Peggy to hold on until she got this case cleared. She really didn't have time to attend a funeral right now. Not that she planned to attend anyway. Oh, who was she kidding? There was no way she could get out of this one. Not if Aunt Sissy, and apparently now Jesse, had anything to do with it.

Her father padded into the kitchen wearing plaid pajamas, a flannel robe, and bedroom scuffs. He greeted her with a kiss on the cheek and soft hug with an arm around her shoulder.

"Reverend Saunders," Jesse said. "Just the person I wanted to talk to."

Ellie cocked an eyebrow and glared at Jesse.

"We had the most amazing revelation today, and I wanted your opinion." Jesse pulled out a chair for Ellie's father then leaned into the table and sipped his tea, quite comfortable.

"Concerning the little boy? Very interesting case. I've been following it some on the news."

"This hasn't made it to the news yet—and hopefully it won't," Ellie said, glaring harshly at Jesse.

Jesse ignored her. "He told Ellie the last thing he remembered before waking up in the morgue was talking with his father. We've established that just wasn't possible."

"We *think*, it's not possible," Ellie interjected. She finally fixed herself a cup of tea and fixed one for her father. Obviously, this conversation was going to happen regardless of how badly she wanted to crawl into her warm bed. She scooted behind Sissy and wedged herself into the chair scrunched between the table and the window. How come she always got stuck beside the drafty window?

"Anyway," Jesse continued, "we've *established* through surveillance video, no one entered or left the morgue while the child was there. He's said his father wasn't with him before the accident, but he talked with him before he woke up in the morgue. We asked him to describe where he talked with his father, what kind of room they were in and—"

"Jesse thinks he described heaven," Ellie said and rolled her eyes. She hated to steal his thunder, but she was really tired, and the rate he was going telling this story, they'd be there all night.

"Really," her father said, looking at Jesse with widened eyes. "How did he describe it?"

Jesse glared at Ellie then turned back to her father. "He said it wasn't a room. He said they were walking along a road, *a beautiful, shiny road*."

"The roads shall be paved in gold," her father mumbled.

"Exactly!" Jesse said. Ellie was waiting for the high five, but her father wasn't exactly a high five kind of guy.

"And then the child woke up in the morgue…" her father said slowly in a slight voice. "After being pronounced dead."

"There's a medical term for it," Ellie added quickly before this thing went much further. "It's called the Lazarus Syndrome. It's more common than people realize."

Jesse stared at her, his face twisted with questions. So she made that last part up about being common. It probably was, though. No telling how many undocumented cases hospitals had every year.

"Did the child say what he and his father talked about?" Her father looked to Jesse for the answer.

Jesse shook his head. "No, all he said was his dad told him he missed him."

Her father sipped his tea, deep thought creasing his forehead. After a moment, he continued the conversation. "I've never personally been involved in a rising, as they're called, but from my research and talks with people who have been involved, most often the risen has a message for someone. It's usually something so obscure no one but who the message is intended for would understand it."

18

"Will you stop all that pacing?" Aunt Sissy said. She poured herself a cup of steaming coffee and carried it into the living room. She sat on the sofa, her legs curled beneath her. "He said he'd be here by seven thirty. According to your clock, he's still got fifteen minutes."

Ellie peered out the window again, her agitation growing by the second. This is why she hated being without a car. She should have never let Jesse *drop her off*. She'd already be in the office digging into Jerome Kenton's life if she had her car.

"I don't know why you didn't just let him spend the night."

Ellie turned around and glared at her crazy aunt. "And where was he going to sleep? This isn't exactly Motel 6."

"You're right. They're a lot more hospitable." She yawned then sipped her coffee. "Don't even get me started about the possible sleeping arrangements. You have no imagination, child."

"Oh, I have plenty of imagination, and I don't like what I'm imagining right now."

Sissy grinned and patted the sofa. "Come. Sit. You're going to be exhausted before you ever get to work."

Ellie sighed heavily then sat down beside Aunt Sissy on the sofa. Sissy lovingly wrapped her arm around Ellie's shoulder and gave her a deep hug. "You're wound tighter than a spring. You need to learn to relax."

Ellie took a deep breath, knowing what Sissy said was the truth. "There's just so many things going on right now, I can't seem to shut off my mind. If it's not one thing, I'm thinking about another."

Sissy ran a gentle hand over Ellie's hair and smiled. "And how many of those thoughts are Mr. Alvarez's doing?"

Ellie sighed then leaned forward, propping her elbows on her knees and resting her chin in her hands. "I don't *want* to think about him. Not like that, anyway. And all this talk about heaven and *believing* and secret messages… I mean, where is all that coming from? That's not the Jesse Alvarez I…"

"Slept with months ago?"

Ellie didn't say anything. She didn't have to.

Sissy tucked a lock of stray hair behind Ellie's ear and gave her another hug. "That Jesse was safe. This Jesse, the Jesse that's grown and matured and shares the same beliefs you do deep in your heart, frightens you because you could actually fall in love with *this* Jesse. And that's scary. Falling in love and wanting to be with someone all the time…it's terrifying."

Ellie cocked her head and stared at Sissy. "But what do you do when they don't want to be with *you*?"

"What makes you think that?"

"He said he wished it'd never happened. And, he never called back."

"He's here now."

"But I don't know how much of that is me—or how much is the case."

"No, I mean he's here. In the driveway."

Ellie glanced outside, and sure enough, the car was in the driveway. "Oh." She grinned sheepishly then gave Sissy a peck on the cheek.

"Go find out what message that little boy came back to deliver."

Ellie grinned. "We might have better luck with a séance."

"Ellie Saunders! Don't even joke about such things."

Outside, Ellie tromped through knee-high snow to get to the car. She tapped her shoes against the doorframe to loosen the snow before getting in. Jesse had the car quite warm and cozy. "Morning, gorgeous," he said, smiling that smile of his that could melt every inch of the snow.

He was wearing an Appalachian State sweatshirt and faded jeans. "Jeans?" Ellie asked. "Obviously you haven't seen the department's dress code, partner."

"Obviously you haven't seen the inclement weather policy, partner."

She laughed. Jack didn't believe in inclement weather. She couldn't wait until they got to the office and Jack sent him home to change clothes. And she *would* remind Jack about the dress code.

Jesse backed out of the driveway easy enough and took his time maneuvering along the short road. "The main roads aren't bad. The plows have them pretty clear."

"Good. I don't know where Kenton's at today, but it'll make it a lot easier if I can actually reach him." She was getting excited at just the idea of talking to him.

"What about this national media thing?" Jesse asked. "Is that still in the plans?"

Ellie had forgotten all about Sara Jeffries and

scheduling an interview. "Let's see what kind of feedback we get with the registry. Now that we have an age and at least a first name, we may not need to go national."

"We'll get a hit. I can feel it in my bones."

Ellie smiled. "Probably just the cold."

Jesse had been right about the roads. They weren't near as bad as she had thought they would be. Traffic was moving at a slow but steady pace through town. She'd be fine driving. As long as she didn't have to track Kenton down deep in the mountains or anything.

Jesse pulled into the parking lot and parked beside his Camaro. Snow was piled at least a foot deep on the hood. He swept off a portion of it with his arm then raced to join Ellie.

"What are we going to do about the desk thing?" he asked as they climbed the first flight of stairs, no indication of any struggle.

"What do you mean?"

"Where are you going to work?"

Ellie stopped mid-step and stared at him. "I'm going to work at *my* desk. Where are you going to work?"

He snickered. "Ah…I see how it's going to be. I'm just the chauffeur."

Ellie wanted to knock him down the stairs. Partly because he wasn't even breathing heavy and she could feel the sweat beading on her forehead. She blew a stray piece of hair out of her eyes. "Fine. You take the desk today so you can get everything loaded in the registry. Hopefully, I'm going to be interviewing Jerome Kenton anyway."

"Whoa—wait a minute. You're going to do that without me?"

"We can get a lot more accomplished in a shorter amount of time if we split up what needs to be done. Right?" Ellie stopped and opened the door to the third floor, fully intending to take the elevator the last two flights but Jesse jerked the door from her hand and closed it. "Excuse me?" she said, forcing much needed air from her lungs.

"Two more flights. You can do it. We'll take it slow." He started up the fourth set of stairs. "Come on. You can do it."

She glared at him hard but followed along. Her legs were on fire. She wasn't so sure she appreciated his encouragement. She wasn't sure what to make of it. Was he telling her she *needed* to work out more? Lose a few pounds? Was that why he never called back? The nerve! She sucked air in through her nose and pushed him aside as she climbed the stairs.

On the fifth floor, she jerked the door open and wanted to crawl to her desk, but she didn't. She fought through the searing burn in her legs and marched to *her* desk, collapsing in *her* chair.

"Now, what were you saying about we could accomplish more if we split up? Sounds like a good idea, but honestly, I'm not real confident in your interview skills yet. That may be something we need to work on." He sat in the guest chair, unwinded.

Ellie caught her breath before tearing into him. "You haven't even seen my interview skills! Every interview we've done together has been the *Jesse* show. My interview skills are fine, thank you."

And to think just a short while ago she had thought she might be, possibly could be, in love with him.

She was seething with anger and barely noticed

Jack standing at the corner of her desk. "Detective Brady Mitchell from Avery County wants you to call him. He said he lost your extension number." Jack handed her the pink message slip with the number scrawled on it.

Brady Mitchell? "Did he say what he wanted?"

Jack raised an eyebrow. "I'm not your personal secretary. And no, he didn't say what he wanted. I assume it's about the kid."

Mitchell didn't have anything to do with *her* missing kid, and Dusty Chambers was safe at home. Or at least he was at home, safe she wouldn't swear by.

Ellie picked up the phone and dialed Mitchell's number. He answered on the second ring.

"Detective Mitchell, it's Detective Ellie Saunders. I had a message you called."

"Yeah, hey, Ellie. Got something you might be interested in. Remember that delivery driver for Bekley's you were looking for?"

"Jerome Kenton."

"Yeah, Kenton. His sister-in-law came by this morning and filed a missing person report on his wife, Becky Kenton."

Ellie sat up straight in her chair then leaned into her desk. "How long has she been missing?"

"The sister couldn't say for sure. Said last time she talked to her was earlier in the week—"

"Kenton was saying something about her going back to New Orleans for a while. I think she was supposed to be staying with an aunt."

"Well, that's where it gets interesting. The sister says Becky would have never gone back to New Orleans. And this aunt down there, she didn't know anything about it."

"Why'd the sister file the report and not Kenton?"

Mitchell chuckled. "My point exactly."

Ellie glanced at her watch. "Can you do me a favor and bring the sister back in. Say around, maybe ten?"

"Will do. I'll call if there's a problem."

Ellie hung up and looked at Jesse. "Kenton's wife was reported missing by her sister."

He smiled. "Road trip! I'm beginning to really like this job."

Ellie shook her head. "We're splitting up what needs to be done, remember? You're checking the registry. I'm heading to Avery County."

"And you're going to be there by ten? Hope they plowed the viaduct."

****

You can do this. You can do this. You can do this, Ellie told herself. *You climbed five flights of stairs this morning. This will be a breeze.* She gripped the wheel, set her mind to the task and steeled her nerves.

With only one slight skid, she pulled into the parking lot of the Avery County Sheriff's Department at 9:45. She sat in the car for a moment and collected herself, rolling her shoulders to release the tension. Her arms and hands were locked in position, frozen stiff from fear. She flexed her hands to bring color back to her knuckles, took a deep breath, and went in to hear what Kenton's sister-in-law had to say about her missing sister.

She registered as a visitor and waited patiently while the receptionist paged Brady Mitchell. Although smaller than the Burkesboro police department, the building housing the sheriff's department was beautiful with high-end décor and framed poster-sized pictures of the various tourist attractions gracing the county. If it hadn't been for the receptionist's uniform and the picture of the solemn-looking sheriff, Ellie would have sworn she was standing in the chamber of commerce.

"Ellie. Good to see you again," Mitchell said as he walked toward her, his hand outstretched.

Ellie shook his hand and smiled. "Good to see you again, too. I hear Richie and Tina Chambers found their missing son, Dusty."

Mitchell grinned. "Yeah. We won't even discuss that case. Come on back here to the interview room. Her name's Karen Moore. Mind if I sit in?"

"No, not at all." Ellie followed him through a maze of hallways and through the squad room. The interview room was at the far end of the squad room with a mirror facing the rows of desks.

Mitchell knocked once on the door then opened it and ushered Ellie in. Karen Moore was sitting at a small table nervously twisting a tissue in her hands. She was a little on the plump side, with mousy brown hair that may at one time have been cut into a fashionable style. Her makeup was a little heavy-handed, but at least she tried, Ellie reasoned.

"Karen—hi, I'm Detective Ellie Saunders with the Burkesboro Police Department." Ellie offered her hand and Karen gently shook it.

"Do you think Becky's in Burkesboro? She doesn't know anyone in Burkesboro," she spoke in a soft voice in rapid bursts, the same Cajun accent as Kenton's.

Ellie sat down in the chair closest to Karen while Mitchell sat across from them. "We don't have any indication that she's in Burkesboro," Ellie said.

"Detective Mitchell called me this morning because I'm working a case that may involve your brother-in-law."

Karen jerked her head up and down like she completely understood. "No telling what he's involved in. I told Becky he was bad news when she married him."

"How long have they been married?"

She sniffled then dabbed the tissue at her nose. "About eight years."

"And what do you mean when you say he was bad news?"

She rolled her eyes and shook her head. "He beat her up one time when they were dating. I told her not to go back to him, but she said he told her he was sorry, that he was drunk when it happened and it wouldn't happen again. But I know it did. I seen the bruises. She was in the emergency room at Tulane so much they could have named a wing after her." Her lips quivered as a stream of tears rolled down her cheeks.

"When's the last time you saw your sister?"

Karen took a deep breath and let it out slowly. "Four and a half years ago. We had lunch for my birthday. She had a black eye, said she'd run into the door."

Ellie's eyes widened. "You haven't seen her in four and a half years?"

Karen shook her head. "After that day, she said it might be best if we just talked on the phone. So we talked every day. Until Tuesday. That's the last time I talked to her."

Tuesday. The day after the accident.

"Did she say anything about being involved in a car accident? Or about the little boy?"

Karen looked at Ellie with questioning eyes. "What little boy?"

Ellie swallowed hard. "Karen, did Becky and Jerome have a son?"

Karen nodded then wiped her eyes. Mitchell handed her a fresh tissue. "They had a little boy. Precious baby." Tears started flowing harder. She covered her mouth with her hand as if that would stop the flow.

"What happened to the baby?"

After a moment, Karen composed herself and wiped her eyes. "He was lost in Katrina."

Ellie leaned in closer and gently patted Karen's hand. "Did he *die* in Katrina, or has he just...never been found?"

Karen took another deep breath. "He drowned. They found his little body still in his crib."

"How old was he?"

"Little over a year." She shook her head again then dabbed at her eyes. "Poor little baby."

Ellie's heart was throbbing in her throat. "Karen, what was the baby's name?

Karen sniffed. "JJ."

Ellie's stomach twisted in deep, constricting knots. She felt the putrid taste of bile rise to her throat. "Karen, do you know if they had any other children living with them? Not in New Orleans, but here?"

She shook her head. "JJ was their only child. They were both devastated when he died. I mean, I don't care at all for Jerome, but no parent should have to go through what they went through. That was one of the reasons they moved up here. To get away from the memories. That's why I know Becky wouldn't have gone back to New Orleans like Jerome said she did.

She told me she'd never go back."

"And you came with them when they moved?"

"No, I was already up here. My husband transferred a couple years before the hurricane. After the storm, and after losing little JJ like they did, they came up here for a while and Jerome was able to get on with that seafood company."

"Becky didn't work?"

She shook her head again. "No, I kept telling her she needed to get out and get a job, even if it was just part-time. It'd at least get her out of the house."

"And during this time, you never actually saw her *in person*?"

"No, but like I said, we talked everyday on the phone."

"And to your knowledge, there weren't any other children in the house? Maybe a nephew?"

"I'm positive. Jerome doesn't have any brothers or sisters, so there aren't any nephews. And if they had adopted or something like that, Becky would have told me. Even if we didn't see each other, we still shared everything. This accident you asked about, do you think Becky was hurt?"

Ellie offered a gentle smile. "We don't know yet. Jerome told me he and his wife were in an automobile accident, and they were a little banged up but they were OK. And apparently, there might have been a little boy with them."

Karen lowered her brows and frowned. "I don't know who he could have been. Becky never said anything about a little boy."

****

217

Out in the parking lot, Brady Mitchell cleaned off the passenger's seat of his Expedition by sweeping fast food bags and empty soda bottles into the floor board. Ellie slid into the newly cleaned seat and buckled up.

"You're sure Kenton's at home today?" Ellie asked.

"I know he's not at work. Ain't goin' to hurt anything to ride out there and take a look around."

"How do you know he's not at work?"

Mitchell offered a slight smile. "I called. He's out sick today."

"So, what's your take on the missing wife?"

He shrugged. "Could be something to it, especially if he has a history of slapping her around. Or it could be she got tired of getting slapped around and took off."

Ellie's heart hurt for little Landon, if in fact he was the same kid Richie and Tina Chambers saw at Bekley's company picnic, and for whatever reason was living with Becky Kenton and her wife-beating husband. She remembered talking to him in the morgue about monsters. She wondered if Jerome Kenton was the monster she was beginning to think he was.

"And tell me again how they're involved with your kid." Mitchell said.

Ellie explained how she suspected they were connected. "We definitely know Landon's not their son," she continued. "What he was doing with them, I haven't quite figured out yet."

"And you're sure the kid was with them when they had the wreck?"

Ellie sighed. There was no physical evidence or witnesses saying he was. And all she had to go on was the word and reactions of a traumatized six-year-old, but in her heart, she believed beyond a shadow of a doubt Landon was with the Kenton's that night. "Without any physical evidence, I doubt it would hold up in court. But yeah, I believe he was with them."

Mitchell grinned. "Mind a piece of advice from an ol' timer?"

Ellie returned the smile. "Not at all."

"Go with your gut. The physical evidence will fall in place."

****

They had driven about three miles outside of town when Mitchell took a left then a right on an unpaved road. Tire tracks were cut deep enough into the snow. The glistening powder scraped the undercarriage as Mitchell slowed the Expedition to a crawl. He shifted the gears into four-wheel drive and soon picked up speed. The houses along the country road were scattered far and between with snow-covered fields separating them by several acres each.

Ellie tried to imagine Landon playing in the fields, chasing rabbits, or hopping over creeks and doing the things little boys do, the sunlight turning his blond hair to gold. But all she could see was Jerome Kenton, red-faced and angry, his menacing fists raised against a helpless victim. She breathed deeply to ward off her rising anger. She needed to be coolheaded and calm when she talked to him.

"Here we are," Mitchell said as he turned into what was supposed to be the driveway. Apparently, Kenton hadn't ventured out since the storm came in. A new extended-cab truck with temporary tags sat underneath a detached aluminum carport beside it, an old, rusted gas grill rested, half-exposed, with a pile of snow accumulating on its cover. There were no footprints leading to or away from the carport, and there were no tire tracks in what she could see of the driveway or the yard. A smaller truck, a single cab, was parked underneath a large oak tree about twenty yards from the carport. The front end was crumpled and the windshield spider-webbed but not busted. An old barn with a lean-to shed that housed an older-model tractor stood about fifty yards beyond the carport. A dilapidated swing set was next to the barn, snow piled high on the broken slide. A set of heavy footprints with wide drag marks leading from the back of the house to the edge of the woods marred the perfect snow-covered yard.

The house was small with an A-line roof and covered front porch. Sheets of plastic covered the windows to keep in the heat and ward off the chill. Ellie traipsed behind Mitchell as they made their way through the knee-high snow to the front porch.

Ellie brushed the snow from her pant legs as Mitchell knocked firmly on the front door. A moment later, Jerome Kenton opened the door.

Mitchell introduced himself then introduced Ellie.

Kenton stared at her hard for a moment then nodded. "Yeah, we met at Shorty McCorkle's the other day."

Ellie forced a smile. "Yes, we did. I have a couple more questions I'd like to ask, if you don't mind."

Kenton looked at Mitchell, sizing him up, then opened the door wide. "Sure. Come on in."

Ellie's eyes immediately found the rifle lying on the threadbare sofa. "Let me get that," Kenton said and quickly removed the gun, propping it in the corner. Ellie's hand twitched and instinctively moved to her hip, resting on the handgun underneath her blazer.

"Been hunting?" Mitchell asked.

"Yeah, got a big buck hanging around. I saw him this morning but couldn't get a clean shot. Didn't want to waste the bullet. I need to get into town and buy another box. That buck sure would look good mounted." He smiled.

In heavy brown hunting pants and a thermal undershirt underneath a flannel shirt, Kenton was a bit over-dressed considering the warmth of the house. The living room would have been a decent size but was monopolized by a massive wood-burning stove protruding from a brick fireplace. The stifling heat felt good on Ellie's skin for all of about a minute. The cheap sofa with worn-down cushions sat opposite an entertainment center holding a large television and video game console. A war game flickered across the screen until Kenton turned it off. He pushed one of the hand-held controllers off the arm of a recliner and sat down, motioning for Mitchell and Ellie to have a seat on the sofa. The room was tidy and neat, no empty pizza boxes or half-full glasses sitting forgotten on the coffee table.

Mitchell squirmed a little on the sofa, probably avoiding the springs that threatened to impale them at any moment. "Jerome, your wife's sister came by the station this morning and filed a missing person's report on your wife," he said as casually as if he were talking about the weather. "I told her we'd hold up a day or two before we actually filed it. Give us a chance to talk to you about it first."

Jerome rolled his eyes then smiled. "Karen's a bit

of a…drama queen. She jumps to a lot of conclusions."

Mitchell nodded understandingly. "So, is Becky around?"

Kenton shook his head. "No. Like I told Karen when she called, Becky went down to visit her aunt in New Orleans for a couple weeks. She…ah…." He took a deep breath then blew it out slowly. "We lost a little boy a couple years ago in Katrina. Tomorrow would have been his birthday. Becky always has a hard time with it so we thought it might do her good to get away for a little while."

But wouldn't a trip back to the place where he died bring back the very memories she was trying to avoid, Ellie thought.

"Well, Karen says their aunt doesn't know anything about Becky coming to visit," Mitchell said.

"She wanted to surprise her. We haven't seen her since we left." He shifted his weight in the chair. "Look…I wouldn't get too worked up about it. Karen likes to blow things out of proportion."

Mitchell nodded. "Yeah, I figured as much. But, I told her we'd check it out. Did your wife drive down to New Orleans?"

Kenton hesitated a moment then shook his head. "No, she took the bus. I took her down to the station Tuesday afternoon."

"Oh, well that probably explains it then. It's a what…two- or three-day bus trip at best?"

Kenton was quick to nod. "At best. And with the weather being what it is, I'm sure that slowed them down even more."

Mitchell bobbed his head up and down. "Probably so."

Kenton looked dead at Ellie, and despite the heat,

a chill ran the length of her spine. "Did you find out anything else about that little boy you were asking about the other day?"

Ellie cleared her throat. "We're making some headway. And now that you've brought it up, one of your co-workers told me that you and Becky had a little boy with you at the company picnic back in the fall. A little boy you called JJ."

Kenton stared at her a moment then quickly looked away and grinned. "It wasn't JJ...his name was *TJ*."

"Oh, OK. Maybe I misunderstood. And TJ is what relation to you and Becky?"

"He's my nephew."

Ellie thought her heart was going to beat right out of her chest. "So you have a brother or a sister?"

Kenton ran his tongue over his lips then smiled big. "No. He's not actually my nephew. He's...ah...what do you call it...my *godson*, if that's what people still call it these days. I went to school with his mom and dad, known them all my life, and we've kept in touch. They came up and visited for a while this summer, and TJ wanted to stay. They were having some problems, finances and stuff, and Becky thought it'd be nice to have a kid around again, so we said sure, he could stay for as long as they needed."

Ellie didn't know what to say. Could what he had said be true? She collected her thoughts then continued. "Jerome, was TJ with you and Becky when you had the car wreck the other night?"

Kenton nodded. "Yeah. Shook the little guy up pretty bad, but he was OK. The truck, as you could probably see when you came in, took the brunt of the damage."

Ellie looked around the living room. There were no indications a child had visited, let alone lived here. "Where is TJ now?"

Kenton didn't miss a beat. "With Becky. That's the other reason she went on back down to New Orleans. To take TJ back."

"Oh, so you put them both on the bus Tuesday afternoon?" Mitchell asked.

Kenton nodded. "Yep," he said slowly.

"And that would be the terminal in Clarksville?"

Kenton thought about it for a minute then slowly nodded.

"What's TJ's parent's names? Just for our records," Ellie said.

Kenton cleared his throat. "Tommy and Susan Baker."

Ellie pulled her notepad from her jacket pocket and jotted down the names. "Do you have a phone number for Tommy and Susan?"

Kenton stared at Ellie hard, an apparent edge rising in his mood. He gnawed on his bottom lip then finally answered. "Yeah, I'm sure we've got it around here somewhere." He pulled himself up from the recliner and started toward the kitchen.

"While you're at it," Mitchell called after him, "We'll need a recent picture of Becky, too."

Kenton stopped but didn't turn around. He just stood there with his back to the living room a moment before disappearing in the kitchen. He was gone a minute or two then returned with a snapshot in a 3x5 acrylic frame with a magnet glued to the back. He handed the frame to Mitchell. "Becky must have taken our address book with her. She said she was goin' to look up some old friends."

Ellie nodded then glanced at the picture. Becky Kenton was a plain-looking woman with curly, dark-blonde hair and lackluster eyes. The smile she wore looked forced. Bone thin with shallow cheeks, she was the exact opposite of her sister, Karen.

"That was taken last summer," Kenton said.

Mitchell stood up and offered his hand to Kenton. "Thanks. We'll return it when we close this thing out."

Kenton shook Mitchell's hand with a firm grip and nodded. "How long do you think that'll be?"

"Well, after we verify Becky's safe and secure in New Orleans, we'll call Karen and tell her everything's fine. I don't really see any sense in filing an official report just yet."

Kenton laughed. "Yeah, give her at least a couple days to get down there. Have you got a card? I'll call you as soon as I hear from her."

"I'd appreciate that. I'm sure Karen will rest a lot easier knowing everything's fine." Mitchell dug one of his cards from his pocket and handed it to Kenton.

Kenton turned to Ellie as they moved toward the front door. "Sorry I couldn't help you with that little boy. I sure hope you find who did that to him."

Ellie smiled. "We will. It's just a matter of time."

19

"What do you think?" Ellie asked as she climbed into Mitchell's SUV and buckled up.

He cranked the engine. "My gut instinct?"

"Considering we have zero physical evidence, yes."

"He's lying through his teeth."

Ellie grinned. "My gut instinct told me the same thing. So, what do we do next?"

"Head to Clarksville and see if Becky got on that bus." Mitchell carefully backed out of the driveway and headed slowly down the road. He headed in the opposite direction from which they came.

"My thought exactly. How far is Clarksville?"

"I'll get you home before dark." He winked at her then settled in for the drive.

Ellie sighed. Not that she didn't enjoy his company, but she was anxious to get back to Burkesboro and see what Jesse had come up with. "And if Becky didn't get on that bus...where is she?"

Mitchell glanced over at her and frowned. "Gut instinct?"

He didn't have to say anything else. Ellie stared out the side window at the landscape creeping by. With each curve, the landscape changed from deep snow-covered ravines to rocky slopes with towering pines close enough to reach out and touch.

If Kenton had killed his wife, finding her body in

this terrain would be next to impossible. But what if Becky did get on that bus and had a little boy named TJ with her? Where did that leave Landon? Ellie would be no closer to finding out who left him for dead now than the night his body was discovered. Even if she was able to get a warrant to search the wrecked truck for hair fibers or Landon's blood, all it would prove was that Landon *was* in the truck. It wouldn't prove Jerome Kenton had beat him half to death and left him in an alley to die. Was it possible that Landon *was* TJ? If TJ even existed. And for whatever reason, he didn't get on that bus, and a total stranger was the one responsible for leaving him for dead?

She wanted to talk to Jesse. She wanted to know if he had found anything on the registry. She took out her cell phone and tried to call, but the call wouldn't go through.

Mitchell chuckled. "You're not goin' to get a signal out here."

Ellie stared at her phone as if by magic, she'd have at least one signal bar pop up. Nothing. She slipped the phone back into her pocket and sighed. "How do y'all communicate up here? You don't even have a dispatch radio in this thing." She looked around the console of the vehicle for any signs of a squawk box but found none.

"We have 'em. Just not in our personal vehicles." Mitchell grinned.

"This isn't the department's?"

Mitchell shook his head. "Ain't no way one of the department cars would make it through all this snow."

"The department doesn't have four-wheel drives?" Even the Burkesboro department had a couple.

"We've got 'em, but they're mostly used for

patrol."

That made sense. She didn't know about Mitchell's department, but investigators like Mike Allistar only left his desk for lunch. Why waste a perfectly good 4x4 on nothing but a burger run?

They had driven about twenty minutes when a small sign welcomed them to Clarksville, population 562. Main Street consisted of a hardware store, a funeral home that shared a parking lot with a diner, and the bus station. The snow had been pushed from the center of the parking lots to the sides where it sat in four-foot-high mounds. Mitchell pulled into the bus station and parked near the front door of the small brick building. Ellie followed him in and looked around.

There were three empty benches lining the far wall. Two vending machines offering soda and snacks stood near the benches. The ticket counter was on the opposite wall, encased in metal bars. An elderly man behind the counter peeked between the bars. "Can I help you?" His voice was crackly and old with age.

"Yes, sir, you can," Mitchell said. He approached the counter and showed his shield. "Detective Brady Mitchell with the Avery County Sheriff's Department, and this is Detective Ellie Saunders from the Burkesboro Police Department. We'd like to take a look at your passenger log for Tuesday afternoon if you don't mind."

The old man nodded obligingly. "Sure, sure. Looking for someone in particular?"

"As a matter of fact, we are," Mitchell said and winked at Ellie. "A lady named Becky Kenton. She may have been traveling with a young boy named TJ."

The old man nodded as he slid the papers through

the small opening under the bars where tickets and money were exchanged. Mitchell scanned the papers then shook his head and handed them back. "And this is the only passenger log you have for that day?"

"Yes, sir. Would you like to see Monday's and Wednesday's? Maybe they were confused on the dates." He pulled more papers from a book and handed them over to Mitchell.

Mitchell scanned through them and again shook his head. He handed them back. "Were you working Tuesday?"

The old man scratched at his head. "Let's see...yes, sir. I worked 10 AM until 6 PM. Gladys Shipman usually works Tuesdays but she was down that day with her arthritis."

"What time does the last bus pull out?"

"Five thirty. The terminal closes at six."

So if Becky Kenton had gotten on that bus Tuesday, the old man would have been the one who sold her the ticket.

Mitchell pulled the picture of Becky from his coat pocket and showed it to the old man. "Do you remember seeing this woman get on the bus?"

The old man tilted his head to get a better look through his bifocals. He slowly shook his head. "No, sir. Don't reckon I've ever seen her before."

Ellie pulled up the picture of Kenton she had stored in her phone and also showed it to him. "How 'bout this man? Have you seen him?"

The man looked at the phone with an air of distrust. "You have pictures in that thing?"

Ellie softly smiled. "Yes, sir. Do you remember seeing him?"

The old man shook his head. "Nope. Never seen

him either."

Outside, Mitchell stood in the parking lot eyeing the diner across the street. "You got time for a bite to eat?"

Ellie had a feeling it didn't matter whether she did or not. "I guess I can spare thirty."

"Good. It's a long walk back." He winked at her then headed across the street with Ellie in tow.

There were two cars and three pickups in the parking lot, and inside the few customers were scattered at different tables or booths as if they were scared a conversation would be overheard or a new strain of the flu would be spread. Ellie suddenly missed the noise and clatter of Caper's.

Mitchell slid into one of the booths and motioned for the waitress. Ellie sat opposite Mitchell and smiled at the elderly woman with her hair under a hairnet who came to take their order.

She handed them two laminated menus, and before Ellie had time to look it over, Mitchell ordered two hotdogs all the way with fries. Ellie didn't see a BLT listed anywhere so she settled for a cheeseburger with mayo.

"Who puts mayo on a cheeseburger?" Mitchell asked and laughed.

Ellie let the comment slide. It reminded her too much of Jesse, and she was really wanting to talk to him—to find out if he had come up with anything on the registry, of course.

"Think we have enough for a warrant?" Ellie asked.

"There's always the possibility Kenton *did* drop her off at the bus station, and she hightailed when he was out of sight," Mitchell said.

Ellie glanced out the grease-spattered window and looked at the knee-deep snow. "That depends on how desperate she was to get away," she said.

"Maybe she had someone pick her up?"

Ellie stared at him a moment. Was his gut instinct floundering? She shook her head, disagreeing with the idea of a third party. "If Becky was as isolated as her sister says she was, she wouldn't have the connections, or the guts, to pull off something like that."

"Maybe she hitched a ride with someone. If that's the case, then it's possible Kenton isn't the one who dumped your kid. Maybe Becky hitched a ride with the wrong person." He obviously saw Ellie's look of surprise, and winked. "I'm just looking at all the angles."

The waitress brought their orders and handed the ticket to Mitchell. He doused his fries with pepper then smothered them with ketchup.

"OK, but hear me out," he said. "Kenton takes them to the bus station, drops them off, and, as far as he knows, his wife and the kid *are* on their way to New Orleans. Becky and the kid get in the car with the wrong person, Becky ends up missing and your kid ends up in an alley beaten half to death."

She guessed it *was* possible. But she didn't believe it. "The kid was with Kenton when he had the wreck. That's one of the last things the kid remembers. He's never said anything about a bus station or getting into a car with someone he didn't know."

"Have you asked him?"

"Not directly, no." She picked at her cheeseburger, her appetite waning.

Mitchell sighed. "Look, I'm not trying to burst your bubble. Just trying to get you to look at the less obvious possibilities."

Was she so focused on Kenton she was missing something? Despite what she believed, she couldn't rule out the possibility Kenton *was* telling the truth and whatever had happened to Landon happened between the bus terminal across the street and the alley beside Shorty McCorkle's. And what if Becky's sister Karen was the drama queen Kenton said she was? What if Karen did have a habit of blowing things out of proportion and jumping to false conclusions? What if…?

"Earth to Ellie?" Mitchell was staring at her, looking deep into her every thought.

"Oh, sorry." Ellie pushed her hands through her hair and sighed. "Look, I know everything you've said is plausible. But gut instinct tells me Kenton's involved with whatever happened to that little boy. The court can prove he's innocent."

"If you're sure about it, then prove he's lying." He finished off his hotdogs then finished his tea. "Make a couple calls and see if Tommy and Susan Baker have a son named TJ."

"*If* Tommy and Susan Baker even exist."

Mitchell smiled. "How long have you been doing this job?" He tossed a dollar on the table then slid out of the booth and paid their ticket at the register.

Ellie waited outside for him and nearly jumped out of her skin when her cell phone rang. She hurriedly dug it out of her jacket pocket and quickly flipped it open, terrified she'd lose the signal in this tiny town. "Jesse?"

"Hey, sweetcakes! Where are you?"

His voice sounded as sweet as a lullaby. "I'm in some little town called Clarksville with Brady

Mitchell."

"What are you doing in Clarksville? The only thing in Clarksville's a bus terminal and a diner."

The man's knowledge never ceased to amaze her. "They've added a funeral home."

"Given the elderly population, I'd say that was a good business decision."

"Hey, listen, before I lose the signal, I need you to run some names for me. A Tommy and or Susan Baker in or around the New Orleans area. They should be around thirty and maybe have a six-year-old son named TJ. I'm sure it's short for Thomas Junior."

"Pretty generic names. There's probably only about half a million Tommy Bakers."

"And probably a couple hundred around New Orleans. Check recent bankruptcy filings, too."

"I checked with the DMV, and they don't have any accident reports on Kenton. He didn't file it with his insurance, either."

How did Kenton know the truck was totaled if he didn't file an insurance claim? Mitchell joined her outside, gnawing on a toothpick dangling from the corner of his mouth. Apparently he didn't feel it was a private conversation and stood close enough she could smell the onions he'd just devoured.

Ellie continued. "Did you get anything off the registry?" She could feel the tension knotting her shoulders as she waited for the answer.

"As a matter of fact, yes."

Her breath stopped somewhere in her chest. "And?"

"Landon Garrett, abducted three years ago at the age of three from Mecklenburg County."

Ellie felt dizzy. Her breath was coming in short,

rapid gasps.

"His mother's name is Ashley. His father's name was Andy. Died two years ago."

Ellie closed her eyes tight. A stream of tears escaped and streamed down her cheeks. "Is she still in Mecklenburg County?"

"According to recent records. She's a graphic artist at a company called Picture This."

Ellie briskly swatted away the tears. Mitchell was staring at her, a puzzled look on his face.

"See if you can get her to meet us at the hospital. I'll be back in an hour and a half."

"You may want to wait until the morning"

"Why?" Ellie sniffled away the rest of the tears.

"There's something else, El. I really hate being the one to tell you."

"What?"

"Aunt Sissy called about an hour ago. She tried your cell but couldn't get it to go through." He hesitated, and Ellie wished he'd go on and say it. She knew what he was going to say, and she didn't know why but her heart was suddenly aching. "Peggy died around eleven this morning."

Ellie turned away from Mitchell to hide the tears she couldn't hold back.

"Why don't we set up a meeting with Ashley in the morning. You go home and be with your dad tonight." Jesse's voice was as tender as the morning dew.

"No. If she is his mother, she shouldn't have to wait. She's been through enough. I don't want to keep them apart any longer."

Maybe her father would forgive her. If she could ever forgive herself.

20

The ride back to Burkesboro was worse than one of those super-duper roller coasters Ellie wouldn't be caught dead on. One that took you to dizzying heights then sent you spiraling into new depths. One minute she was frantic with excitement in the possibility they may have found Landon's mother; the next, she was troubled by Peggy's death. Her heart ached for her father in his loss; her heart pounded with joy for Ashley Garrett's gain—if Landon was truly her son.

They were meeting Ashley at the hospital at 6:00 and had less than an hour to kill. She parked beside Jesse's Camaro and sat in her car a moment, getting up the nerve to call Aunt Sissy. Finally, after a couple of deep breaths, she dialed Sissy's cell phone.

"Hey," she said when Sissy answered. She fought to keep her voice from cracking. "Jesse told me."

"I'm sorry, honey. When he told me where you were, I knew you'd be checking in with him sooner or later."

"No. No, don't apologize. It's fine. How's Daddy?"

"He's good. He's very, very tired, but otherwise OK. They had already made the arrangements, so at least he doesn't have to deal with all that." Aunt Sissy sounded tired, too, and it reminded Ellie of her aunt's age. Sometimes it was easy to forget the woman was seventy years old.

"Y'all are staying at the house tonight, aren't you?"

"Oh. Well, thanks, honey, but I guess there really isn't any need. We'll probably just head on back home."

Ellie batted back tears. "Please stay. Just for tonight," she said, her voice barely above a whisper.

Sissy didn't say anything for a moment then Ellie heard her sniffle. "OK. I'll call you back if your dad insists on going home."

"Tell him I really want him to stay. We've got to go meet someone at the hospital, but I'll be home right after."

"All right. Go get that hunk of a partner of yours and get going. I don't want to be up all night again." Sissy laughed, and the sound was as comforting as a warm cup of tea.

Ellie hung up and headed inside. She stopped at the ladies' room to see how bad her face looked. Her eyes were bloodshot and the skin underneath puffy and dark. She wet a paper towel and dabbed at her eyes, hoping the coldness would help with the swelling. Maybe she needed one of those cold cucumber packs she had read about in one of those magazines.

Jesse was at *her* desk, concentrating hard at the monitor. She didn't have the strength to argue with him about the desk situation and sat down in the visitor's chair instead.

He looked up and smiled the softest smile; her heart nearly melted.

"Rough day, huh?"

She shrugged. "A lot of mixed emotions, I guess." She pulled her desk phone around to where she could see it and dialed Marc Deveraux's number. It was a long shot, but she hoped he could pull some strings.

"Doctor Deveraux," he said after the first ring.

"Hey, Marc. It's Ellie. I'm glad you're still there."

"Paperwork. It'll be the death of us all. What's up?"

"Mind hanging around for a little while longer? There's a good possibility we've found Landon's mother."

There was silence on the other end of the line. After a long moment, he finally spoke. "You're serious?"

The joy in her heart brought a smile. "Yeah. I'm serious. She's meeting us at the hospital at six."

She heard him sigh heavily. "Wow," he said. "What an answered prayer."

It didn't surprise her. She would've been more surprised if he *hadn't* said a prayer for little Landon.

"If it pans out, I'd like for you to talk to her about the medical issues. And also, can you arrange a private meeting room where I can talk with her before I let her see him? I've got a lot of questions, and I'm sure she'd like some privacy."

"Sure, no problem. We have a small conference room behind the nurses' station. I'll make sure it's unlocked for you."

"Thanks, Marc." She started to hang up but decided to press her luck. "Oh, and one more thing...didn't you graduate from Tulane?"

"You're very observant."

"Thank you. It helps that I get paid to be. I need a big favor, and I don't really have time to go through the proper channels. Do you still have contacts at Tulane?"

"Some, yeah."

"I know this is asking a lot, but I need to verify if someone was seen in the ER."

"Uh-huh. And the proper channels you don't have time for I'm assuming involves getting a warrant or subpoena?"

Ellie squeezed her eyes closed. "Sort of, yes."

"Is this related to Landon?"

"In a roundabout way, yes. I can't really tell you the whole story yet, but I need to know if a woman named Becky, or maybe Rebecca, Kenton was seen in the ER any time prior to Katrina, or maybe even right after. She would have been seen maybe multiple times for injuries consistent with spousal abuse."

"How do you spell the last name?"

Ellie spelled it for him. "I really do appreciate it." She hung up and looked at Jesse. "Want to grab a bite?" She had barely touched the lunch Mitchell bought, and her stomach was now rumbling.

"As long as you don't eat all the chips again."

She grinned and grabbed Landon's file from her desk then headed toward the elevator with Jesse right behind her.

"You going to tell Jack about Ashley Garrett?"

Ellie shushed him then leaned against the wall as they waited for the elevator. "This is going to be a jurisdictional nightmare as it is. I've come too far for him to pull the plug. We'll let the different DA's offices figure all that out."

Jesse shook his head. "Second day on the job, and I'm already breaking the rules."

Ellie couldn't help but smile. "We're not breaking the rules. Besides, Jack doesn't like to be bothered with the little details. He's more of a results-type man."

Outside, Ellie tossed Jesse the keys and settled into the passenger seat. She was too tired to drive. Hopefully after their meeting with Ashley, she could wrap this thing up with one more trip to Avery County.

"What'd you find out with Tommy and Susan Baker?" she asked.

Jesse shook his head. "Found plenty of Tommy Bakers and Susan Bakers but no Tommy *and* Susan Baker in or around New Orleans. And none with a kid named TJ."

It didn't surprise her. She knew Kenton was lying as sure as he was breathing. Her gut tightened, wondering what happened to Becky. She closed her eyes and leaned her head back against the headrest. She'd have to leave Becky to Brady Mitchell.

"Did you talk to Aunt Sissy?" Jesse asked.

Ellie slowly nodded. "They're going to stay tonight at the house, then go home tomorrow."

Jesse nodded. "You know...you can take a couple days. I mean, I'm sure there'll be a funeral and all, and it's perfectly acceptable if you wanted to—"

"And let you make this arrest? Over my dead body. I'm seeing this one through to the end."

"Go ahead, take all the glory. Even if I've done most of the legwork," he mumbled.

"Ha! Legwork? Only if it involves a computer. Who's run their butt off all over half the state?"

He was furiously fighting off a smile. "Oh, I see how it's going to be, *partner*. I get stuck with all the desk work because you barely know how to send an email."

Ellie burst out laughing. "I know how to send email, thank you."

"You sure don't know how to delete anything or put it in folders."

He had her there. She huffed and stared out the window. "Fine. You're a little better on the computer than I am."

He glanced at her. "A little?"

"OK, don't push it. You're an invaluable partner. Besides, you've got contacts, too. I think you know everybody under the sun."

"Not quite, but close. Comes from years spent in vice." He grinned at her.

Ellie shifted in the seat and stared at him. "Speaking of vice...why'd you leave?"

He didn't say anything for a moment, just stared straight ahead at the road passing by then finally shrugged. "It's a long story."

Ellie glanced at her watch. "Well, if I've calculated the time correctly, we've got about an hour before we meet Ashley."

He smiled a soft smile then sighed. "I didn't like the lifestyle anymore. Not that I ever really liked it. I just reached a point I didn't want to be a part of it anymore."

Jesse Alvarez was too good at what he did to have just walked away from it. "What happened?"

He took a deep breath then shrugged again. "I made a choice. I saw an opportunity, and I took it."

Ellie furrowed her brows and stared at him. She wasn't letting him off that easy. "And the rest of the story? What was the choice?"

He sighed heavily then a gentle smile slowly spread across his lips. She didn't know if it was a memory or resignation that she wasn't giving up that triggered the smile but he had her full attention.

"There was a girl, Brittany. She was fifteen and had been hooking for drug money for about six months. Her family life was awful. Dad ran off when she was a kid; mom was on her fourth husband and didn't care if Brittany came home or not. We knew Brittany was involved with Eddie Mako, making buys for him, and we'd been on his trail about two years. She started showing up to make her buys, and I noticed a bruise here or there. Mostly on her upper arms, on her legs occasionally. She told me she had a john that liked it a little rough. Then she showed up one day and her face looked like a punching bag that had been hit one too many times." He shook his head, shaking off the memory, then continued.

"It started happening more and more—her showing up with the crap beat out of her. Busted lips, black eyes. And she used to have the prettiest hair, long honey blonde, and one day she shows up and it's all whacked off—no style, it just looked like someone had taken a pair of scissors and hacked at it. I asked her if her john did it, and she told me no, that she had done it. Got mad one night and just lopped it off. I never really knew whether to believe her or not.

"She was a pretty girl. You know, the kind you imagine being on a high school football field leading the cheerleading squad every Friday night. I took an interest in her and got to know her pretty good, trying to gain her trust—for all the wrong reasons. We were using her to get to Eddie Mako, and she was slipping further and further into a world she didn't belong in. We were looking right through her, looking at the big fish and couldn't see the little fish dying right in front of our eyes." He shook his head again, took a deep breath then continued.

"She didn't show up for a buy one day, and I got worried about her. I found her at a crack house. She'd done a couple hits then slit her wrists."

Ellie's stomach knotted. She swallowed the bile in her throat. "Was she dead?" she asked, her voice a small whisper.

Jesse shook his head. "She'd lost a lot of blood, but the razor was old and rusty. She didn't get a clean slice."

Ellie sucked in a deep breath, allowing it to fill her lungs with much needed air. "What happened after that?"

Jesse smiled. "I witnessed to her. I introduced her to Jesus Christ." He looked over at Ellie and his eyes sparkled like dark chocolate diamonds. "I told her the truth about who I was and told her what God had done in *my* life and what he could do for her. She gave her life to Christ and hasn't looked back."

Ellie stared out the front window. She swallowed the knot lodged in her throat. "But if she wasn't in the life anymore, then your cover wasn't blown. Right?"

Jesse looked at her as if he didn't understand her theory. "My cover didn't have anything to do with me leaving. I didn't want to be a part of that life anymore. Do you know how much sin I saw every day?"

Ellie glared at him, an edge of resentment creeping into her thoughts. "I see the same sins, Jesse. We all do. It doesn't matter whether you're in vice or wearing a uniform. It's part of the job."

He nodded. "But you've never had to *act* like selling dope to a kid was cool."

She'd give him that one. Apparently, he was very good at acting. "Have you talked to Brittany since?"

"Oh, yeah. Her mom gave up custody of her so I

set her up with a family at church that takes in hard-to-place foster children. She's been with them ever since. She's back in school, Academy Christian, and is going on her first mission trip at spring break. Costa Rica, I think. She needs to raise about twelve-hundred dollars to go, so she got a job after school cleaning the church."

"And how much have you donated to the cause?" Ellie asked with a slight grin.

He laughed. "Let's just say she's halfway there."

****

After a quick bite, they headed to the hospital. Ellie's stomach was in knots, and it had nothing to do with the greasy burrito she'd just devoured. What if Ashley Garrett wasn't Landon's mother? What if she *was*? Ellie tried to imagine what was going through Ashley's mind at the moment. Had she saved his little toddler clothes and toys? Or were they packed away in a storage tote in the far corner of an attic, out of sight, the memories too painful to bear. Had she left his bedroom untouched, if she even lived in the same house? Perhaps she had moved? It would surprise Ellie if she had. It had been her experience that parents of missing children seldom left the house the child called home, fearing authorities, or even the child, wouldn't know how or where to find them. Ellie assumed Ashley hadn't remarried; her last name was still the same as her late husband's. Did she *want* to remarry? If she *was* Landon's mother, would there be a stepfather in the future? Would he love Landon like his own? Would he play ball with him? Would he take him fishing?

"Ellie?" Jesse was staring at her. "You OK?"

They were parked outside the Emergency Room. Ellie stared at the red neon sign. "Yeah, I'm fine."

"Thinking about the meeting?"

She nodded. "Yeah, a little. You ready?"

"Are you?" He looked at her, a look of genuine concern shadowing his perfect face.

She forced a smile. "I'm always ready." She removed the photo of Landon from the file, smiling and happy and laughing at Leon then slipped it into her jacket pocket.

Inside at the ER check-in, a young woman stood alone, leaning against the wall for support, her face conflicted with anxiety. She was quite pretty with blonde hair cut pixie style and ocean-colored eyes framed by just a touch of makeup. Her petite frame was hidden beneath a pair of baggy jeans and a loose-fitting sweater.

"Are you Ashley Garrett?" Ellie asked.

She looked from Ellie to Jesse then nodded. "You're Detective Alvarez?" she asked, her voice shaking with emotion.

"Yes. And this is Detective Ellie Saunders."

"It's a pleasure to meet you, Ashley. We'd like to ask you a couple questions before we take you to Landon."

She nodded quickly. "But he's OK?"

Ellie smiled softly. "He's fine. Why don't we go upstairs where we can talk privately?"

The receptionist buzzed them through. They led Ashley through the Emergency Room and to the elevators. Ashley's gaze darted back and forth to each person they passed, reminding Ellie of a tiny, confused mouse. "And you're sure he's OK?" she asked again in the elevator.

Ellie nodded. "He's been thoroughly examined."

"Then why is he here in the hospital?"

Ellie didn't quite know how to explain that one. That one may have to wait until Ashley was sitting down. Jesse jumped in and offered a temporary explanation. "Standard procedure," he said and smiled.

Ashley accepted it with a nod.

When they reached the fourth floor, tears spilled from Ashley's eyes as she tenderly touched a mural. She gently ran her fingers over a painted teddy bear and cried.

Ellie approached the nurse's station and told a nurse Deveraux had arranged for them to use the conference room.

"Oh, yeah, you're Detective Saunders. Right this way." She led them down a short hall then opened a door and showed them in. "Dr. Deveraux wanted me to let him know when y'all arrived."

"Tell him to give me about thirty minutes and then he can join us."

The nurse nodded then closed the door on her way out. The room was about the size of an average living room, split in half by a large table surrounded by mismatched office chairs. Medical journals, women's magazines, and grocery-store tabloids were scattered on one end of the table.

Ellie pulled a chair out for Ashley then one for herself and sat beside her while Jesse took a seat on the other side of the table. Ellie pulled her chair closer to Ashley then reached in her pocket and took out the picture of Landon. There was no sense in putting the poor woman through a barrage of questions and the gory details of how he was found if Landon *wasn't* her son. "I want you to look at a picture, and I understand Landon has grown, but I want you to tell me if you think there is a possibility this is your son." She laid the picture on the table in front of Ashley.

There was little reaction. At first. Then Ashley slowly picked up the picture and held it as if it were a fragile piece of china. She gently ran her finger over the image of Landon, as if she could actually feel the softness of his hair, the smoothness of his skin. A tear fell from her eyes and splattered on the picture. She burst out crying and slammed the picture hard against her chest, cradling it as if it were the real thing, not just an image. "Oh thank You, God," she sobbed over and over again. "Can I see him? *Please*, take me to him. Please? Oh thank You, God."

Ellie fought back her own tears as each tear Ashley shed tugged at Ellie's heart. "Of course, but we do need to go over a few things first, OK?"

Ashley quickly nodded and furiously wiped her face with her hands. "But he's OK?"

Ellie softly smiled and nodded. "Yes. He's fine, and you'll get to see for yourself in just a few minutes."

Tears streamed down Ashley's face as her lips quivered with emotion.

Ellie's heart was tied in knots, and the raw emotion radiating from Ashley tugged the knot tighter.

Ashley sniffled, then took a deep breath. "Where was he found?"

Ellie's chest tightened. How was she going to tell this mother her six-year-old son was found *dead* in an alley—but now he was *OK*?

"Ashley," Jesse said, "do you believe in miracles?"

She looked at Ellie then at Jesse. "I've prayed every day that wherever he was, he was safe. And that one day, I would find him."

"Your son is *truly* a miracle," Jesse said, his smile warm and sincere. "Landon was found in an alley. And when he was found, he was clinically dead."

Her hand flew to her mouth. "But you said he was fine?"

"He is fine," Ellie said. "He's in perfect health. But, he *was* pronounced dead on arrival at the hospital."

Ashley sprung from the chair and moved away from Ellie, away from the table, pacing around the room. She was breathing so hard Ellie feared she was going to hyperventilate. Ellie got up quickly and moved toward her. "Ashley, I promise you, he's in perfect health. We don't know what happened, or how it happened, but Landon is *alive,* and that's what matters right now. Look at the picture, Ashley—it was taken yesterday. He's laughing, he's smiling. He's in perfect health."

"What...what happened...to him?" she stuttered, backing herself into the corner.

"We think he may have been involved in a car accident, and rather than being brought to the hospital, whomever he was with...left him in the alley."

Ashley stared from Ellie to Jesse, her face an open plain of emotion. "He was left to die in an alley?" With her back in the corner, she slowly slid down the wall, crumpling into a small knot, deep gut-wrenching sobs wracking her entire body. Ellie went to her and sat beside her, cradling her in her arms, stroking her hair. They sat like that for a while, Ellie fighting back her own tears. Finally, Ashley wiped at her face with the backs of her hands. "I prayed every day that whoever had him would love him and not hurt him," she said, choking on her words. "How could they leave him like that? He must have been so scared."

Ellie turned Ashley's face toward her own. "None of that matters right now. What matters is he's alive."

Ashley nodded quickly, like she finally saw the bigger picture. "Please take me to him. I want to see him."

Ellie stood and offered her hand to help Ashley up. Whatever questions she had, could wait. This mother *needed* to see her son.

There was a slight knock on the door and Deveraux gently pushed it open. Ellie smiled softy. "Ashley, this Dr. Marc Deveraux, chief of pediatrics. He's been very involved in Landon's care."

Deveraux looked at Ashley with eyes so warm, Ellie fought to keep her own heart from melting. "You're sure?"

"We'll have to confirm with a DNA test," Ellie said. "But, yes, it looks like it may be."

"I'm very happy for you," he said. "You have a very remarkable son."

"Detective Saunders said he was...dead? When he was brought to the hospital, is that true?"

Deveraux looked at Jesse then Ellie and nodded. "Yes."

"We can't explain how or why," said Ellie. "But he woke up in the morgue, and any trace of the accident had vanished."

Ashley shook her head. "What do you mean, any trace of the accident?"

Deveraux propped himself on the edge of the table. "When he was brought in, he was bruised, bloody. He had suffered severe trauma."

Ashley fell into the chair, tears rolling down her cheeks. "And he was...dead."

Deveraux nodded. "Yes. He was clinically dead."

"And he *woke up* in the morgue?" Her face was a collage of questions.

"Without any bruises or trauma or any memory of what happened to him," Jesse said.

Ashley looked at each of them, her eyes still wet with tears. "If he doesn't remember what happened, do you think he'll remember *me*?" Her voice was soft, childlike.

"Ashley," Jesse said, "Landon said the last thing he remembered before waking up was walking and talking *with his dad*."

"With Andy? That's im...possible." She stared off into space, looking at something only she could see. "Isn't it?" she whispered.

"We believe," Jesse said, "in that time between when he was clinically dead and when he woke up, that he saw his dad in heaven."

"We believe Landon had an after-life experience," Deveraux said.

They believe, Ellie thought. She still wasn't sure about the whole thing. She was reluctantly leaning that way, but it was something she would have to come to terms with herself, regardless of her dad's or Jesse's or Marc Deveraux's beliefs.

Ashley stood and moved slowly around the room as if she were carefully navigating through a dense fog. "This is all so...hard to...understand."

That's an understatement. Ellie was used to dealing with facts, with everything black or white, no in-between. She was out of her comfort zone dealing with things that couldn't be explained.

"Ashley, I need to prepare you for what to expect when we take you to Landon," Deveraux said.

Ashley spun around and stared at Deveraux. "But you said he was fine…"

Deveraux smiled. "He is, physically. Mentally and emotionally, there appears to be some delays."

She shook her head, confusion evident on her face. "What kind of delays?"

"We've estimated his age to be around six. Is that correct?"

She nodded. "He turned six in October."

"Given that, he doesn't necessarily have the maturity other children his age would have."

Ashley shook her head. "I don't understand. How mature *is* a six-year-old?"

Marc smiled, understanding her concerns. "Developmentally, he's not where he should be for a child his age. For instance, he struggles to count to ten, he enjoys activities older toddlers might enjoy, and he sometimes confuses his colors."

"He knew his colors. Andy used to color with him every night."

"What Dr. Deveraux is saying is there doesn't appear to be anything wrong that can't be fixed," Ellie said, wanting to reassure her. "We know he didn't attend school. And if we're right about his abductors, they kept him pretty isolated. He hasn't been exposed to other children or given the opportunities to learn and develop like he should have been."

"It's pretty common with child abductions," Jesse said. "The abductors are scared the more people who know about the child, the better the chance someone will find out."

Tears streamed down her face again, and she brushed them away. "And you don't think he was abused?"

"There's no indication of physical or sexual abuse," Marc said. "Mentally, there's no real way to tell just from observing him. I do recommend that he continues to see a child psychologist for a little while. There may be things buried quite deep that a trained therapist can bring to the surface."

"Ashley," Ellie said, "can you tell me what happened the day Landon was abducted?"

Ashley took a deep breath then spoke in a soft voice. "We were at the grocery store. I had finished my shopping and put Landon in his car seat while I loaded the groceries in the trunk. When I got through, I went to put the cart back and there was this lady...an older lady...and she had fallen there at the front of the store. I stopped and helped her up and made sure she was OK then I helped her gather up the groceries that had spilled out of her bag. When I got back to the car..." Tears streamed down her face again. Her red-rimmed eyes were distant, staring at a vivid memory. "He was gone," she whispered. "Even his car seat was gone."

"Do you remember seeing anyone around the car, or even in the parking lot, that looked suspicious?"

Ashley shook her head then looked at Ellie then Jesse. "The police took all this information. We went over it and over it and over it, again and again and again. They never could come up with a suspect. They listed Landon with all the registries, and I was getting updates every day and then...it was like the interest just faded away."

Ellie understood the frustration, but knew there came a time when you had done all you could do. Unfair as it seemed.

"Ashley, was your husband already deceased when Landon was abducted?"

She shook her head. "Andy was diagnosed with a brain tumor about six months before Landon was…taken. He lived a year and three months after Landon was kidnapped. The day it…happened…Andy was feeling good and wanted me to leave Landon at home with him. But I didn't feel comfortable leaving him with him. Andy had just finished a round of chemo and sometimes it made him so sick. Maybe if I had left Landon…."

"Did the police find any fingerprints on your car?" Jesse asked.

Ashley nodded. "But they never could find a match."

"Do you know if the police ever interviewed anyone of interest?"

"There were a couple of people, I think. Mostly the sex offenders in the area." She shuddered.

"Did the police interview anyone else?" Jesse asked.

"I told them about this one guy. He kind of gave me the creeps, but I don't know if they ever interviewed him or not."

"What guy?" Ellie asked.

She half shrugged. "It was probably just my imagination, but there was this delivery guy that came by the office once a week to fill the vending machines in the break room. He was just…weird. He kind of flirted with me a couple times, and it gave me the creeps. Then I saw him a couple times at the grocery store, filling the machines outside, and he'd speak, say hello or something like that."

"Was he there the day Landon was taken?"

Ashley shook her head. "I don't remember seeing him. That's why the police didn't think too much about it, I suppose."

Ellie pulled her cell phone from her pocket and scrolled to the picture of Jerome Kenton. She then turned the phone so Ashley could see. "Ashley, was this man the delivery driver?"

Ashley stared at the picture for a long moment then slowly nodded.

****

Deveraux escorted them down the hall toward the playroom. Before they reached the one-way mirror, he stopped and turned to Ashley. "He may not recognize you right off. I want you to be prepared for that, OK?"

Ashley quickly nodded then wrung her hands and wiped the moisture on her jeans. She batted away the tears clinging to her lashes then took a deep breath and stepped up to the mirror. As soon as she did, she gasped then nearly collapsed. Jesse moved quickly and caught her in his arms, holding her while she sobbed. "I never thought I'd ever see him again," she said between deep, gasping sobs.

Landon was playing smash-up cars again with Leon, oblivious to the scene on the other side of the window. Ellie watched him a moment, wondering if all this miracle talk might be true. Even the medical examiner couldn't explain why this child was alive. Whether or not it was a miracle he was alive, Ellie couldn't deny it *was* a miracle they had been able to reunite him with his mother.

Ashley reached out and touched the glass with trembling fingertips. "Please," she begged. "I want to hold him."

Deveraux nodded then opened the door to the

playroom and escorted them in. Ashley stood in the corner, trembling, tears pouring down her face, her hands cupped over her mouth. Leon stood and took a step away from the small table, apparently aware this wasn't a good time for his usual antics.

The smile on Landon's face disappeared as he stared at Ashley, then, all of a sudden his glacier-blue eyes reamed with tears. "Mom?"

Marc gently pushed the door open and followed her into the room. "Hey, sport," he said.

Ashley ran toward him as he leapt from the chair and ran toward her. She swept him up in her arms, his arms wrapped tightly around her neck. "You came for me," he sobbed, his cheek pressed hard against hers.

"So much for not recognizing her," Jesse whispered.

"Shut up," Ellie whispered back as she brushed away her own tears.

Ashley found her way to the rocking chair and cradled Landon in her arms, rocking him back and forth like a new mother rocking a baby. She alternated between cradling him fiercely and pulling away, gazing at him, lovingly touching his face, his ears, counting the fingers on his hands.

"I knew you'd find me," he said, his arms wrapped tight around her neck.

"We'll never be able to thank you enough," Ashley said, turning to Ellie and Jesse. She brushed the hair out of Landon's face and smothered him with kisses.

"Landon, I do have a few more questions to ask, if you feel up to it," Ellie said hopefully.

He glanced at Deveraux then at his mom. Deveraux gave Ellie the evil eye then sighed. Ashley looked at Landon protectively. "Do you feel like answering some questions?"

He stared at Ellie then nodded and settled into his mother's lap. Ellie took her phone out and flipped through the pictures to the one of Becky Kenton that Brady Mitchell had forwarded to her. "Landon, have you ever seen this woman before?" She turned the phone around and showed him the picture.

Landon nodded quickly and without fear. "That's Becky."

"How do you know Becky?"

"She lived with us in that house with the big stove."

"She lived there with who? Who else lived there with you?" She already knew the answer, but she wanted to hear him say it.

He scooted down in his mom's lap but showed no signs of shutting down like before. "Jerome. He's her husband. She's nice...but he's not."

Ellie knelt down beside the chair, eye-level with Landon. "Remember you told me the night of the accident, y'all hit a deer? Do you remember anything else about that night? Especially after the accident...anything at all."

He burrowed a little deeper into Ashley's lap and shook his head. "I remember Becky crying. She was screaming really loud."

"Why was she screaming?"

"She was screaming 'cause I was hurt."

Ashley tightened her hold on him and closed her eyes. She rested her chin on the top of his head.

"You were hurt in the accident?" Ellie asked.

He nodded. "And there was a lot of blood, too."

"Your blood?"

He nodded again. "Becky was bleeding a little,

too, but not as much as me."

"And she was screaming because you were bleeding?"

"She was screaming, 'We've got to get him help! We've got to get him help!'" He wiggled away from Ashley's grip and flayed his arms about in an animated demonstration. "But Jerome told her to hush. He said they couldn't take me to the hospital 'cause then people would know."

People would know he wasn't their child.

"Do you remember anything else?"

He shook his head. "I went to sleep after that." Then suddenly he turned toward Ashley and smiled a smile that lit his entire face. "And I saw Daddy. I saw Daddy, Mom. That's how I knew you'd find me—he told me you would. And he told me to tell you he didn't blame you. He said it wasn't your fault."

Stunned, Ashley looked at Ellie then Jesse.

"What wasn't your fault?" Ellie asked, as confused as Ashley looked.

Ashley stared at Landon for a long while then mashed him to her, her tears spilling onto his round cheeks. Finally, after she had regained enough composure to speak, she whispered, "I always blamed myself. If I had just left him with Andy that day..."

Ellie suddenly felt light-headed. She braced herself on the arm of the chair. *That was the message.* Jesse, Deveraux...her father. They had all been right. This child *had* seen heaven.

21

The drive back to the office was quiet, a product of the emotional exhaustion Ellie felt. Jesse tried occasionally to make small talk then eventually gave up and accepted the silence. He pulled into the parking lot, sat there a moment, then finally cut off the car. "You OK?" he asked, looking over at Ellie.

She nodded. "Just a little drained."

"Yeah. It was a pretty eventful day. Scenes like that in the playroom, that's what makes the job worthwhile."

Ellie stared out the windshield, watching the snow flutter in the lights. It had tapered off to scattered flurries, but not before leaving about two feet accumulated on the ground.

"I'm glad we were able to reunite them," Ellie said, her voice faint, like an echo. "But it makes me mad that we *had* to. What made Jerome Kenton grab that little boy out of his own car, raise him as his own? I'm sorry the Kenton's lost their son, but it didn't give them the right to take someone else's. If they had never hit that deer…"

"But they did. And because of it, Landon is back with his mother."

Ellie shook her head. "More Divine intervention, huh?"

Jesse grinned. "I hate to think that poor deer was sacrificed, but yeah. Divine intervention."

Ellie sat there a moment, too tired to argue. She wasn't so sure she could argue with him about it anymore. All these *miracles* did give her pause.

"You want me to drive you home?"

She considered it then shook her head. "No. The roads aren't bad. I just hate it's so late. I told Aunt Sissy I wouldn't be long."

"I'm sure your dad will understand. I know he'll be happy about Landon."

Ellie knew Jesse was right. Despite her father's current heartbreak, he'd be overjoyed to hear about Landon and his mother. That's just how he was. So sacrificing. So godly.

****

Ellie sat in her driveway and brushed the tears from her face before going in. Her heart had been tugged in so many directions in the last few hours she wasn't sure who or what she was crying for anymore. From the car she could see the soft yellow glow of a light on in her living room, but at this hour wasn't sure her father would still be up.

She sucked up her tears and headed inside, trudging through the snow still packed along the walkway. Aunt Sissy was curled on the sofa reading one of her romance novels, and her father was in the kitchen fixing himself a cup of hot tea.

Sissy glanced up from the book and glared at Ellie over the rims of her reading glasses. "You look like crap."

"Thanks. You look wonderful, too," Ellie said as she tossed her coat in the chair. She went into the kitchen and wrapped her arms around her father. He embraced her tightly, surprising her at his strength. "I'm so sorry, Daddy. I'm sorry I wasn't there." She choked back another onslaught of tears.

Her father gently stroked her hair as he shushed her. "Hey, it's all right. I know you had work to do...and Peggy knew it, too."

"But I should have been there for *you*."

He pulled away from her and cupped her face in his hands. "Sweetheart, you're forgiven. It's time you forgive yourself."

She wished she had an ounce of his strength. And faith. He gently wiped away her tears and smiled tenderly at her. "She went very peacefully. If I were to mourn her death, it would be selfish of me. She's rejoicing in the arms of the Lord, and as much as I'm going to miss her, I wouldn't ever wish it any different."

He took another cup from the cabinet and fixed Ellie a cup of tea. "Come. Tell me about the case. I assume there's been a new development?" He led her into the living room. Sissy sat up to make room on the sofa.

Ellie sat between them and reveled in the closeness. She told them about Ashley Garrett and her husband Andy, and about Jerome Kenton. "I'm going back up to Avery County tomorrow. Jerome Kenton has some serious questions to answer."

"Did the little boy recognize his mother?" her father asked.

Ellie nodded. "He knew who she was immediately. And...remember you told Jesse the child probably had a message for someone...apparently, the message was for his mother." There. She had said it. She had finally acknowledged God had been involved in this case from the beginning.

"What was the message?" Sissy asked.

Ellie told them about the guilt Ashley had carried and how in one simple sentence, she had received the release she needed.

Her father slowly nodded and smiled. "Amazing how liberating forgiveness can be. You should ask Jesse about that sometime. He's forgiven." He gave her a teasing wink.

Sissy craned her neck to look out the window. "Speaking of Jesse, he didn't drive you home tonight?"

Ellie couldn't help but grin. "There wasn't any reason for him to. The roads are pretty clear."

"Shucks. I was wanting to see him again before we left." She winked at Ellie.

"Oh, I'm sure we'll be seeing more of Mr. Alvarez," her father said, patting Ellie's knee. "And if you'll excuse me, I believe I'm going to turn in now." He gave Ellie a peck on the cheek then rose and padded into the kitchen.

"I love you, Daddy," Ellie called after him.

He turned and smiled at her. "Love you, too, sweetheart," he said then disappeared down the short hallway.

"I wish I had his strength," Ellie said in a soft voice.

Sissy smiled at her. "You do. You just don't know it yet."

Ellie doubted it but was too tired to argue the point. "What kind of arrangements have been made?"

"The visitation's tomorrow night, and the funeral's the day after. Sam Pearson and your daddy's going to preach."

"Daddy?" Her father hadn't preached since he left

Valley View Baptist Church.

Sissy smiled and nodded.

Ellie curled up on the couch and laid her head in Sissy's lap. "Aunt Sissy, do you think my mom's in heaven?"

Sissy softly stroked Ellie's hair. "Child, what makes you ask that?"

"I remember Daddy preaching and saying suicide was a sin." Ellie couldn't believe she had said it. It was the first time she had verbally admitted to anyone her mother had taken her own life. She was surprised at how easy it was to say. Surprised that the world hadn't stopped with a crier shouting her shame from the rooftops.

"The way I understand it, and I may be wrong because Lord knows I'm not as up on all that stuff as your daddy, but God gave us life, so it's not up to us to dictate when that life ends."

"So what about my mom?"

Sissy sighed heavily. "Sweetie, your mom was not a well woman. She had a sickness that we didn't really understand at the time."

"Why didn't Daddy ever get her help?"

"It's hard to get someone help when they don't think they need it. Sweetie, truth is, your mama had these frequent episodes. She'd be fine and happy, then she'd fall into fits of depression so deep there was no reasoning with her. An idea would take root, and she'd be like a dog with a bone. Wouldn't let go until she saw it through or came to a moment of clarity." Aunt Sissy shook her head. "She took her own life, that's true, but who of us is to even say whether she knew what she was doing? Who of us knows if she found a moment of clarity right before she died and begged His forgiveness? Only God knows, sweetie, and I have no doubt He judges justly—and mercifully." Sissy patted Ellie's leg. "Is she in heaven? I don't know, sweetie, but one day, I'm sure we're going to find out."

Ellie batted her eyes, fighting back the sleep that threatened to overtake her at any minute. "Do you think the rumors were true about Daddy and Peggy?"

Sissy lightly chuckled. "Peggy was an easy target. She was an attractive, single lady who was hungry for God. She loved talking theology with your father, and since she *was* the church secretary, they saw each other nearly every day."

Ellie pulled herself up and turned to face Sissy. "You didn't answer my question."

Sissy stared back at her. "Do I think they were having an affair? No. Your father loved your mother very much, despite all she put him through."

"But the rumors—"

"Ellie, your mom started the rumors herself." Sissy let out a deep breath then continued, "She started the same rumor at the first church they were at, too. Back before you were born. Your dad just quietly resigned, and a couple of months later, took the position at Valley View. Back then, it was an older congregation, and I guess your mom didn't feel as threatened by little gray-haired ladies in their sixties. Your dad worked hard at building the church and bringing in more young people, and I guess, that was the beginning of the end."

Ellie pushed her hands through her hair and took a deep breath. Somewhere deep inside, she had known the truth all along. But it had been easier to blame it on Peggy than to accept her mother wasn't well.

"Peggy was a good woman, Ellie. And despite all

the troubles y'all had, she loved you very much."

It wasn't the first time she had heard it, but for the first time, Ellie believed it. And now it was too late to do anything about all the pain and hurt she'd caused her father's wife...her stepmother. She wondered if she ever *would* be able to forgive herself.

****

The next morning at the office, Ellie sipped her third cup of coffee while talking to Brady Mitchell on the phone. She told him about Ashley Garrett and the delivery driver Ashley identified as Kenton. "She doesn't remember seeing him at the grocery store the day Landon was kidnapped, but she said she wasn't paying much attention, either."

"Did they get fingerprints off the car?" Mitchell asked.

"Yeah, but they were never able to find a match."

"All that means is he wasn't in the system at the time. Maybe it's time we bring Mr. Kenton in for a formal interview. I'll head back out there. Maybe he'll come willingly." Mitchell said, his voice not very hopeful sounding.

"Mind if I ride along?"

"Not at all. Can you make it up here around eleven?"

"I'll be there." As she told him goodbye and hung up, Jesse plopped down in the guest chair. The look on his face was dire.

Ellie's heart leaped into her throat. "What's the matter?"

"Jack wants an update."

"Oh." This wasn't good.

"My sentiments exactly," Jesse said.

Ellie stared at him, wondering how he…she didn't have time right now to wonder about his mindreading abilities. "Let me do the talking," she said, rising slowly from her chair.

"Oh, you don't have to worry about that. I'll even give you the rope to hang yourself."

Ellie glared at him then squared her shoulders and headed into Jack's office with Jesse tagging along behind. Jack was elbow-deep in paperwork, glanced up then motioned the both of them to come in. He motioned toward the chair but Ellie continued to stand. She didn't plan on being in there long enough to get comfortable.

"Sara Jeffries called the chief's office complaining about the lack of information coming from this department on the Johnny Doe case. What happened to the interview you were supposed to schedule with her?"

"We were chasing a good lead, and I wanted to see how it panned out," said Ellie.

"And?"

Ellie took a deep breath then forced a smile. If she told Jack the whole story, he'd pull the plug on the investigation. He'd consider it over. Ellie wouldn't consider it over until Jerome Kenton was behind bars whether in Burkesboro, Avery County, or Mecklenburg County. "We were able to locate his mother."

Jack raised his brows. "Really?"

Ellie quickly nodded. "We're bringing the suspect in this afternoon for a formal interview."

"You have enough to charge him?"

"He'll be charged." She didn't lie. *Someone* would

charge him.

Jack nodded his approval, indicating the conversation was over. Ellie turned and hurried out of the office with Jesse on her heels.

22

Ellie sat at her desk and ran it over again and again in her mind. Daddy said he didn't blame you. He said it wasn't your fault. How could a six-year-old know the guilt Ashley felt? He was three years old when he was taken from her car. What does a child know about guilt? The knot in her chest told her to believe...just believe. Even her gut instinct was telling her to believe. There was absolutely no medical explanation for Landon even being alive. The only logical explanation was the one thing she couldn't admit. It was a miracle. A true miracle in every sense of the word. Through all the years in church, all the years hearing her father preach the Word, she had never felt as close to God as she felt now. So why was she still filled with so much doubt?

"You sure you don't want me to go with you?" Jesse asked, interrupting her thoughts. He was sitting in the visitor's chair, his elbows propped on her desk. "The roads may still be in pretty bad shape up that way."

Reminded of the evil that was Jerome Kenton, Ellie pushed the thoughts of God and miracles from her mind. "The roads are fine," Ellie reassured Jesse. "I didn't have any trouble yesterday. Besides, you need to get back up to the hospital and go over witness procedures with Ashley. I don't want her to think it's the end of it when they walk out of the hospital."

"You think Deveraux's going to release him that quick?"

"Not until they get the DNA results back, which he's rushed. But I just want her to be prepared."

"And tell me again why you're going back to Avery County to interview Kenton? I hate to tell you, sweetcakes, but we really don't have a dog in this fight."

Ellie stared at him. "What do you mean we don't have a dog in this fight? Landon was dumped in our jurisdiction."

Jesse laughed. "You're right, he was *dumped*. After he was in a bad car accident. Kenton didn't beat him to death in that alley. And he was kidnapped in Mecklenburg County. And the whole missing wife thing, that's in Avery County. Our charges are going to be pretty low on the totem pole."

The charges in their jurisdiction didn't really matter. She just wanted to be there when Brady Mitchell questioned him again.

"You're still going, aren't you?"

She looked at Jesse and grinned. "Do you really have to ask?"

He sighed. "I just don't like you going by yourself."

His concern was flattering. "I'll be fine. Besides, I won't be by myself. Brady Mitchell's bringing him in."

"Hmph. Brady Mitchell should have retired ten years ago."

Ellie glared at him, her jaw hanging open. "And how do you know Brady Mitchell? No, don't answer that. I don't even want to know." She shook her head, unbelieving.

****

"I'm happy for you. Real happy for the little fella and his momma, too," Brady Mitchell said as he settled into his SUV. Ellie climbed into the passenger seat and buckled her seat belt.

"It was a pretty emotional scene. If Jerome Kenton had been standing in front of me, I'd have choked him."

Mitchell laughed. "You'll get your chance. Not to choke him, but at least to formally question him."

"I appreciate you letting me tag along, considering the charges I have against him are pretty minor compared to yours and Mecklenburg County's."

Mitchell slowly nodded, knowingly. Letting her know he understood the craving to finish a job whether you had *a dog in the fight* or not. "I hope we're wrong about Becky," he said, his voice solemn. "But I don't think we are."

Ellie stared out the window at the passing snow-covered landscape. She hoped they were wrong, too. Not just for Becky's sake, but for Landon's, too. Although Becky had no right to him, she was kind to him. It made the pain and suffering of his abduction a little easier to swallow.

"What are we going to do if Kenton doesn't want to come down to the station?"

"He'll come. He's got all the answers, remember?" Mitchell said. "He'll be anxious to share 'em."

The main roads had been pretty clear, but the road leading to Kenton's was still almost impassable. Mitchell shifted into four-wheel drive and crept forward in the snow. He carefully moved around a mail carrier's truck stopped at one of the mailboxes.

Mitchell threw up his hand and waved and the carrier nodded. The guy didn't look like he was enjoying his job very much. "Rain, snow, sleet, or hail," Mitchell said and chuckled.

The closer they got to Kenton's, the more knots Ellie could count in her stomach. She was already having to remind herself to breathe. She rolled her shoulders, releasing the tension, then reached around behind her and pulled the pistol from her waistband. She checked the clip then patted her jacket pocket for the extra. Mitchell glanced at her and grinned.

"You plan on shooting someone?" He chuckled.

"Only if I have to."

He slowly nodded, still grinning. "Ever fired it?"

"Sure." The gun was incredibly heavy in her hand.

"Outside the shooting range?"

She glared at him hard then rolled her eyes. "I'll have you know I shot a perfect score."

Mitchell eased into Kenton's driveway. "Well, hopefully we won't mess up your perfect record."

She could feel the bile churning in her stomach, her heart racing. "Yeah, let's hope so."

Mitchell parked about halfway up the drive and cut off the engine. "We're just going to talk to him, Ellie. No matter how bad you want to string him up, our mission is to get him to come down to the station for an interview. Hopefully before he lawyers up."

He reached for the door but Ellie grabbed his arm. "You have your gun, right?"

Mitchell reached in across her and popped open the glove compartment. "Sure. I've got it. It's right there."

"You're not going to carry it?" Her eyes were wide, the fear suddenly gripping her as tight as her grip on the door handle.

Mitchell shook his head. He got out of the vehicle. "You coming or am I going to have to do this interview alone?" he asked before he closed the door.

Ellie took a deep breath and willed her hands to stop shaking. She didn't know why she was so nervous. She'd done hundreds of interviews like this before, carted many off to the jail. Why was this one different? Why was that butterfly in her stomach fluttering like a two-ton elephant? *God...if you're listening...*

The sun glistening off the snow cast a painful white glow. Kenton's new truck was parked where it had been the other day, and judging by the untouched snow around it, it hadn't been moved.

Ellie joined Mitchell and headed toward the house. "Since you're a bundle of nerves, why don't you let me do the talking," he said, winking at her.

"I'm not nervous. I'm perfectly calm." They were about twenty yards from the porch and that elephant in her stomach started doing somersaults. She stuffed her hands in her pockets to hide the trembling.

Mitchell chuckled and turned to smile at her.

Suddenly, Ellie heard the ear-shattering pop. Blood spattered against the freshly fallen snow, turning it bright crimson.

"Brady!"

Ellie hit the ground hard, covering her head, scrambling to get to Brady. Another blast tore through the deafening silence. "Oh, God...Oh, God...Oh, God, help me!" she prayed.

Brady was on his back, a stream of blood seeping from underneath him. He was wide-eyed, blinking furiously, and wheezing for breath. Ellie stared at the hole in his side. "Hang in there, Brady...hang in there."

Tears stung her eyes, her fear beyond reason. She jerked her cell phone from her pocket and hurriedly punched in 911. There was no familiar dial tone. There was nothing. There wasn't even a dispatch radio in the Expedition!

Brady moaned and tried to speak, but Ellie shushed him. "You're not going to die on me, Brady Mitchell." But she knew if she didn't get him help and get it soon, he *would* die on her, and if Jerome Kenton had his way, she'd die too.

Brady shook his head. "Listen," he said, his voice a shallow whisper. "Listen."

Ellie tried but couldn't hear anything above her heart thundering in her ears.

"Did you hear the click? He's out of bullets." Each word was wrapped in a noisy breath. "The truck hasn't been moved."

Ellie stared at the little house, the shattered front window where the shots had come from. She wanted Jerome Kenton more than anything, but she couldn't leave Brady. Not like this. Not to die alone. There was no way to know for sure if he *was* out of ammo, and she couldn't risk a stand-off. If she were to get into a stand-off with Kenton, all he'd have to do was wait it out—there was no help coming and Brady would certainly die right there in Kenton's front yard.

She had to get help, and she was running out of time. She looked over at the shiny new truck and rusted grill under the little carport. The propane tank was still attached to the grill. Had God really heard her prayer? Could there still be gas in it?

With every ounce of strength she had in her, she wedged her arms under Brady's shoulders and pulled as hard as she could, dragging him backwards toward his SUV. He groaned in pain as she tugged at him again and again. "Hang in there, Brady. Hang with me, man."

Ellie dragged Brady's dead weight until they were behind the vehicle and near the road. With one final heave, she fell backwards, exhausted, every muscle in her body crying in pain. She frantically wiggled out from under Brady and crawled over him, keeping an eye on the house. She heard noises, snow crunching under foot and suddenly, she spotted Kenton running from the back of the house toward the little shed.

Ellie covered Brady as best she could with her own body then drew her gun and sited the propane tank, blinking away the tears so she could see. She took a deep breath to steady her hands. One shot and the tank exploded into an orange ball of fire, flames shooting a hundred feet into the air, blowing the carport and truck into giant shards of flying metal. There was no way the mail carrier they had passed earlier could miss the fireball now raging.

Ellie scrambled over Brady then crawled to the Expedition and slid in, grabbing his gun from the glove compartment. Unless the shed had a back door, Kenton was still in it. She dropped Brady's gun in her pocket then crouched beside the rear quarter panel to catch her breath. With her pistol in her hand, she gave another quick peek at the shed then burst into a full run toward the house. She crouched for cover at the porch, gasping for breath. The air was frigid and burnt her lungs as she sucked it deeply in. "Jerome," she yelled as loudly as she could. The sound echoed in the stillness, reverberating off the snow-laden trees. "Jerome," she yelled again. "I know why you did what you did with JJ. You had no choice."

Despite the freezing air and wet clothes, sweat trickled from her brow, dripping into her eyes. The sun glaring off the snow was blinding enough. She quickly wiped her brow and squinted. "You had no choice, Jerome. You couldn't take him to the hospital. There'd be too many questions."

"You don't know nothing!" Kenton said, his voice faint but angry. He was still in the shed.

Ellie's eyes followed the trail of blood where Brady had fallen to where he lay at the edge of the driveway. Black plumes of smoke from the burning truck rose high into the pale colored sky. Help would be coming soon. She peeked around the edge of the house at the shed, took a deep breath then sprinted as hard as her legs would go toward the shed. She dove under the lean-to and rolled quickly into a crouch against the wooden wall. Her heart felt like it was going to explode and shatter her chest like the carport had when it blew apart. "Jerome, I know it was an accident. I know you didn't mean for him to get hurt."

She heard rustling in the shed and waited to hear the sound of Kenton reloading but it never came. He *is* out of bullets. She slowly stood and pressed her back against the wall, terrified to move, terrified not to. "Jerome...JJ's alive. He told us everything. He told us how Becky loved him and how good she was to him."

"She wouldn't shut up. She wouldn't stop screaming."

By the sound of his voice, he wasn't deep into the shed. He was close. The only thing separating them was the rickety wooden wall.

Slowly, she moved one foot in front of the other as quietly as she could.

All of a sudden, she was knocked backwards, completely off her feet as Kenton plowed into her head-first, slamming her hard into an old tractor. Her gun spiraled through the air. A white-hot pain shot through her whole body as she felt her left arm snap below the elbow. She grabbed for it, screaming in agony, but Kenton slammed her head hard against the cold metal. He pounded at her face with brutal fists then drove them deep into her stomach. She tasted blood, her own blood, and wondered how often Becky Kenton had tasted *her* own blood.

With a fury fueled by adrenaline and anger, Ellie kicked furiously at him with the strength of a kick boxer and landed a strong blow to his crotch.

Kenton spiraled backwards, giving her just enough time to scramble away from the brutality. Her head spinning with pain, she fell to her knees and clutched her arm then tried to crawl to safety. Kenton was on her again. He drove her face deep into the snow as he pummeled the back of her head, handfuls of her hair wrapped around his fingers. She bucked like a wild horse until he jerked her over onto her back, the pain raging in her arm so intense she feared passing out. He drew back his fist, her face the target, but she wrestled out from under him and drove both her feet deep into his chest. She reached for Brady's gun in her jacket pocket... *Please, God, let it be loaded...*

Kenton regained his footing and towered over her. When he saw the gun, he grinned and the evilness in him sent shivers down her spine. "You ain't got it in you." He smirked.

Ellie pulled the trigger.

23

Ellie's eyes fluttered open for a moment then she squeezed them closed. She remembered the coldness of the snow, the way it stung her skin, the way it bit at her face. She slowly opened her eyes again, allowing her vision to adjust to the brightness. She tried to focus and get her bearings, but the pain was excruciating. Each breath brought a crushing feeling to her chest. She tried to swallow but her throat was painfully dry. She tried to cry out for help but the only sound she could make was a breathless moan.

"Don't try to talk," Jesse said. He was there beside her, his beautiful face slowly coming into focus.

Suddenly everything was coming into focus, and she knew where she was. She wasn't in the freezing snow fighting for her life anymore; she was alive and safe in a warm hospital bed. Tears rolled from the corner of her eyes, stinging her face as they pooled in the cuts and scratches.

"You had me worried," Jesse said as he gently dabbed a soft tissue at her tears.

"Jesse…." Her voice was crackly and shallow.

"You're at Avery County Memorial Hospital." He pressed the nurse call button then continued softly wiping away Ellie's tears.

The last thing she remembered was Jerome Kenton standing over her and then…it all came back to her. She tried to lift her left arm and felt the heaviness of the cast.

"They had to put a pin in your wrist. They just operated yesterday so it's probably goin' to hurt pretty bad today."

"Yesterday?" Her throat felt like she had swallowed a pail of sand. She swallowed hard, trying desperately to wet her throat. "What day is it?"

"You've been here three days, baby."

A nurse padded into the room and stopped beside the bed. "Well, good morning, Miss Saunders. It's good to finally see you awake." She smiled then did a quick scan of the various monitors. "I'm Ruby, and I'll be your nurse today. How's your pain?"

"Hurts," Ellie whispered.

Ruby nodded then checked the IV bag. "You took quite a beating. But I want to hold off just a little bit on the morphine and see if we can't get you a little more awake, OK?"

"Can you give her something maybe not as strong?" Jesse asked.

Ruby winked at him. "We're not going to let her hurt too long. Think you could handle some ice chips?"

Ellie nodded. Anything to take away the tightness in her throat. Ruby left and returned a moment later with a small cup of ice chips. She handed the cup to Jesse. "Start slow. Give her just a little bit at a time." She raised the head of the bed to a forty-five degree angle. Ellie grimaced at the movement of the incline. "I know it hurts, but I want you to sit up for a little while. I'll let the doctor know you're awake, and he'll probably be in shortly. Call me if she needs anything," she said to Jesse before she left.

Jesse gently placed the spoon in Ellie's mouth. The ice was cold and burned sliding down but felt good to her parched throat. She took another small bite then slightly turned her head away from the spoon.

He set the cup on the table then pulled a chair up beside the bed. He looked as if he hadn't shaved in a week, his hair a mess of tangled waves. His clothes were wrinkled and loose fitting and Ellie wondered how long it had been since he had been home. Had he been there the whole time? Had he been there since…?

"Brady?" she asked, the moisture slowly coming back to her voice.

Jesse nodded. "He's down the hall. The shot really wasn't that bad. He's on blood thinners. That's why he bled so bad. I think they're going to release him tomorrow."

Ellie closed her eyes and slightly nodded, then silently thanked God for his grace and mercy.

"He said you blew up Kenton's truck to signal for help."

Ellie slowly ran her tongue over her lips and nodded. "There was no radio. No signal on the cell phones. I had to do something."

Jesse smiled. "Well, it worked. The mailman heard the explosion and saw the flames and called it in. The paramedics said if it had been another ten minutes, Brady would have bled out. We'd be going to a funeral instead of a retirement party."

Funeral…oh, no.

"Peggy's funeral…."

Jesse slightly nodded then grinned. "Aunt Sissy said you'd do anything to get out of going."

"Daddy—"

"They'll be here after lunch."

Ellie took a painful breath and asked about Landon.

"Deveraux released him yesterday. Leon went home with them, to help them get settled."

"Leon?"

Jesse chuckled. "Apparently, he and Ashley hit it off, and the next thing we know, Leon's taking a day of vacation and going home with them."

Ellie cracked a smile then the smile, although painful, led to a giggle. "Leon?"

"Yeah, I know. Stranger things have happened, I suppose."

"Poor Ashley."

"See what happens when you're not around to micro-manage everything? Poor unsuspecting Ashley falls for Leon. I told you, you should have let me go with you."

Ellie smiled, reluctantly admitting to herself this was one time she wished she had listened to him.

Jesse's expression suddenly turned solemn. He said quietly, "They found Becky's body."

It didn't surprise her. "In the woods behind the house," she whispered.

Jesse nodded. "How'd you know?"

"The first day we went out there, there were footprints in the snow leading to the woods. There were drag marks beside them." Her heart ached for Becky Kenton and the hell on earth she lived through. Maybe God would forgive her for her part in Landon's abduction, and she'd be able to live a peaceful life in Heaven.

"Kenton?" Ellie asked in a small voice.

Jesse looked at her for a long moment then slowly shook his head. "You hit him dead center."

****

Ellie looked out her living room window, and, through the approaching dusk, gazed at the daffodils poking their heads up through the soft ground along the walkway. She admired their resilience. Year after year, they came back. Sometimes blooming underneath a heavy snow or an early spring cold spell. They never gave up or gave in to what seemed like unbeatable odds. She wondered if God was that way. Never giving up on troubled souls, waiting patiently for them to come around and reach their full bloom.

She went into the bathroom and pulled out her newly bought items of makeup. She opened the women's magazine she'd bought at the grocery store to the how-to page and propped it on the back of the toilet. Moisturizer, check. Concealer, check. Foundation, check. Green eye-shadow (to make her eyes *pop*), eyeliner, mascara, an eyelash curler, check, check, check. Lip-liner, lipstick, cream blush, and finishing powder, check, check, check, and check. She stared at the assortment of makeup, wondering if each piece was *really* necessary to achieve the light and natural new look for spring the magazine boasted. Maybe she should have allowed more time to do this? Jesse was picking her up in about half an hour.

She read the instructions on the small tube of moisturizer then applied a dab on her cheeks, under her eyes and on her forehead. Next came the concealer, guaranteed to hide imperfections and flaws. It looked like a tube of yellow lipstick. Was it really that easy? She'd been hiding her imperfections and flaws for years. Or maybe hiding *behind* them was a better choice of words. *For all have sinned and fallen short of the glory of God... He still loves me despite all my flaws.* She put away the concealer and foundation, the lip liner and that odd-looking lash curler. Keep it simple, stupid, she told herself, then applied a thin dusting of eye shadow and a small amount of eyeliner. She accidentally poked herself in the eye with the mascara brush. "Ouch," she cried, using a tissue to dab away the tears. She wondered if women who carried mascara in their purses should be required to have a concealed weapon permit.

She put away her collection of makeup then glanced at herself in the mirror. The bruises on her face had faded, and all that remained was a slight scar under her bottom lip. If you didn't know it was there, you wouldn't even see it. But Ellie knew it was there. It would always be there. But it wasn't a bad thing—it was a reminder of a mother who found her son, and a little boy's miracle that saved Ellie from herself.

She went into the bedroom and looked at herself in the pedestal mirror. She was wearing a lightweight sweater and jeans. Jesse had told her to dress casual, to wear jeans, but she wasn't so sure about this wearing jeans to church thing. It had been so long since she had set foot in a church, she wasn't sure of the protocol. Why she ever agreed to go with him she'd never know. But like those stupid little daffodils, he was nothing if not persistent.

It was CrossPoint Baptist Church's spring revival, and she guessed there'd be no harm in going with him to one service. Besides, she liked the name—CrossPoint. She wondered if its members were all at a cross point in their lives, too?

She heard a knock on the door then Jesse's familiar voice. "Hey, sweetcakes, you ready?"

She took one last look at the mirror, took a deep

breath then joined him in the living room. He was wearing faded jeans and a long sleeve t-shirt with a CrossPoint emblem on the chest. Ellie liked the logo, a compass with a cross in the center, indicating a new direction. A new direction suited her just fine.

"Wow," he said, smiling softly. "You look *great.*"

"And you're sure about the jeans?"

"Have I ever led you astray? OK, don't answer that." He laughed as he closed the door behind them.

Ellie buckled her seat belt then asked, "Who's preaching tonight?" Like she would really recognize the name of any preacher!

"Just a visiting preacher. I hear he's pretty good. Brittany's going to be there. She's really looking forward to meeting you."

"When does she leave for her mission trip?"

"Three weeks. She's two-hundred dollars short, so hopefully she'll get it in the love offering."

Love offerings, mission trips, spring revivals...it was all so foreign to her, yet so familiar. Even despite a bad case of nerves, she was comfortable with it.

"You ready to come back to work Monday?"

She chuckled. "Are you kidding? I'm so bored I thought about taking up knitting."

"Hey, my mother's a knitter. Don't knock it," he said and laughed.

"Has she ever knitted you anything?"

"Best pair of socks I've ever had. They don't fit at all, but they make wonderful pot holders."

Ellie laughed. "Does she know you use them for pot holders?"

Jesse shook his head. "And she'll never find out, will she?"

"Your secret's safe." She grinned. She wondered if

she'd ever meet Jesse's mother? She wondered about this whole *relationship*...what made him appear that day at Caper's? Why'd he take such an interest in the case *she* was working?

They'd been almost inseparable since that day he'd eaten all her chips, but the only time they had spoken about their one night together, Jesse had said he *wished it had never happened*. For someone who wished it had never happened, Jesse Alvarez had integrated himself so deeply in her life, she couldn't imagine life without him now.

"Jesse," she said in a quiet voice, deciding now was as good of a time as any to confront the subject.

"Yeah?"

"About...*us*. You said the night Dad and Aunt Sissy came over that you wished *it* had never happened. Why?"

He didn't say anything for a long moment, then finally smiled softly. "It was *almost* perfect."

Ellie raised her brows. "Almost?"

"Take away the fact we weren't married and it *would have been* perfect." He glanced over at her and grinned.

"But you never called back."

He sighed. "I was ashamed. Ashamed I'd let myself down, ashamed I'd let God down, and ashamed I'd dragged you down with me."

"If I remember correctly, I went pretty willingly."

He smiled at her then reached over and gently stroked her cheek. "I *want* a relationship with you, Ellie Saunders, more than anything else. A real relationship. But not on my terms, or your terms...I want it to be on God's terms."

****

The parking lot of the church was packed and Jesse circled a time or two to find a parking space. Ellie did a double take at a blue Buick parked near the front. "That's my daddy's car," she said, her voice rising slightly.

"Oh, yeah. I invited him and Aunt Sissy."

"Jesse, why didn't you tell me they were going to be here?" Her heartbeat rose a notch.

"What difference does it make if they're here or not?" He glanced at her then parked beside a Toyota compact. "You don't want them here?"

Ellie wasn't sure she was ready for all this. She didn't know *what* she wanted. "No, I just...I'm just surprised, that's all."

"Surprised to see your aunt and your father at church? He's a preacher, Ellie."

Ellie shook her head, hoping to clear some of the confusion she was feeling. "He's a *former* preacher. He hasn't preached in...I don't even know how many years."

"That doesn't mean he gave up on God. God certainly doesn't give up on us, does He?"

"I suppose not," she said in a small voice, not really wanting to admit Jesse was right again. Just because her father wasn't standing in a pulpit every Sunday didn't mean he had turned his back on God. She knew that for a fact. He had never really stopped preaching at all. He seized every opportunity he had to share God's grace with someone, anyone. "Do they know I'm coming?" she asked as they walked up the front steps.

"I told them to save us a seat."

Great. She swallowed hard, trying to force the knot

in her throat down into her stomach where it could play with the butterflies. Jesse held the front door open then stepped up behind Ellie as she entered. "Wow. Get a load of that," he whispered in her ear. "Ellie Saunders's just walked into a church, and it didn't crumble beneath her."

Ellie glowered at him, a smirk crossing her lips. Although, truth be told, she was a little surprised the building was still standing. Aunt Sissy spotted them and waved them over.

The church sure wasn't anything like Ellie remembered churches being. There were no rows of cloth-covered pews. Instead, roll out stadium seats were pulled out from the walls in an octagon shape. The pulpit was down front, slightly elevated with three rows of risers behind it. Choir members dressed in jeans and white shirts filled the risers.

"No robes?" Ellie whispered to Jesse

"We're not a robe kind of church." He smiled then offered her his hand as she climbed the bleachers to where Sissy was seated.

Ellie sat down beside Sissy and immediately looked around for her father. "Where's Daddy?" she asked Sissy.

"He'll be out in a minute. I'm so glad you came," Sissy said as she wrapped an arm around Ellie's shoulder. "I know he's going to be tickled to death you're here."

Jesse sat on the other side of Ellie and chatted loudly with everyone around. After a minute or two of greeting everyone within shouting distance, he leaned across Ellie toward Aunt Sissy. "I think she was a little surprised the building didn't fall when she walked in."

"We're not out of here yet," Ellie said and grinned.

Ellie searched the crowd for her father but didn't see him anywhere. A young man in a CrossPoint t-shirt and jeans stood at the pulpit reading announcements into a microphone. He made the announcement about Brittany's mission trip and a special offering and about an upcoming bowling outing. Suddenly Ellie spotted her father and her heart raced. *What was he doing down there? What was he doing at the pulpit?* The young man making the announcements introduced the church pastor and then turned to Ellie's father and welcomed Reverend Ferrin Saunders as their guest speaker.

"Keeping with our revival theme," the young man said, "Reverend Saunders will be speaking on new beginnings and God's power of redemption."

Ellie couldn't take her eyes off the pulpit and met her father's gaze when he glanced up at Sissy. He smiled the kindest, proudest smile Ellie had ever seen. She felt the forgiveness start at the top of her head and like a gentle, steady rain, felt it spread from the top of her head to the bottoms of her feet, washing her clean of the past. She sucked in the comfort, relishing in the joy it brought and knew she had found her way back home.

Jesse gently took her hand as her father began to speak again, "Jesus said to her: I am the resurrection and the life: he that believeth in Me, although he be dead, shall live…"

Ellie bowed her head, and she prayed for a fresh start, a new life. A new life like Landon's. She felt God's loving arms wrap around her, felt His miraculous hands breathe new life into her heart and soul. And finally, she believed.

The Lazarus Syndrome was real. It had brought her back from the dead, too.